Seven Games in October

Seven Games in October

CHARLES BRADY

Little, Brown and Company — Boston – Toronto

FIRST EDITION

LIBRARY OF CONGRESS CATALOGING IN PUBLICATION DATA
Brady, Charles.
    Seven games in October.
    I. Title.
PZ4.B8117Se   [PS3552.R238]   813'.5'4   79-14345
ISBN 0-316-10594-5

BP

Designed by Susan Windheim

Published simultaneously in Canada
by Little, Brown & Company (Canada) Limited

PRINTED IN THE UNITED STATES OF AMERICA

*For Beverly, who was there at the
beginning so many years ago; and for Lawrence S.
Cruikshank, a film executive
and former writer's agent,
who never stopped believing.*

1.
The Fix

FRIDAY
Eight Days before the World Series

You should have seen the fans last year. There were dudes who waited for hours after the game for me in the parking lot. They were there ready to cut me up. People were threatening my life all the time here.

—REGGIE JACKSON, New York Yankee outfielder

1.

Roosevelt Chad's long legs glistened in the late afternoon sun as he jogged around the high-school track a block from his home. He moved effortlessly around the curve and down the stretch. He was running a gentle two miles to burn off nervous energy. Shortstop for the Los Angeles Dodgers, he and his team opened the playoffs tomorrow, in Dodger Stadium against the Chicago Cubs. Chad was burning off nervous energy because he didn't want to lie awake half the night thinking about the game.

Ahead of him was his eight-year-old son, Billy, whom he'd already lapped twice. Billy wore short pants, tennis shoes, and soccer-length socks. The left sock had lost its elasticity and drooped over the boy's ankle.

When Chad finished his eighth lap he ran off the track and headed toward his son, who was stealthily tiptoeing toward a butterfly resting in the grass. A moment before the boy pounced, the butterfly took wing. While the boy watched the fluttering insect Chad came up silently and swept his unsuspecting son into his arms. "I got ya. I got ya." Chad laughed, and covered his son's face with kisses.

Hand in hand, father and son left the school grounds and headed down the street for home.

As they reached the deep, wide lawn that surrounded the two-story brick house, Chad said, "C'mon, Billy. I'll race you to the back door."

The boy clenched his fists in front of him and began running as fast as he could. "I'm gonna beat you, Daddy. I'm gonna beat you."

"No, you're not." Chad laughed.

"Yes, I am, Daddy. Here I go. I'm gonna sprint now. I'm really gonna go."

The boy pulled away as Chad, seemingly making great effort, slipped behind.

The long driveway curved behind the house, and the two rounded it, Chad several paces behind his son.

"I'm beating Daddy, I'm beating Daddy," Billy shouted. "Look everybody. Look, Grandma!"

Mrs. Chad, hearing the commotion, stepped out of the back door to watch the end of the race. Billy ran ahead by three paces, and when he got to his grandmother he threw himself in her arms.

"I beat Daddy," he cried and kissed his grandmother, who kissed him back.

Chad walked up, laughing, and put his arms around his son and the tall, slim woman. The three laughed at the race.

The door opened and Camilla, Chad's nine-year-old daughter, came out. She was tall for her age, and slim. Her hair was in pigtails and she wore a dress. She was leaving the tomboy stage and becoming a lady.

"I beat Daddy in a footrace," Billy boasted to his sister. He was still excited and breathing hard from running.

"Only because he let you," said his sister, acting very grown-up. "You don't honestly think that a little boy like you could win a footrace from the shortstop of the Los Angeles Dodgers?"

"No. But it's a good story," the boy said seriously.

"All right," Mrs. Chad said, "if we're going to the pizza shop, you men better hurry and dress." She opened the door and Billy tore through it.

"Last one out of the shower is a New York Yankee," he shouted over his shoulder.

"That boy!" Camilla said, still in her grown-up pose. She shook her head.

The telephone rang then, eliminating Chad from the race and condemning him to be a hated New York Yankee.

He took the call in the den. "This is Roosevelt Chad," he said into the receiver.

He waited for the caller to speak. Western music came faintly through the earpiece. Then he heard breathing and a giggle and then another. They came from different persons. Men. He heard an impatient, whispered "go ahead."

"Is this the ball player?" a reluctant voice asked.

Chad's heart sank. A fan, probably a drunk one, had gotten hold of his telephone number. It was going to be one of *those* calls.

"Yes, it is," he answered in a tight voice.

"I'm from Chicago, see," the voice said, trying to sound threatening. "I'm calling from Chicago."

Chad heard a giggle and guessed the call was coming from a bar in downtown Los Angeles.

"If the Dodgers beat the Cubs tomorrow you and some of your teammates are going to be in big trouble, buddy."

The voice sounded drunk.

Chad didn't answer and there was a silence on the line.

"Hey!" the voice shouted. "Did you hear what I said. I'm no goddam Hollywood fairy calling. I'm from Chicago. My uncle was Al Capone."

"He's dead," Chad commented, and wished he'd kept his mouth shut.

"That's right," the voice snapped back. "And you're gonna be dead, too, if you beat the Cubs. Remember that tomorrow during the game. There are ways of getting a rifle into the ball park. Any of you hit a homerun, I'm gonna drop you with a deer slug the moment you round third base. Remember that."

Chad heard some more giggling in the background and then the line clicked dead.

He hung up the receiver and stood a moment in the den. He hated those calls. He got one or two a year like that. All the better-known players did. His phone wasn't listed and the Dodger office never gave out numbers, but, still, there were ways. Security guards, grounds keepers, deliverymen, workers. A lot of people could get numbers if they really wanted to.

A psychiatrist hired by the league had written a paper on how the players should conduct themselves during such calls. You were not supposed to hang up. That could enrage the caller, provoking a flood of hate letters and telephone messages. It usually satisfied the caller· to speak his piece. The hate calls came mostly from men. Women made obscene calls.

You were supposed to inform both the team management and the commissioner's office of such calls. But Chad guessed that only about half the threats were actually reported. He personally turned in only the ones he thought serious and he didn't even like to do that. Someone in the police department or the commissioner's office would invariably leak the information to the press. This had upset his mother and frightened his children. Chad knew that most of the players felt the same way. The players's reps were in the process of developing a better way to handle threats.

Legislation recently had been passed permitting the FBI to intervene. Of course, you couldn't expect them to investigate every drunk phone call. But Chad preferred the FBI. They didn't talk. And the commissioner's office couldn't push them around like they did the local cops. The commissioner's office simply wished the threats would go away. They liked to pretend they weren't real. Most of them weren't.

Someday one would be real though, Chad thought. It was only a matter of time before some nut smuggled a rifle into a stadium and took a shot at a player. Some of this generation of fans were throwing bottles and steel balls. Some of the next generation would start shooting.

The door to the den burst open, startling him. It was Billy. The boy had come directly from the shower, a towel wrapped around him, his hair wet, water dripping to the carpet. "You're the last one out of the shower," he screamed. "You're a New York Yankee."

Chad faked a look of extreme hurt. "A New York Yankee!" he echoed. "Oh, no. Anything but that."

Chad grabbed the boy and tossed him over his shoulder. Father and son left the room laughing uproariously.

SATURDAY
One Week before the World Series

The December 8, 1976 issue of the *New York Times* reported that a London businessman confessed to selling 2.5 million dollars' worth of stock in a family business to cover gambling losses. The story continued that he began gambling as a youth. He was described as a "lonely and sometimes friendless man."

2.

Robert Hencill glanced at his watch. In one hour the Notre Dame–Southern Cal football game would be televised from South Bend. He walked to the bar of his Beverly Hills home and dialed a number. On the second ring his bookie answered.

"Hey, kid," Carmichael's voice rasped, sympathetic. "That was a tough one you lost last night in Dallas."

Hencill had bet seventy-five thousand dollars on Southern Methodist against Iowa and lost. "It's not whether you win or lose that counts," Hencill answered, forcing a lilt in his voice; "the main thing is to be in action."

Carmichael's chuckle came over the line. "You're all right, kid. Who do you want today?"

Hencill started to say Dodgers and then changed his mind. "Notre Dame," he blurted, his voice tight with fear. "For a hundred thou."

"Gotcha, kid. Notre Dame even. One hundred thousand American dollars. You're going for a bundle, kid."

"Easy come, easy go," Hencill said. He gave his voice a casual tone, fearful to let his anxiety show to the bookie. "I made it in the drug traffic."

It was an old joke between the two. Carmichael knew that Hencill was the president of a pharmaceutical company. Again the bookie chuckled. "You're all right, kid."

Hencill pictured Carmichael recording the bet.

There was a pause and then the bookie's gravelly voice came through the receiver. "I don't say this often, kid . . ." He hesitated and Hencill suspected the bookie was looking over his shoulder to make sure no one heard him. ". . . but I hope you win today," Carmichael said finally. "You been having a tough run of luck lately."

Hencill's face flushed with embarrassment. He didn't like to be pitied. For anything. He heard his wife come down the stairs and he was thankful for the excuse to terminate the conversation. "Got to run," he told the bookie.

"Sure thing, kid."

People called Hencill kid because of his size. In his built-up shoes he was not much over five feet four inches tall. He had thick black hair and a handsome face that at thirty-five was still boyish and unlined. "A midget John Travolta," an insensitive person once had called him.

Hencill was president of Doctor's Prescriptions (The Medicines Doctors Prescribe for Themselves) Pharmaceutical Company. The company had been founded by Robert Hencill, Sr., who seven years earlier had died of a heart attack. To Mrs. Helen Sanders, who had kept house for him for more than a quarter of a century and who had raised his son, Robert Jr., the senior Hencill had willed an annuity of twenty-five thousand dollars, plus lifetime free residence in the coach house located on a corner of his Beverly Hills estate.

To his only child, Robert Hencill, Jr., he left cash and stocks valued at six million dollars.

The hundred thousand dollars Hencill had bet on Notre Dame was the last of his fortune. If Notre Dame lost he would be dead broke.

His wife tapped on the double door.

"Herein," Hencill called out. He had met his wife, Ilka, when he

• 9

was in Germany, fulfilling his ROTC commitment in the Army Chemical Corps. He spoke German to her when he wanted to be playful, but now his voice was tight. It was the bet.

The doors parted and Ilka entered. He had married her eight years ago, when she was twenty-one. She was attractive then; now she was on her way to becoming a great beauty. She had a Nordic face, clear-complexioned, with delicate bone structure. Her blond hair was cut short. She had the slim body of a gymnast, firm and tight-skinned without being muscular, and her breasts bobbed slightly as she walked. She wore no bra under a beige short-sleeved jersey. Her medium-brown suede skirt had a wide leather belt that matched her boots. The clothes were expensive, bought during annual, sometimes semiannual, trips to Europe. She didn't like American fashions — she didn't like anything American.

She smiled, showing small very white teeth, as she walked toward Hencill, who waited on the bar stool for the expected good-bye kiss. "Are you leaving now?" he asked.

"Yes, darling," she answered with a husky German accent.

He turned his cheek to her and she touched it with her lips in a kiss that was habitual rather than affectionate.

"Are you going to win today, darling? I hope so. Win us five hundred dollars and we go tonight to Vegas, *nicht?*"

Hencill nodded and smiled a thin smile. His wife had no idea of the sums of money he bet and he was frightened to speculate what she would say, or do, if she knew. "Say hello to Renata for me," he told her. Renata was Ilka's best friend. They had been schoolmates at Wiesbaden. Renata had followed Ilka to the States and Hencill had found her a job as a receptionist for a group of doctors. Now she was the mistress of one of them.

"She is just coming back from Germany. Did I tell you? She had dinner with Mutti."

"Give her a *Gruss* from me." Hencill spoke the half-German, half-English dialect he sometimes used with her. *Gruss* was the German word for greeting.

"I do it." Ilka turned and looked at the darkened television screen. "Who plays today?"

"Notre Dame and South Cal."

"Which team did you pick?"

"The winner," Hencill answered and waited for her to leave.

"And who is that?"

"Notre Dame."

"Good." Ilka smiled and kissed him again. "Then you win for sure five hundred dollars and tonight we go to Vegas."

"Perhaps," said Hencill.

"*Tjuss,* darling," Ilka said. "I see you later."

"*Tjuss,*" Hencill called after her.

At the door she turned and smiled and formed her lips in a kiss. "I be back after the game, darling."

Ilka's car was in the drive. As she walked to it she automatically threw a glance at the coach house even though she knew Mrs. Sanders had gone shopping.

When she got to her car, a blue Porsche Carrera, she looked again at the coach house and muttered an oath under her breath. "Torturer," she hissed at the coach house.

She got into the car, started the engine, and drove quickly down the long, palm-tree-shaded drive. Twenty minutes later she parked in front of Renata's apartment house.

She smelled fresh, strong German coffee when she exited from the elevator. She touched the door bell, and in a moment Renata was there, a small, dark woman voluptuously built. The two embraced. "Come," said Renata, "you can carry the cakes to the table. We eat on the balcony. Just like at home."

Ilka followed her through the large modern apartment to the kitchen. Renata had already filled a tray with pastries, and Ilka carried them to the table on the balcony. Renata followed her carrying a coffee service.

In a moment the two German women were sipping coffee and sampling the variety of cakes. "Don't you see Bjorn today?" Renata asked.

Bjorn was a Swedish actor with whom Ilka had been having an affair for several years. Normally she met Bjorn on Saturday afternoons before coming to Renata's.

"I see him later. He had to talk to a producer about a film."

"How is it with him?"

"*Ach*, it's all getting so boring. If I wasn't leaving so soon I would get another lover," Ilka answered truthfully. She told Renata everything.

"Does he know yet you are getting a divorce?"

"*Nein*," said Ilka. "Nobody knows. Only you. I see the lawyer Wednesday or Thursday."

"And Robert. When do you tell him?"

"This weekend. I can't wait any longer."

"Do you go to Vegas?"

"Yes. I make him go. It will be easier to tell him there."

"And how much do you get?"

The worry left Ilka's face and she smiled. "Plenty. I get plenty from the impotent little bastard. I am married eight years to him. For this I get plenty. Maybe a million."

Kickoff was only fifteen minutes away and still Hencill hadn't turned on the TV. He hated the pregame shows. He paced around his bar, glancing every minute or so at his watch.

It was a long room with the bar at one end and a color television set built into the wall at the other. The south wall was a sheet of glass with louvers at the top, to let in the occasional fresh air still to be found in southern California.

The north wall was paneled in oak, most of which was covered by schedules of sporting events, blown up to poster size. The largest was the schedule of television events, and it served as a centerpiece. Games that already had been played were blacked out by a crayon attached to a string hanging at the side.

Hencill walked to the wall and stared at the sports listings. Earlier in the morning he had considered three betting possibilities. To take the Dodgers in their game against the Cubs, the Washington Senators in their opening playoff game against the Angels, or Notre Dame against Southern Cal.

The problem was odds and risks. The Dodgers were a heavy favorite and he would have been betting his hundred thousand to win only sixty-five thousand. On the other hand, the Senators were the underdogs against the defending American League Angels. He could get back one hundred eighty thousand for his hundred thousand if he won. But the risk was great. The football game was a toss-up. He could take either team even by laying eleven to ten. He'd had trouble picking football winners and he knew he shouldn't have bet the game.

His eyes shifted aimlessly over the placards, finally stopping at the team photo atop the Dodgers schedule. He wished he had bet them. He scanned the photo, focusing at last on Roosevelt Chad, their All-Star shortstop. He was a good-looking man. His Afro was clipped short, emphasizing his high forehead; he had an intelligent face with alert eyes and a strong chin. Sportswriters called him a superperson as well as a superstar.

Hencill remembered when Dodger scouts had discovered Chad playing ball at a small community college near St. Joseph, Missouri. The following year Chad had started at shortstop for the Dodgers and won Rookie of the Year honors. In the ten years since, he had twice led the league in batting average, runs batted in, and home runs. He had seven Golden Gloves as the league's best fielding shortstop. And, to crown it all, he had three times been named Most Valuable Player. Twice he had been named first on all twenty-four ballots.

Hencill turned away. It was almost game time and he turned on the television set. The kickoff came a minute later. He almost swallowed his tongue when a Southern California player ran ninety-two yards for a touchdown.

The Dodger–Cub game didn't start until four-thirty, so Chad ate a late breakfast with his family. He had awakened at eight o'clock. He liked to move around before breakfast and he puttered about the lawn doing minor gardening. At nine o'clock Billy appeared sleepily at the front door in his pajamas. Chad sent the boy in to get dressed and then the two of them did some weeding in the flower bed and shortly before breakfast they turned on the lawn sprinkler.

The smell of bacon and eggs cooking brought their work to an end. They washed up in the exercise room in the garage. When they came into the kitchen the table was set and Camilla was taking blueberry muffins from the oven. She had made them herself from her grandmother's recipe.

"Boy, am I hungry," Billy shouted, slamming himself onto a chair. "I could eat a horse."

"We haven't got a horse," Camilla said haughtily. "There is only bacon and eggs and some *very* good blueberry muffins."

"Okay," Billy agreed. "If there's no horsemeat I'll eat pigs and chickens."

Camilla made a face at this grossness.

"Drink your juice, you two," their grandmother reminded them.

"Definitely drink your juice, darling," said Chad, taking his seat at the table. "It is Golden C orange juice, and the famous Roosevelt Chad ..."

"And his fast-running son," chipped in Billy.

"And his beautiful and charming daughter," added Camilla.

"... drink Golden C orange juice every day," Mrs. Chad finished, laughingly.

Billy began singing a commercial. "This is the time we drink our juice, drink our juice, this is the time we drink our juice, each and every morning."

The others chimed and sang the second verse with Billy. At the end the boy shouted, "Down the hatch!"

They all drank their orange juice.

"When are we gonna make another juice commercial, Daddy?" asked Billy.

"One of these days, son. Pretty soon, I think."

"I thought we were supposed to make one each month," Camilla said. She liked making commercials.

"They'll be here soon," promised her father.

Mrs. Chad filled everyone's glass again with the orange juice.

"I think it would be a good idea to photograph us drinking juice from champagne glasses," said Camilla.

Billy picked up his orange juice glass and holding it daintily as he imagined a champagne glass should be held, shouted, "Down the hatch."

"One doesn't say, 'down the hatch,' " sniffed his sister.

"I do," retorted Billy.

"One says, 'cheers,' " Camilla corrected him.

"How do you know?" asked her father interestedly. "Have you been serving champagne at your mud-pie parties?"

"I saw it on television," Camilla informed him. "In a film. The ladies drank champagne and everyone said . . ."

"Down the hatch!" shouted her brother.

Despite her newly acquired dignity Camilla joined the others in laughter.

They ate a leisurely breakfast, spicing it with conversation and laughter. Afterward Chad sipped a second cup of coffee. "Do you want to come to the game today?" he asked his children.

"Father! For just a *playoff* game?"

"We'll come for the World Series," Billy promised.

Chad and his mother exchanged humorous glances.

It was a team rule that the players show up in the clubhouse three hours before a game, so Chad left home around noon. He had plenty to do at the stadium. He had interviews to give, balls to sign, and a hurried but important meeting with his business agent. Afterward, time permitting, he had a baseball game to play. Chad sometimes thought that the game was incidental to the business spin-offs.

A mile from his home he stopped to fill up at a service station where he was a regular. The owner was Tom Barry, a good-natured, red-faced man of Chad's age. Barry came from the garage wiping his left hand on a rag.

"Hey, Rosie, the football game is on." He faked indignation. "Can't you buy your gas somewhere else?"

"Absolutely," Chad replied. "And if I'd known you approved of violence, I'd never have become a customer here in the first place."

Barry laughed and unhooked the gas hose.

"What's the score?" Chad asked.

"Notre Dame just tied it seven–seven," Barry told him. "Hope it stays that way. I got number four in the scoring pool." He inserted the gas hose in the tank.

"Notre Dame will win it," Chad said.

"How much you want to bet?" Barry had been a local high-school hero and had played freshman ball at USC.

"Bet! Don't talk like that." Chad pretended to shudder. He looked around him. "You'll get me in trouble with the commissioner's office. Next year I'll be playing for the Chop Suey Giants in the Japanese League."

The men laughed. "You going to beat the Cubs?" Barry asked.

"Yup. And Washington is going to beat the Angels."

"The Senators!"

"They're the team."

Shaking his head in disbelief, Barry pulled the hose from the tank. "I'll tell you one thing — if you pick Notre Dame and Washington, you're no threat to Jean Dixon."

"How much do you want to bet?" Chad deadpanned.

Barry broke into laughter and then Chad joined him.

On the dresser facing the double bed in Bjorn's bedroom was a portable television set. The sound was off. It was halftime at Notre Dame Stadium. A score flashed on the screen: Notre Dame 14, USC 7. Ilka got out of bed, took her handbag from the dresser, and continued out of the room.

A moment later Bjorn heard the shower go on. He lit a cigarette and then another until he heard the shower go off and the toilet flush. A moment later the bathroom door opened and Ilka appeared, nude, coming down the hallway. Her body glistened from the shower and the toweling off and Bjorn felt desire rise in him again.

Ilka smiled coldly as she came into the room. She collected her clothes, which she had neatly folded on the dresser, and began dressing.

It was a sensuous thing, Bjorn thought, to watch a woman dress or undress. To watch the body slowly covered or uncovered. He gazed at her with pleasure, and after she was dressed he watched her brushing her hair in the mirror. She looked very desirable, the brush in her right hand, her arm crooked at the side of her head. Her breasts rose and fell as she brushed. He saw her looking at him in the mirror. "What are you thinking?" she asked.

"That I like basketball better than football," he answered.

She looked quizzically at him in the mirror. "Why? Did you play basketball as a young man? Do they play that in Sweden?"

"That has nothing to do with it."

She turned from the mirror and looked directly at him. "Why, then?"

He ran his eyes over her. "Because in basketball they are always having overtimes. Sometimes two and three overtimes."

Understanding appeared on Ilka's face. "Perhaps then we could make love again, *nicht?*"

"Yes."

Ilka looked at the television screen. USC had tied the score fourteen to fourteen. "Be thankful it is not the Kentucky Derby today. Then we have to make love in two minutes."

Bjorn exploded with laughter. "That's good. I can just see us in bed, racing the horses. But this time we'd leave the sound on and make love to the roar of the spectators. Louder and louder. Tens of thousands of people urging us to copulate faster than the horses run."

"Who would win?" Ilka asked him, her eyes amused. "The horses, or us?"

"Oh, the horses, of course. Who can make love in two minutes?"

"My husband," Ilka replied acidly. "And for him that would be a long race."

Bjorn walked Ilka to her car. She raised herself on tiptoes and pecked him on the mouth. "I call you maybe next week, *nicht?*"

She touched his lips again, then got into the Carrera and drove off.

On her way home she tuned in the football game. Notre Dame had gone ahead, seventeen to fourteen. She half-listened to the radio as she made plans to tell Robert she wanted a divorce.

She had been a travel bureau employee in Wiesbaden when she met Robert on a Rhine River cruise. She had not been attracted to him because he was too small. But when they came ashore, he offered her a ride home. To save a long bus ride, she accepted.

When she saw his car, a Lamborghini, she became interested in him. Only someone with much money, more money than a first lieutenant in the American Army Chemical Corps earned, could afford such an auto.

She began dating him. She recognized very quickly that he had little experience with women and had no confidence. She seduced him quickly and was not surprised to find him little better than impotent. He could not withhold his orgasms.

She married him for his money. A girl friend of her older sister had married and divorced an American major and lived now in Munich like a princess.

Ilka decided to do the same with Robert. That was eight years before. Now she wanted her reward.

The football game caught her ear. It was in the final moments. She turned up the volume and listened as Southern California scored a touchdown and won the game.

She hoped the loss would not put Robert in a bad mood. Recently he had been moodier than usual. No matter, tonight she had to tell him about the divorce.

3.

Fear drove Hencill's heart. It raced in his breast like a propeller gone wild. Pacing quickly back and forth in the bar he fought down panic. The past year he had watched coolly, almost as a third person, while he lost bet after bet, the figures in his bank account plummeting toward a row of zeroes. Now he was broke.

The baseball playoffs had begun, the World Series was upcoming, the entire pro football season spread before him, and he was broke. He had achieved the gambler's nightmare: he had lost his stake and was out of action. He was an alcoholic without a drink, with the fear that this horrible thirst would go on and on and never be quenched.

He tried to think positively. He felt relief that no one knew he was broke. That could be a big help in getting a new stake. The thought momentarily occurred to him that if he gave up gambling and made certain other temporary financial adjustments, he could continue living a comfortable life. He dismissed it.

He could not quit gambling. He had no desire to quit. What did people do who didn't gamble? Where did they find excitement? Besides, his problem was not gambling, but losing, indiscriminately gambling large sums of money.

That's why he had gone broke! He had stopped betting the good bet. Bet the good bet and he'd get his money back. Gambling was not his problem. Losing was his problem.

It hadn't always been that way. In the beginning he often had won. Somewhere along the way he had lost the winning habit. But he had won some big ones.

Baseball was his best game, a sport he consistently had beaten. He never talked about it, but he had been a very good high-school player himself. A little bit taller and he would have played varsity. He put it out of his mind. It did no good to think of past hurts.

He walked to the bar, went behind it, picked up a Scotch bottle and a glass, and then took a seat at the front of the bar. He poured a double shot of whiskey into the glass and took a sip. It burned his throat and made him feel alert.

He needed a stake to make one bet to get started on a comeback. It had taken him eight years to go broke, to tap out. He wasn't going to spend eight years getting it back. One big bet of five or six hundred thousand dollars to get him going again.

Where could he get the money? His house and property would be worth that much. Involuntarily he shuddered with distaste at the thought of the formalities of a mortgage: the questions, asked and unasked, it would raise, the embarrassment. But it was certain money. He'd think about it.

He dropped off the bar stool and walked to the window and

looked down at the garden. Uncle Fred was another possibility. Fred was his father's older brother. He and Hencill were the surviving members of the family. The old man was rich as Midas and lived in a twenty-one-room mansion in Santa Monica. The problem was they weren't very close and Uncle Fred was a meddler. If he went to him for money he'd better have a good reason and proof of the reason.

He turned from the window. How else could he get money? The easiest way would be to embezzle it. He was president of a company which the previous year had grossed one hundred twenty-seven million dollars. Getting a bundle of cash through the company would be no great problem. Doctor's Prescriptions was a leading American supplier of medicines to South and Central America, and the firm had paid its shares of bribes. It wouldn't be the first time he requested the bank to fill a suitcase for him with hundred-dollar bills. The last time he had gotten two hundred fifty thousand dollars for a payoff in Argentina. And he had gotten four hundred thousand dollars for a payoff in Chile after Allende's government had been toppled. American firms had rushed to regain their former markets. The competition in medicines was ferocious and Doctor's Prescriptions had paid large bribes.

There were no revolutions now. He'd have to find another excuse. A bigger one, even, because he wanted more than four hundred thousand dollars.

The California legislature was debating a law that would make it a criminal offense for a California firm to make a payoff, kickback, or bribe. Well, he'd tell the bank he needed one big sum of money to beat the new law, to prepay several years of bribes. He'd bet some companies were doing just that.

How much could he get? Six hundred thousand was within reason. It would have to be covered with a company check and resolutions mandated by his board of directors specified that the treasurer countersign any check over fifty thousand dollars. He shrugged nonchalantly. Forgery was no worse than embezzlement. He'd simply sign the treasurer's name. "And if I personally bring the check in," Hencill said aloud, "no one will even look at it."

He walked back to the bar. He felt loose. If he thought about it, it might have occurred to him that he was feeling the freedom of the damned. The impending disaster of being broke, going broke, had hung over him for months, weighing him down. Now it was done and the emotional load had been lifted.

He had three sure sources of money. Which one he would tap could be determined later. First, he had to decide on the bet.

His mind quickly reviewed the possibilities. The Dodgers would be in the Series for sure. And he thought the Senators would beat the Angels. But if they didn't, and the Angels met the Dodgers, he'd bet the Dodgers. He wouldn't get great odds. But by betting at least half a million, he'd win back a quarter million.

What if the Senators got in the Series? That was another question. He might bet them. He'd like to bet them. They were an expansion team, formed only two years earlier. The odds on them as a Series team would be phenomenal. If they upset the Angels in the playoffs, they'd go into the Series a two-to-one underdog. He clenched his fists and shook them in front of him. A half million at two to one . . . a million dollars! *That* was maximum action, pal. It was an exhilarating thought, and he couldn't stop himself from laughing.

He walked to the Dodger poster and looked again at the team. Could the Senators beat them? The Dodgers were a superteam, but the Senators were a miracle team. They had gone with youth and had won. They were like the Miracle Mets of 1969. He felt it. But did he feel it enough to bet five or six hundred thousand dollars?

He returned to the bar for another Scotch. Better not, he told himself. Not if he was going to fly to Vegas. Ilka would be home soon and she wanted to go. So did he. He had to think about teams and odds. To do that there was no better place than Las Vegas.

4.

He took off from Santa Monica airport and headed north for twenty minutes before he banked the plane and flew on a straight eastward course to Las Vegas.

He had learned to fly after his army stint. Ilka liked traveling and flying, which was why she had gone to work for a Wiesbaden travel agency. Hencill once had heard her express admiration for pilots, and it was partly that that had gotten him into the pilot's seat. Later, however, the airplane had proven a great convenience in both his work and the frequent pleasure flights they made to Vegas.

The clear sky over Los Angeles was the aftermath of a huge frontal system and the visibility was perfect. Behind them the sun lowered to the sea, the shadows on the desert floor grew longer. But Hencill did not look at the scenery below. He ran over in his mind the plans to get the six hundred thousand dollars from the bank if he decided to embezzle. He knew exactly which bank officer he could use to arrange the so-called bribe money. George Butts had been a personal friend of his father's. Butts was from the old school, a gentleman who would ask no questions and not bother to verify signatures. Getting the money from the bank would be no problem. Still, for losing his own money he only went broke. For losing embezzled money he went to jail. A mortgage was the safer way.

In Las Vegas he would determine whom to bet the money on. The World Series began Saturday, though the playoffs, if either of them ran the full five games, might not be over until Thursday. He had to start figuring the possibilities now. It had to be done expertly, the way he used to do when he was winning.

Ilka didn't notice the beauty of the changing colors of the desert below them, either. Her mind was on the conversation she absolutely must have with Robert in Las Vegas. She wanted to be home for Christmas. She wanted to ski in the Alps and make love by a fireplace. She had traded most of her youth to this man beside her; now she wanted to collect her money and go home. She did not have much youth left, and she was anxious to begin living it. Her mind sought a way to tell him about the divorce.

It was after six o'clock when they checked into Caesar's Palace. The bellman showed them to their room. Hencill told Ilka to meet him at ten in the cocktail lounge next to the lobby, and hurried out.

His goal was the Horseshoe Betting Parlor. In the rear of the room were four long wooden benches bolted to the floor, each having a seating capacity of six or seven persons. In front of the benches a scoreboard was attached to the wall. Next to it was a TV set tuned to the Dodger–Cub playoff game. Hanging from hooks on the scoreboard were nameplates of college football teams followed by the scores, and at the bottom were nameplates for the four playoff teams. Washington had beaten the Angels four to three.

Next to the scoreboard was a ticker tape machine, which clicked out Saturday night football scores. The scores were posted by a gangly youth wearing Adidas track shoes, Levi's, and a sweatshirt lettered with the name of a Las Vegas college. The boy wore horn-rimmed glasses and had a serious countenance. He looked very much out of place in the Horseshoe Betting Parlor.

There was one person seated on each bench at the end of the room. The one on the fourth bench didn't count. He was an old rummy asleep in a sitting position. He could remain so long as he did not snore.

On the third bench Hencill smoked a cigarette and alternately watched the playoff game and leafed through a sports magazine. The Dodgers were leading five to nothing at the top of the seventh inning. Hencill had already reflected a dozen times that had he bet on the Dodgers instead of Notre Dame he would have been sixty-five thousand dollars richer instead of a hundred thousand poorer.

The magazine he was reading featured a story on one star player from each of the playoff teams. Each had been chosen because the writer believed the player would mean the difference in his team's winning or losing. Hencill skipped the Angel and Cub stars. He read about Elmer Verban, the Washington rookie infielder sensation. Then he read about Roosevelt Chad. The sports statistics he knew; he concentrated on the part about Chad's private life.

There were pictures of the ball player with his mother and two children and one of him with his former wife. There were cuts of old newspaper headlines of the Chads' sensational divorce.

The *Daily News* had printed:

CHADS DECLARED FREE AGENTS

Another paper had written:

ROSIE CALLED OUT AT HOME
EX GETS 500 THOUSAND

The former Mrs. Chad was an actress who, the gossip columnists hinted, had married the innocent young baseball star from Missouri to escape the oblivion of a dead-end film career. She had left him for a nightclub owner. Chad had paid the huge settlement for his wife to relinquish any claim on the children, whom she hadn't wanted anyhow.

Hencill turned his attention to the TV screen. The Dodgers were at bat. The first player singled. The next man was safe on an infield error. The third batter grounded out, moving the base-runner to third. Chad came to bat and rifled the first pitch through the pitcher's box, scoring the runner from third and making the game six to nothing. Hencill bit his lips and thought about his stupid bet on Notre Dame.

He turned a page of the sports magazine. On one side was a portrait of Chad and his mother and two children. Chad's mother was a handsome woman in her middle fifties. It was a good-looking family. The opposite page had an ad for Golden C orange juice, which featured a picture of the Chad family around the breakfast table drinking the advertiser's product. Central casting couldn't have done better.

Hencill got to his feet and walked a few steps to a waste can and dropped the magazine in. He returned to the bench, lit a cigarette, and watched the football scores being posted.

The door opened, letting in the sounds of the street. Hencill looked up and watched the new arrival come to the back of the room. "Hey, Wiener," the man called out, "you givin' any odds on mah Senators?"

The man called Wiener was seated on the first bench. He was in his forties, had thinning black hair, a pencil-thin mustache. He was wearing a yellow sports jacket several sizes too large for his narrow shoulders. He contemplated the newcomer. "You rebel son of a bitch," he said finally, "I wouldn't give you anything."

The rebel let out a shriek of high-pitched laughter. "You scared, boy?" the rebel asked. "You 'fraid mah Senators, mah wannerful Washies, gonna eat up your Disneyland Dollies?" He let out another shriek of laughter and slapped a thigh.

"Your Senators ain't going to win nothing," said Wiener. "It's a goddam miracle they got in the playoffs."

"Whooooeeee," cried the southerner. "Sheeeet. They gonna wipe up California and then they gonna put the blocks to the Dodgers. Boy, they gonna win the World Serious."

"I don't believe that shit," Wiener shot back. "The last Washington to win anything was George, and he can't make the double play anymore."

"The Senators have been in three World Series, won one of them," a third man said, entering the conversation. "In nineteen twenty-four they beat the Giants in seven games. In nineteen twenty-five they lost to the Pirates and in nineteen thirty-three they played the Giants again and lost," the man said, detailing his knowledge. He was alone on the second bench. An old man with long, gray hair, and a mean, thin face. His eyes were sunk deep behind high cheekbones. He wore a worn tan summer jacket made of poplin. The greasy collar covered a frayed white button-down shirt. He looked like an educated man who had surrendered to life, a professional man gone bad. He was chewing gum, his jaws churning furiously.

"I don't believe that," scoffed Wiener.

Hencill did. It was obvious the old guy was a student of baseball.

"And I'll say this," Wiener added, "'if they ain't been in a Series since nineteen thirty-three, they goddam sure are due for one. But I ain't betting on them."

"I wouldn't bet on a World Series," said the old man dogmatically. "They're too easy to fix."

"Get this guy out of here," spat Wiener. "In the other part of town you have to listen to these old farts talk about lost gold mines and over here they try to sell you gambling fixes."

Now the student posting the scores entered the argument. "Gamblers tried fixing the Series in nineteen nineteen and they didn't get away with it because it was obvious to everyone that a lot of players weren't playing their best. Today there is television and the public is even more sophisticated. I don't see how players could intentionally lose four games."

The old man smiled tolerantly. He had the air of a condescending professor talking to a class of dullards.

"No, no, no," he told the student. "You're making it too complicated. Forget about losing four games. In a World Series, games two, three, and four are crucial. Teams which have found themselves down two games to none have come back only six times to win the World Series. Since nineteen twenty-five only two teams down three games to one have come back to win. That was the Yankees against Milwaukee in nineteen fifty-eight, and Detroit against St. Louis in nineteen sixty-eight. And no team down three games to none has ever come back to win."

The old man paused and looked around. The group waited expectantly. He enjoyed the attention.

"The World Series is the easiest event to fix," he went on, "because there are so many chances to lose. No other sport championship has so many games and so many plays. All a man has to do is wait. He has time to overcome his bad luck and time to wait for good luck. And when the right time comes, the man can lose the second game, or the third game, or the fourth game or, if need be, the seventh game."

The old man looked directly at the student. "A gambler does not need to fix four games, he needs to fix only one. But it has to be the right one."

The room was quiet except for the click of the sports telegraph wire. The sneer had left Wiener's face. His cynical eyes were fixed shrewdly on the old man. The rebel chewed thoughtfully on a toothpick. The student fidgeted with his glasses. As the old man continued his theory, Hencill stared intently at the back of his neck.

"In every Series games have been won by a single player. Some have done it with their bat. Reggie Jackson, Carlton Fisk, Mantle, and Mazerouski. The list is long. Other players have won games with their glove. Graig Nettles, Brooks Robinson, and Bobby Richardson. This, too, is a long list."

The old man bent forward on the bench. His voice became low and confidential. "And then there are the players who fail. The ones who, in a critical situation, misplay a pop fly, throw slightly off base, are slow getting the jump on a ball, are late throwing out a runner, drop a throw, lose an outfield fly, strike out to kill a rally, miss a hit-and-run sign, break slowly or stumble and are thrown out trying to steal a base, hit into a double play, take a pitch they can hit well, swing at one they cannot."

A look of self-satisfaction appeared on the old man's face. "There are many ways to lose a game and players lose games all the time. In every World Series."

"But those players are what the sportswriters call goats," the student argued. "Are you saying they're really losing games intentionally, that they're throwing the World Series?"

"Not at all." A smile appeared on the old man's thin lips. "That's my whole point. Don't you see, how do you know which player is just a goat, and which player is losing the World Series?"

The old man got to his feet. He looked around the group, into each of their faces. Wiener stared at the floor. The rebel nodded his head slowly. The student was deep in thought. Hencill's face had colored with excitement.

"To fix a World Series," the old man continued, "all you need is just *one* player to be on your side for just *one* play, to interrupt the rhythm or to reverse the momentum, of just *one* game. . . . And the deed is done."

The old man turned and walked out.

Hencill's heart was pounding. Excitement forced up his blood pressure and a sharp pain shot through his torso. He got up from the bench. Dizziness struck him. He steadied himself on the seat back. He took a deep breath and started for the door. He turned suddenly and walked back to the wire basket where he had dropped the sports magazine. He pulled the pages out until he found the one with the feature story on Roosevelt Chad. He stuffed it into his coat pocket and headed for the door.

5·

At nine o'clock, an hour before she was to meet her husband, Ilka emerged from the elevator and walked through the lobby of Caesar's Palace. She was dressed in a St. Laurent black satin jumpsuit. The gold zipper that closed the front was pulled down suggestively, leaving open enough suit to reveal the absence of a bra and the beginning of the roundness of her breasts. Her blond hair and pale complexion contrasted brilliantly with the suit. Within a minute every man in the lobby had turned.

Two men, traveling companions from Chicago, registering at the desk, stared at her. The clerk and the bellman momentarily neglected their duties to join in. All four wordlessly watched Ilka walk by. When she had passed they exchanged wistful looks. One of the men sighed. "Yes," he said, the meaning of the word clear only to him.

Ilka went into the lounge for a drink. To discourage passes from men on the make, she sat at a table rather than at the bar. A waitress approached her.

"I drink a sherry while I wait for my husband." Ilka told her in a voice that she hoped carried to two men at the bar who were eyeing her. "A dry sherry. No ice, please."

In *Amerika* you always had to say, "No ice, please." *Die Amerikaner* put ice in everything. *Die Amerikaner* couldn't stand to taste things. They liked to swallow and to eat but they couldn't stand flavors and tastes. They were all fat and hadn't even had any pleasure to show for it.

The two men at the bar continued to stare at her. The waitress brought the sherry and Ilka said thank you. She took a sip. It was too cold. They must keep it in the freezer, she thought. She shrugged. This, too, was coming to an end.

She became aware again of her purpose in Las Vegas. The divorce. To tell Robert it was all over. But how? When? After dinner? Bedtime? She shrugged again. When the time came, she would know. The time would be right and she would instinctively know it. What to say, that was the problem. She could not just simply say at dinner, "Pass the salt; I want a divorce."

She turned over different phrases, different openings. "Darling . . ." Leave out darling. You don't say "darling" to a man when you tell him it's over. "Robert, you know I've been unhappy in the United States." That was no good. He *hadn't* known she was unhappy. All he knew was pharmaceutics and games.

It would be better, she reasoned, to lead him into the conversation, to get him to talk. She couldn't stand to have him just sit there with that ridiculous smile covering his emotions, staring at her while she babbled away. "Robert, I've decided to go home."

Ah, that was it. She would say that and stop, and let it dangle. Then he'd have to ask when, and then she'd tell him when. And why. Yes. That was it. She liked that idea. "Robert, I've decided to go home." She took in a deep breath and smiled. One of the men at the bar saw her smile and smiled back. For a moment she didn't notice him. When she did, the smile left her face and she looked coldly at him. He stopped smiling and turned back to the bar.

"Robert, I've decided to go home." She said the line over and over to herself, like an actress rehearsing for a play. "Robert, I've decided to go home." At that instant he entered the bar.

He looked around for her and she waved. He came toward her, moving quickly, like an anxious bird. "Have you been here long?" he asked her.

"A half hour," she answered. He sat down beside her. The waitress was there.

"Shall I order a drink," he asked Ilka, "or do you want to go to dinner?"

"Let's go to dinner." The sherry was inferior; when it warmed, she understood why it was served cold.

"Have you paid?" he asked Ilka.

"Two dollars," said the waitress. Hencill gave her three singles.

"Let's eat in the French restaurant," Ilka said as they walked out of the bar.

They ate dinner in silence. Ilka saw that her husband was withdrawn, preoccupied. He sat there, that thin smile on his face, and said nothing. He ate indifferently. Then, he always did. Food, whiskey, sex. They didn't interest him. What did? Only his weekend afternoons in front of the television watching games. How could children's games interest a grown man? She realized suddenly that she had been married eight years to a man she had never really known. I know him no better today, she told herself, than the day I met him on the Rhine. But then she hadn't really wanted to know him.

She ate her dinner, from time to time stealing looks at him. He seemed completely *abwesend*, absent. She wondered what his reaction would be when she asked for the divorce. "Robert, I've decided to go home," ran automatically through her mind. She shrugged.

"What?" he said, seeing her shrug.

"Nothing," she replied, and looked at her plate. The thin smile reappeared on his face. That's what she would see when she told him she was going to divorce him. He would smile the thin smile and say ... what would he say? She caught herself before she shrugged again. In a few hours she would know what he would say.

When they finished coffee he asked: "Do you want to see Dean Martin or Heidi Bruhl?"

"Heidi Bruhl."

"Of course."

She looked quickly at him. The thin smile was on his face. She knew he had no desire to see Heidi Bruhl. She didn't give a damn.

He called for the check, signed it, and they left the dining room.

In the lobby she saw a tall, thickset man approach them. Ilka immediately found him immensely attractive. He wore a pale blue suit with a cream shirt open at the neck. Dark hair pushed out through the open collar. He looked very European.

Ilka glanced at her husband and then she looked again at the man. She was pleased to note that he was eyeing her. She felt desire flood her body. Eight years in *Amerika* had not killed the German woman within her. When she liked a man she did not ignore him or hide her feelings like an American woman. When she knew that a man desired her, and she desired him as well, she told him this with her eyes. She stole a look at her husband. He was paying no attention. She looked at the man and her glance told him she wanted him. Then she saw that he wasn't simply strolling along, but that he actually was coming to meet them! She feared it was because of the inviting look she had given him and she became nervous as he neared.

Robert still hadn't taken any notice of the man. He did, though, when the man spoke. Ilka thought her husband was going to faint right on the spot. She felt light-headed herself.

"Hello, Mr. Rogers," the man said familiarly to her husband. "We're a long way from Nashville."

Confused, Ilka turned to her husband, whose face, after a fleeting moment of panic, had become expressionless again.

This had happened once before in Las Vegas. A stranger had addressed her husband by another name, "Mr. Hawkins." Ilka had expected Robert to tell the man he was mistaken. Instead, he had carried on as if he really were Mr. Hawkins. The incident had puzzled her, even made her apprehensive. Afterward, Robert told her it was a question of mistaken identity and he had gone along with it so as not to embarrass the man in front of his wife. Ilka was not so sure. This time she was — she knew this man and her husband knew each other. She wondered under what circumstances. She saw her husband force a rare, broad smile on his face.

"Hello, Mr. Saccente," he said, and put out his right hand.

Ilka noted the false joviality in Robert's voice.

"I don't believe you've met my wife, Ilka," Hencill said.

Ilka looked at Saccente, who gave her a look a man should not give another man's wife. Again she felt sexual desire. "Hello," Saccente said in a bass voice.

"Hello," she answered, her own voice more sultry than usual.

"Are you just up for the weekend?" Hencill asked.

"Right. How about you?"

"We're going back tomorrow."

Saccente looked at Ilka then at Hencill. "Have time for a drink?" he asked.

Ilka hoped her husband would say yes. But she knew he wouldn't.

"We're late meeting friends," Hencill lied.

"That's a pity," Saccente said.

"But nice running into you," Hencill said.

"My pleasure," Saccente answered. He turned to Ilka. "It was nice to have met you, Mrs. Rogers. I'll look forward to seeing you one day in Nashville."

"Thanks," Ilka said. "I hope so." She felt Robert's hand press her elbow.

"Well, good-bye," Saccente said.

Hencill and Ilka said good-bye and walked away.

In a mirror Ilka saw Saccente watch her. She felt his gaze on her back. It was *ein schönes Gefuhl,* a nice feeling.

"I never saw the guy before in my life," Hencill was saying.

"Really! And right away you call him by his name." Ilka's manner was half amused, half sarcastic. "How clever you are. Now be so clever and tell me who I am when I am Mrs. Rogers?"

"You are the wife of Mr. Rogers," Hencill said, steering her out the door to the taxi stand.

"And who is Mr. Rogers?"

"Me."

The doorman put them into the taxi and gave the driver the destination.

Ilka's curiosity would not rest. "Who was that man?" she insisted.

"A business associate," Hencill answered.

"And he calls you Mr. Rogers?" Ilka's curiosity turned to perplexity.

Her husband didn't answer. He stretched out his short legs and slid deeply into the back seat of the taxi.

"You have other businesses?" Ilka persisted.

"No."

"But you have other names?"

"Yes."

"Do you have more names than Hawkins and Rogers?"

Hencill didn't answer. As Ilka opened her mouth to ask him another question, he looked up at her. "Forget it," he said. "It's none of your business."

Ilka obeyed. It was all very strange.

They were barely on time for Heidi Bruhl. They were just able to order drinks and to begin sipping them before the show began. Hencill played with a weak Scotch and soda and she sipped white German wine.

"How is it?" Hencill asked her, as she took the first sip.

"Too cold," she complained. "In *Amerika,* when something is supposed to be served at room temperature you serve it cool, when something is supposed to be served cool, you get it cold, and when something is supposed to be served cold, it's frozen when you get it. What a country!"

Hencill sipped his drink, smiled his thin smile, said nothing.

Ilka sipped frigid wine and listened to Miss Bruhl's songs. In particular she enjoyed one sung in German. She closed her eyes and listened to the lyrics and pretended she was where she soon would be. *Deutschland.*

She applauded very hard when the show ended.

"Shall we go into the casino?" Hencill asked.

All evening she sensed his desire to be alone. Now she gave him the chance. "You go. I watch television."

"I won't be long," Hencill promised. "I feel like playing some blackjack."

"I go to the room," Ilka said.

She got the key from the desk and went upstairs.

There was a *TV Guide* atop the set and she looked at the listings. At 2 A.M., there was a Bergman film. She looked at her watch. Only a while to wait.

She turned on the set. Cowbows and Indians were on the screen. She slipped out of the St. Laurent jumpsuit and put on a robe. The television cowboy was now in a saloon and was arguing with his girl friend. Through Ilka's mind ran the line "Robert, I've decided to go home."

She had to tell him when he came up. It will be better to tell him now, she thought. Nighttime is the best time to give people bad news. At night one is tired and resistance is down and bad news has more effect. She wanted her husband to know that it was for real, that her decision was not a recent, wavering one, a decision that could be changed by argument. She had waited eight years for this moment and she wanted him to know it was real and final.

When the Bergman film came on she watched the credits for Bjorn's name. She didn't see it. The encounter with Saccente, plus the tension of waiting to tell her husband about the divorce, made her very desirous of sex. She wished she was in bed with Saccente. Or Bjorn.

The room was cold and she got into bed and pulled the covers over her. "The gott-am air conditioning," she muttered. "We pay one hundred fifty dollars to sleep in the clean air of the desert and we can't open the gott-am windows."

Hencill forsook the gambling room for the bar. He ordered a Coke. He'd had enough gambling and booze for one day. His head ached. "Got any aspirin?" he asked the bartender.

"Righto," he answered. "How many, sir?"

"Three. And a glass of water. No ice." That was Ilka's influence.

He tried not to think of everything he had to do. If he considered the whole campaign he knew he would never be able to make the first march. He must approach one battle at a time. Each one would be harder, but the farther along he plunged, the less chance he would turn back. There would be no turning back once the money was bet. That was the point of no return.

He had decided to embezzle the money. If he was going to fix a World Series he might as well bet the money that was most accessible to him. To mortgage his property would not only be embarrassing but it could raise questions. More important, it would be time consuming and time now was going to be severely limited.

To borrow money from his uncle was also out. The old man meddled too much. He'd make phone calls around the city, stirring up trouble, drawing out the whole process.

Embezzlement was the best way. The money could be gotten easily and paid back easily. Hencill breathed in deeply, held it, then blew out a lungful of air. Once the money, the embezzled money, was bet, the rest would follow no matter how hateful. Once the money was bet he'd have to fix the Series.

An aphorism stuck in his mind. "Desperation is the father of courage." Who said that? he asked himself. Perhaps it was original. It certainly was true.

He spent an hour at the bar sipping Coke and thinking about his scheme. When he left, his headache was worse.

He winced as he entered their suite and heard the television. He absolutely didn't want to talk. He saw Ilka in bed, her back against the headboard, watching television. She put a finger over her lips when he said hello. "It's almost over," she whispered.

He nodded and picked up his pajamas, went into the bathroom, turned on the shower, and closed the door.

He felt better, though not by much, when he came out of the shower. He took two more aspirins and a long drink from the Maalox bottle and went into the bedroom. The set was off and he hoped Ilka was asleep. She wasn't. She was seated in bed reading *Constanze*, a German fashion magazine. "What film was on television?" he asked.

"One by Bergman."

"Good?" He lit a cigarette.

"The commercials ruin it." She closed the magazine and turned to him. "I don't know how you Americans stand these stupid *Werbungen*."

Hencill didn't like being lumped with "you Americans" as if he were one of the mass. But he felt too lousy to take up the point.

He blew out a puff of smoke and walked across the room and looked out the window at nothing. "Spanish sherry. French food, German wine and songs, and a Swedish film. You've had a very European evening."

"Robert, I've decided to go home."

He wasn't prepared for that.

His head hurt, his stomach was upset, he was frightened, and at that moment he felt he didn't owe his wife a goddam thing. She had been home in the spring. Every time she went it cost him at least five thousand dollars. He could afford it before. Now he couldn't. He looked at his wife. Her face had an arrogant expression.

"You can't go," he said bluntly.

Immediately he saw that his answer shocked her. Her mouth opened in a gasp. Her arrogance disappeared.

"Why not?" she demanded. Her surprise turned to scorn.

He fixed a smile on his face and didn't answer.

Her reaction was immediate. Her lips curled back from her teeth. He thought of the expression "bared fangs." She got up from the bed and strode toward him, her eyes cruel and angry. "Why not!"

He did not like her tone of voice. Who did she think she was?

"I'm waiting." Her voice rose, cold and arrogant.

He turned his back to her. Suddenly her hand was on his shoulder and he felt himself being twisted around to her.

"I tell you something, Robert . . ." Her voice was loud and close to his ear. "I *am* going home!" It was a shout.

She was standing close to him, and he looked up at her and hated the scorn he saw in her eyes. He could tell her why she couldn't go. That would scare her to death. And why shouldn't she be frightened? Why should he be frightened alone? She was his wife. She had had eight good years. If he hadn't come along she'd still be selling Rhine tour boat tickets in Wiesbaden. In Beverly Hills she lived like a goddam German queen.

"Do you hear me, Robert? I wait no longer. Why can't I go home?" Her face was twisted with hate. "Answer me! YOU LITTLE BASTARD!"

The taunt slapped him and loosened his final constraint. He felt the anger rise in him. It bubbled and whirled and he felt it rising, forcing its way out. The anxiety, the fear, the frustration, the hopelessness, the anger, the pain, and now, finally, this insult. He stopped trying to hold back. It all came out in a scream. "I'M BROKE! YOU CAN'T GO HOME BECAUSE I CAN'T AFFORD IT! DO YOU UNDERSTAND? I'M BROKE! *VERSTEHST DU, FRAULEIN? ICH HAB' KEIN GELD MEHR! DU KANNST NICHT NACH HAUSE DENN ICH PLEITE GEMACHT HABE!* YOU CAN'T GO HOME BECAUSE I'M BROKE! BROKE! BROKE! BROKE! *PLEITE! PLEITE!* BROKE! *PLEITE!* BROKE! *PLEITE!* BROKE!"

At last it was there in her eyes, the fear he so much wanted to see. Her face paled. The color disappeared like a shadow struck by the sunlight.

He bent forward, gasping for breath. The sickness in his stomach was gone. Now there was a tightness around his chest and he bent forward to breathe. Ilka was close in front of him. He looked up at her. She was shaking her head dumbfoundedly.

"Where . . . ?" She didn't know how to say it. He knew the question she wanted to ask and he answered it for her.

"I lost it gambling."

"Six million dollars!" It was a whisper.

"And more."

She shook her head. "The company?" Her voice began to rise. "The money?" It was a shout now. "The stocks?" She screamed, "EVERYTHING FROM YOUR FATHER?"

He nodded.

For a full thirty seconds she stared at him in disbelief, her mouth open, her head shaking. Then her face registered belief and she let out one long, piercing scream.

He fixed a smile on his face.

She slapped him. She slapped him with the strength of all her fitness and exercising, and all the emotion of her hate and scorn.

His head jerked to one side. She slapped him again and again and again and again.

He was afraid he would cry, so he kept the smile on his face.

"YOU GOTT-AM FOOL. YOU GOTT-AM FOOL. YOU GOTT-AM FOOL." She shouted and struck him and he smiled at her until she was too exhausted to strike him again.

SUNDAY
Six Days before the World Series

"They're really pressing this game like crazy," a bookie in midtown Manhattan reported. "People who usually bet $20 are up to $500. The hundred-dollar guys are betting a thousand."

— A *New York Times* story on betting
for a championship game

6.

They did not sleep. Hencill lay on the bed and smoked one cigarette after another. Ilka sat in a chair facing the window and looked out at the darkness. The stillness of the room was broken occasionally by the muffled sound of footsteps in the carpeted hallway. Once the whine of an emergency vehicle penetrated the tomblike silence.

Hencill's throat was dry and raw from cigarettes. He lit yet another.

Muffled voices came from the hallway. A loud laugh. The voices passed.

"What are we going to do?"

Ilka's voice startled him. He looked at her, her back to him, rigid and straight. He put his feet on the floor. He crushed out a cigarette, lit another. There was only one more left in the pack. "I have a plan," he said at last, "to get back some of the money."

Slowly Ilka turned in the chair and faced him. "How much is 'some'?" she asked quietly. Her face was emotionless.

He did some quick mental calculations. "A million, at least. Probably more. Maybe even a million and a quarter."

Interest flickered in her eyes. "How?"

He blew out a cloud of smoke. "I am going to make a bet."

"With what?"

"I can get half, maybe three-quarters, of a million dollars."

Ilka's mouth dropped open. "Jesus Christ! You are going to bet hundreds and hundreds of thousands of dollars on a gott-am game!"

He nodded. She looked at him for a moment. "If you can get so much money, why do you bet it? Why don't you, for once, just keep it?"

"Because I am borrowing it. I have to pay it back."

"And if you lose?"

"I am not going to lose," he said determinedly.

Ilka laughed. It was not a pretty laugh. She got to her feet. "You tell me you have lost six million dollars betting on games and now you tell me you can't lose. If you can win this, why did you lose the other?"

"Because I was dumb."

"And now you are smart?"

"Desperate is a better word."

She looked closely at him and nodded. "Yes. That is a word I understand."

"Good," he said, "because I need you to help me bet the money."

"Me! Make bets! I think you are crazy out of your mind. What do I know?"

Hencill had already thought it out. He could get rid of $300,000 in Vegas and Los Angeles. He'd bet another $100,000 in New York. The rest he'd have to bet with bookies spread around the country. The time frame was too limited and Ilka would have to help.

"I'll tell you what to know," he told her. "I'm going to send you to four cities. You get off the airplane and take a taxi to an address I'll give you. There you ask for a man whose name I'll tell you. He'll be expecting you. I'll make the necessary phone calls. You hand him the money. It will be in a package."

"How much money?" Ilka interrupted him.

"Fifty thousand dollars."

"In each package!"

"Of course. I can't bet hundreds of thousands of dollars in five-dollar amounts."

"Jesus Christ! What if I'm mugged?"

Hencill sighed. "That unlucky I can't be."

"Don't bet on it," Ilka said bitterly.

"All right," Hencill snapped, closing off the debate. "What's done is done. Now the problem is getting it back."

Ilka nodded vigorous agreement. "I give him the package."

"And he gives you a slip of paper, which is the receipt, the record of the bet. Don't worry. It'll go smoothly. The bookie will know you're my wife. Bookies are nice guys. They ought to be. They're in a business where they rarely lose."

"And that's all I do?"

"Yes. Just don't forget your names. In each city you use a different name."

Ilka's eyes showed puzzlement.

"That man you met tonight," Hencill explained. "Saccente. What did he call you?"

At the mention of Saccente's name a flash of pleasure struck Ilka. Again she saw the dark hair from his chest pushing through his open shirt. For a moment she forgot to answer her husband's question. "Mrs. Rogers," she said finally. "He called me Mrs. Rogers."

"Right. And that's what he'll call you Friday in Nashville when you hand him a package with fifty thousand dollars."

So that was how her husband knew Saccente. "He's a bookie!" she said. "And so was the other man. The one who called you Mr. Hawkins?"

Hencill smiled. "You're catching on."

"And who really is Mr. Rogers? The man I supposedly am married to in Nashville."

"He is the district manager for Doctor's Prescriptions. We paid him sixty thousand dollars last year."

"Does he know you are using his name?"

Hencill laughed. "Hardly. But there is little chance he'll find out."

Ilka shook her head in confusion. "I don't understand the names. Why not your own name?"

"Two reasons. One, if I bet all the money with a single bookie it might draw suspicion to me later. I don't want the Mafia to know about it. Second, a few years back I began to lose a lot of money with Carmichael — he's a big bookie in Los Angeles. I got a veiled hint that I could recoup my losses . . . earn a lot of money . . . by cooperating with the Mafia, going into business with them."

"What kind of business?"

"Drugs. Not medicines. Or not just medicines. But hard drugs as well. They didn't mention specifics. It was just a hint. I can imagine that the Mafia would like very much to gain control of a pharmaceutical company. It would be a perfect cover to import hard drugs into the country, not to mention the laboratory facilities that could be used to manufacture LSD and other drugs.

"So, for a while, I cut down on the amount and frequency of bets I made in Los Angeles. Instead, I began setting up new identities around the country. It was easy to do. I know how the betting system works, and through my salesmen I had built-in identities and credit ratings. I had the great advantage through personnel records and long business relationships to know the men whose names I was using. That minimized the risk of being found out."

"This Mr. Rogers, does he have a German wife?" Ilka asked.

For a moment Hencill didn't make the connection. "No. She's American."

"But that man Saccente will know I'm German."

Hencill waved a hand. "He doesn't know if the real Mrs. Rogers is American or from the moon. And doesn't care. He probably figures you're my girl friend anyhow. No one brings their wife to Las Vegas. All Saccente will be interested in is the money."

Ilka thought her husband was wrong on that. She guessed Saccente might be interested in something else. And she hoped they would have time for it.

Hencill looked at his watch. It was five-thirty. "I'm going down to the lobby. Should I send up some coffee?"

Ilka shook her head. "Just tell me when I do these things."

"I don't know. It depends when the playoffs are over."

"Who do you think plays in the World Series?"

"Los Angeles for sure and, I hope, Washington. The odds will be higher on Washington. That's the team I want to bet on."

"You are sure it is the best team? If it is, why is Los Angeles favored?"

He considered telling her he was going to fix the World Series and then rejected it. "Just take my word for it," he said. "I know Washington will win."

He left the room and went down to buy cigarettes.

Ilka ran a bath and lay in the warm water pondering her future, trying to make a plan. Without a plan, without order in her life, she couldn't exist.

One thing was certain: she had to divorce Robert the moment he won his bet. She had to get her money before he lost it again. And he would lose it again. A lawyer would know how to get the money for her. It occurred to her that she could use her husband's gambling sickness to her advantage. What better reason for divorce? She would get less money now. No matter. She trembled to think of how close she was to getting nothing at all.

What if he didn't win? The thought pierced her optimism and released her German angst. Why was he so sure he would win? What proof did she have that he would? He had lost all this money and now he was telling her quite casually that he would win it back.

He obviously had gone a bit crazy in eight years, and she wondered if she wasn't a bit crazy to believe him. But what were her choices?

She had none.

If he didn't bet, he didn't win and then he was broke for sure. She didn't know how he could win, but if he bet the money there was at least a chance.

Yes, she would carry the money for him. It would be no sacrifice to visit Nashville. She thought of Saccente. He wanted to go to bed with her. Well, she would let him. And with pleasure.

Desire engulfed her and she let her body slide deeper into the warm water. She stroked her body and fantasized about Saccente as she did so. She pictured him making love to her in many positions. She ran her hands over her breasts and between her legs, all the while imagining herself and Saccente making love. She ran the film a long time before her closed eyes, all the while stroking herself. After a while her body shuddered and she relaxed.

They checked out of the hotel early and flew back to Los Angeles.

When they got home Hencill got out of the car and opened the door for Ilka. "Make us a nice dinner. I'll be home about eight o'clock."

Ilka thought he was going to get back in his car. Instead, he turned and walked to the coach house.

On the second floor of the main house was a sitting room. Ilka had converted it to her private use shortly after arriving in Los Angeles. She called it her German room. On the walls were paintings of German landscapes. The chairs and writing desk were heavy pieces that an immigrant German woodworker had made for her.

She sat at the desk and wrote to her mother. She mentioned nothing about the divorce or that she soon would be home.

An hour later her thoughts were interrupted by the sound of voices. She looked out the window and saw Robert and Mrs. Sanders walking from the coach house toward his car. Mrs. Sanders's face was worried. Ilka wondered if Robert had told her about the money. She was certain he had. Ilka was frightened of the woman.

She was sure her little dog had been brutally murdered by Mrs. Sanders. She would never forgive the woman that. The dog had barked, to be sure. And Mrs. Sanders hated noise. But Ilka had not permitted the dachshund she had named Sassy to run free in front of the house.

Mrs. Sanders lived on the front side of the estate. She had planted a large flower garden between her coach house residence and the main building. Once, when the dog was a puppy, it had run into the flower garden, destroying some newly sprouted plants. Also, it had left its waste at the edge of the garden. Mrs. Sanders had been furious. The incident had led to the first open fight between the two women. Mrs. Sanders had kicked the puppy several times. Angrily, Ilka had ordered the woman never to do that again. They had not spoken for days after that.

Afterward, Ilka had a small kennel built for the dog on the swimming pool side of the house. A neighborhood boy walked and fed the pet when she was gone on weekends, and for longer absences she left the dog with Renata. Mrs. Sanders complained that the dog barked when left alone on weekends that Ilka and Hencill spent in Las Vegas. Ilka asked several neighboring estate owners, who said the dog did so occasionally, but it wasn't disturbing.

Once it happened that they went to Las Vegas on Friday and Mrs. Sanders was scheduled to leave on a trip to Minnesota on Saturday. When Ilka returned from Las Vegas the dog was gone.

The neighborhood boy said the dog had been there Saturday afternoon, but was gone on Sunday morning. The boy also told her that Mrs. Sanders had not left on Saturday as she had planned, but on Sunday.

In the middle of the night Ilka had been awakened by the sound of a whining dog. She found Sassy in front of the house, blood coming from its mouth. In the morning her pet was dead.

Ilka asked a vet to do a postmortem on the dog. He had found broken double-edged razor blades and undigested hamburger in the dog's stomach. Enraged and in tears Ilka had searched Mrs. Sanders trash cans. She found four empty blade packages and the wrappings of a pound of hamburger.

For one of the rare times in their marriage Ilka had gone to Robert's office. She charged past his secretary and burst into his suite. He was holding a meeting with the company's marketing and sales managers who quickly excused themselves as Ilka wept hysterically and talked about her murdered dog.

When Mrs. Sanders returned from her trip, Robert gave her a severe tongue lashing.

Besides writing to her mother Ilka wrote several letters to girl friends. In the late afternoon she tried to take a nap, but her mind was too active and she couldn't sleep. She made dinner, and just before eight o'clock her husband came in. His face was pale and the boyish look was gone from it. She wondered where he and Mrs. Sanders had been.

Ilka put his dinner on a tray and carried it into the bar. They spent the evening there watching the playoff games on TV.

Both the Dodgers and Senators won and took leads of two games to none. Monday was a travel day. The playoffs resumed Tuesday, with the Dodgers playing in Chicago and the Senators playing in Anaheim.

TUESDAY
Four Days before the World Series

We get strange letters all the time, threatening our lives. Letters, really scary letters. Spooky, actually. I haven't opened my mail for the last three weeks. I won't until after the Series is over. I don't want to become scared.

—Graig Nettles, New York Yankee third baseman, in an interview

7·

Mrs. Chad had just finished putting breakfast on the table when Roosevelt called from Chicago. The children clamored to talk with him, so she let Camilla use the kitchen phone and sent Billy to use the extension in the study. Mrs. Chad heard Camilla promise to watch the game on television. It began at eight o'clock in Chicago, six o'clock Los Angeles time.

Afterward Mrs. Chad talked a few moments with her son. He was in excellent spirits and confident that the team would end the playoffs that night.

Excitedly, the children ate breakfast and left for school.

Mrs. Chad spent the day as she spent most days. She collected the children's laundry, which she would do later in the day, straightened the house, ate an early lunch, napped, and then went shopping. She was home at two-thirty. The children came home from school at three o'clock and she always had a snack ready for them before they did their homework. They did homework before they watched television or went out to play.

The children arrived on schedule. Mrs. Chad joined in their

snack by eating a peanut butter sandwich with them. Halfway through the meal the telephone rang. Mrs. Chad answered. "Hello," she said cheerfully into the receiver. An equally cheerful female voice came back at her.

"This is Mrs. Norton from Golden C orange juice. Well, not exactly from Golden C. I'm from Burton and Jarston, the advertising firm which represents them. I think our Mister Sieboldt was in charge of the last photography session. Do you remember him?"

Mrs. Chad was not certain what the woman was driving at. She was uncertain if the name of the man who had conducted the last picture session was Sieboldt. But she said, "I think it was him."

"Well, no matter," the voice assured her. "I'm calling to verify the photography session we have scheduled at four-thirty this afternoon in your home."

"Now that I don't know anything about," Mrs. Chad admitted.

There was a pause on the phone. "You weren't expecting us?" Mrs. Norton's voice was filled with puzzlement.

"Not exactly," Mrs. Chad told the advertising woman. "We knew you were coming; we just didn't know when. As a matter of fact, we were talking about it at breakfast a few days ago."

"And no one has telephoned you?" Mrs. Norton persisted.

"Not that I know of." Mrs. Chad chuckled. "Unless they talked to Roosevelt and he forgot about it. Which is possible, because during the playoffs he tends to be that way."

Mrs. Norton's understanding laugh came over the line. "Oh, my," she said, "this is confusing. Can you hold on a moment while I make an inquiry here in the office?"

"Go right ahead," Mrs. Chad said. Mrs. Norton had a nice voice. She probably was a very nice person, Mrs. Chad thought. She put her hand over the receiver and spoke to Camilla. "It's the orange juice people, Camilla. They thought they were supposed to take pictures today."

Camilla's face lit with anticipated joy. "Oh, goody!"

"I said *supposed* to, honey. How can they take pictures without your daddy here?"

Camilla calmed down and a look of disappointment appeared on her face. "But it's so much fun," she moaned.

Mrs. Norton was back on the line. "The mystery is solved, Mrs. Chad. You were not expecting us because no one telephoned to tell you to expect us. It's our fault. If I've disturbed you, I'm sorry."

The woman's voice was filled with concern and regret and Mrs. Chad was quick to assure her that no harm was done. "You haven't bothered us at all."

"Aren't they coming?" Camilla said, her voice filled with disappointment.

"Sssssh," Mrs. Chad shushed her.

"Then if we've not disturbed you, and it's no bother," Mrs. Norton went on, "we'd like to come over as scheduled."

"I certainly wouldn't have any objections," Mrs. Chad said, "but Roosevelt is in Chicago with the team."

"That's no problem," Mrs. Norton assured her. "The contract calls for sessions of the family alone. We use the shots for children's and women's magazines. Mr. Chad would not appear in them anyway."

"You just want the three of us?" Mrs. Chad confirmed.

Camilla began to jump up and down. "Oh, yes, yes, yes, yes," she cried.

"Hush, child!" Mrs. Chad ran a hand affectionately over the girl's head.

"We'll be there in an hour," Mrs. Norton said. "And it'll go much smoother if you keep the neighborhood children away."

Mrs. Chad chuckled. "I know what you mean," she said.

An hour later they arrived. Instead of coming to the front door they came around to the back. From the laundry room Mrs. Chad saw the van come around the drive, which curved to the rear of the house, and stop by the kitchen door. From the driver's side emerged a young man with three cameras strung around his neck. A good-looking woman of Mrs. Chad's age got out of the passenger side.

Mrs. Chad left the laundry room and hurried to the kitchen to greet them. Billy and Camilla were in the living room watching cartoons and she called to them, "They're here, children. Get ready."

The two persons from the advertising agency had seen Mrs. Chad come into the kitchen and they waited at the door for her. The woman Mrs. Chad took to be Mrs. Norton smiled and waved. Mrs. Chad smiled back and then she was at the door.

"How very wonderful of you to let us come over," the woman said. "I'm Mrs. Norton and the photographer is Ed Daniels."

The photographer was young. Mrs. Chad guessed him to be in his late twenties. He had stylishly long brown hair. He wore high-heeled cowboy boots, Levi pants and shirt. When his name was mentioned he gave a quick nod of his head.

"I'm pleased to meet you, Mr. Daniels," Mrs. Chad said, and showed the two into the kitchen.

"Hurray! Hurray!" Camilla and Billy ran into the room.

"Camilla wants to have her picture taken drinking juice from a champagne glass," Billy said, telling on his sister.

"I was just playing," Camilla protested.

"What were you doing before I came?" Mrs. Norton asked.

"We were watching cartoons," Billy answered.

"And you, Mrs. Chad?"

Mrs. Chad laughed. "Doing the laundry."

"Perfect!" cried Mrs. Norton. "Everyone back to what they were doing. Only this time you'll be drinking a golden glass of Golden C orange juice."

Billy held an imaginary glass in his hand. In a falsetto voice he said, "Camilla and Billy Chad always drink orange juice when they watch cartoons."

"Golden C orange juice," Mrs. Norton corrected him. They all laughed except the photographer, who was busy bringing in a case of Golden C orange juice.

"All right, everyone take their places," Mrs. Norton ordered.

"Back to the cartoons," Billy shouted. Laughing, he ran into the living room, his sister chasing after him.

"And I'll be in the laundry room," Mrs. Chad said.

The photographer carried the lights into the kitchen.

"We'll do the children first," Mrs. Norton told him.

"Can I be of any help with them?" Mrs. Chad asked.

"Just go on with your work and don't let us bother you," Mrs. Norton told her. "In fact, it'll be better if the children are alone with us. We've found that they're more natural if no older family members are present."

"Then they can clown around more," Mrs. Chad added chuckling.

"Don't I know it," laughed Mrs. Norton. "I had three myself. Show them a camera and they were a regular circus."

The women smiled in mutual understanding. Mrs. Chad liked the woman — she was so friendly and natural. "Well, I'll be in the laundry room if you need me," she said again.

"We'll get to you next," Mrs. Norton said.

Mrs. Norton positioned the children before the television set while the photographer arranged his lights. When everything was ready, the photographer disappeared into the kitchen. A moment later he returned with a pitcher of orange juice and two glasses.

"Yummy, yummy," Billy shouted.

"Not so fast," Mrs. Norton laughed. "Save the enthusiasm for the photographer."

She filled the glasses and handed one to each child. "Now, when I say the word, I want you to drink all the juice down without stopping. The photographer will be hopping about taking pictures. Don't look at him."

"What's the word you're going to say?" Camilla asked.

"Down the hatch!" yelled Billy and looked quickly toward the door to see if his grandmother heard.

Mrs. Norton laughed. "Okay. That will be the signal. When I say, 'Down the hatch,' you two do just that."

She looked at the photographer to see if he was ready. He nodded his head that he was. "All right, children," Mrs. Norton cautioned. "Get ready." The children raised their glasses. Mrs. Norton moved away from the lights. "Down the hatch!" she cried.

And they did just that.

Mrs. Chad looked up when Mrs. Norton and the photographer came into the laundry room. "Any problems?" she asked.

Mrs. Norton shook her head vigorously. "Perfect. And now for you."

"What do you want me to do?" Mrs. Chad asked.

"Well." Mrs. Norton put her chin in her right hand and looked inquiringly around the room. "Let's do this. You stand by the open washer. Like you're getting ready to do a load of the children's clothing. You're taking a break, drinking a glass of orange juice." She turned to the photographer. "How about that?"

He shrugged indifferently. "Whatever."

Mrs. Chad thought that Mrs. Norton gave the photographer a look of disapproval. He seemed a queer sort. She accepted the glass of orange juice offered her by Mrs. Norton.

"You've got to drink it all down," Mrs. Norton warned. "Can you do that?"

"That's all I have to do?"

"Just drink it all," Mrs. Norton emphasized.

The cameraman snapped on the kleig lights. Mrs. Chad blinked her eyes. "You'll get used to it in a second," Mrs. Norton assured her.

"I'm all right," Mrs. Chad said.

"Are we ready?" said Mrs. Norton.

The photographer nodded his head.

"Ready," said Mrs. Chad.

"All right," laughed Mrs. Norton. "Down the hatch."

Mrs. Chad laughed at the advertising woman's using Billy's remark, tipped the glass to her mouth, and drank the juice slowly. All the while, the photographer moved about the room taking pictures from different angles.

"Well, it's done," exclaimed Mrs. Norton after the glass was empty.

"Is that all?" asked Mrs. Chad.

"That's it," said Mrs. Norton. "Just a few questions. We can do that at the kitchen table while the cameraman carries the equipment out."

The two women went into the kitchen and sat down at the kitchen table. Mrs. Chad yawned. "Excuse me," she smiled. "The excitement is making me sleepy."

"It's the drug," said Mrs. Norton.

"The what?" asked Mrs. Chad.

"The drug," repeated Mrs. Norton. "You'll be all right. We've drugged you. It won't hurt."

Mrs. Chad half rose in the chair. Her eyes fluttered and she sank back, missing the chair and falling to the floor. Immediately the photographer was at the doorway. "What's wrong?" he hissed.

The woman who called herself Mrs. Norton got up from the table. "She's out."

"Let's get the hell out of here," the photographer said anxiously.

It was in the betting parlor that Hencill had gotten the idea to kidnap the family. He had believed the old man's argument about the World Series. Not that a World Series had been fixed before, but that it was possible to do so by using one key player. Hencill had chosen Roosevelt Chad.

The next step was to find a means of getting the player's cooperation. Bribery was ridiculous. Threats equally so. Kidnapping was the only way. Besides coercing the player, it put a strong restraint on him from going to the police or contacting the baseball commissioner. Both steps would lead to news coverage and that, the player must know, would be fatal to them all.

Once deciding to carry out the kidnapping, Hencill was faced with a group of logistical problems. With two university degrees (chemistry at Cal Tech and a masters in business administration at Stanford) and honors in both, Hencill approached the kidnapping in a logical and disciplined manner, reviewing the possibilities open to him and selecting those that presented the greatest security.

He first gave thought to kidnapping just one of the children. To do so would greatly simplify the housekeeping problem of hiding the victim away. But also it would leave behind two more persons (besides Chad) who would know of the crime, increasing the risk that it could become news.

Once he decided to take both of the children, it followed that he had to take Mrs. Chad as well. Her inclusion was actually an advantage if not a necessity. It would give Chad a feeling of security to know his mother was with the children. (Hencill didn't want the man to feel everything was lost and call the police.) And it certainly would calm the children.

The housekeeping problem was settled early in his thinking. The Chads would be held captive in the coach house and Mrs. Helen Sanders would be their warder. She knew how to administer drugs, and from the germination of the idea he planned to drug the family. That was his profession and he knew how it could be done safely and easily.

He knew Helen would object. There was even the possibility she would not go along. He had no way to force her. But he knew she was vulnerable when her financial security was threatened. He thought he could use this successfully.

The coach house would be a perfect hideout. The downstairs, which once had been a three-car garage, still retained its spaciousness. When Mrs. Sanders remodeled the building she had not permitted the architect to divide the floor space. The garage itself became one huge living–dining room area with a fireplace at one end, the kitchen at the other. Next to the kitchen there was a bath, then stairs leading to the second floor, where Mrs. Sanders had a sitting room, a bedroom, and a second bath.

The house was well insulated and set back from the street, which was sparsely traveled. The afternoon before the kidnapping, Monday, Hencill had two carpenters install metal shutters on the inside of the windows, explaining that he feared burglars. Then, with Mrs. Sanders's help he'd put up heavy draperies.

The following day, before they drove to the Chad house, Hencill stood on the street while Mrs. Sanders turned the television in the coach house to full volume. He hadn't heard a sound.

The final problem had been when and where should the kidnappings take place. He considered and rejected the idea of separate kidnappings. That is, getting the children going to or from school, or devising a plan that called them out of classes and, then, earlier or later, kidnapping Mrs. Chad from the home.

The best plan, Hencill knew, would be the simplest plan, and the simplest was to get the family together.

Getting Chad's address and phone number was no problem. A celebrity service, to which Hencill had access because of the Doctor's Prescriptions advertising accounts, provided Chad's address. To be safe, Hencill asked also for the addresses of several other baseball players, two football players, and some film stars. He wasn't overly concerned. He didn't expect the kidnapping to be made public.

He went twice to look at the house. The first time was Sunday afternoon, after returning from Las Vegas. He took Mrs. Sanders with him. Twice they drove by the house. It was ideally situated for a kidnapping. It was enclosed on three sides by a high U-shaped wall. Behind the wall was a golf course. Only the front of the house was exposed. And that was compensated for by the driveway, which hooked around the back of the house. From there one could enter or leave the house and not be seen from the street. The wall prevented anyone else from watching. Hencill reflected that if Chad had bought the house for privacy, he certainly had succeeded.

On Monday Hencill kept a close eye on the neighborhood, taking great care not to be conspicuous. He saw the school bus drop the children off shortly before three o'clock. That determined the time when he would put his plan into motion.

One part of the plan was definite from the beginning. It had to take place Tuesday while Chad was playing in Chicago. Hencill planned to use the orange juice advertisement as a ruse for entry and at three o'clock it would be too late for Mrs. Chad to verify the story with her son, though Hencill doubted if Mrs. Chad would have the sophistication to see through the ruse. And using the picture-taking session as a cover prevented interruption by friends or neighbors. Finally, he and Mrs. Sanders could disguise themselves against the casual sidewalk passerby who might glance at them as they entered or departed the driveway.

It was a good plan. If any step went wrong they could retreat. Only the last step was irrevocable: drugging the family and carrying them to the van. There would be no retreat or explanation after that point.

Mrs. Sanders stood at the corner of the house and watched down the driveway as Hencill carried out the children. First he brought Camilla and then Billy and laid them gently on sleeping bags in the back of the van.

"Do you need any help with Mrs. Chad?" Mrs. Sanders asked him.

"Just keep your eyes on the street," he said tensely.

A moment later he returned carrying Mrs. Chad in a fireman's hold. "All right," he said anxiously when he got her in the van and had closed the doors.

"Have you got everything?" Mrs. Sanders asked.

"Everything," he snapped. "I double-checked."

"Let me look," said Mrs. Sanders.

"Then let's get the hell out of here," Hencill said.

Once out of the neighborhood it was all right. They rode silently back to the coach house. "Is Ilka home?" asked Mrs. Sanders as they came up the drive.

"No."

"And she knows nothing about this?" Mrs. Sanders jerked her head toward the rear of the van.

"Nothing. She knows I'm going to make the bets. I had to tell her that. She has to carry money for me."

"She'll be good at that," Mrs. Sanders said bitterly. "She's carried enough of your money to Europe. The German bitch."

Mrs. Sanders was born Helen Bjorklund in Bingen, Minnesota, population 728. When she was nine years old a tornado struck the town. Seventeen persons were killed, among them her mother, whom she loved very much, and her alcoholic father, whom she detested. Helen was in school when it happened.

Her maternal grandmother, a woman of nearly seventy, took her in and raised her. The old woman lived on a small acreage ten miles out of town. Scandinavians, especially those of rural stock, develop quickly, and at age fourteen Helen was a well-built, exceptionally pretty girl. In the summer of her fourteenth year a young man working the harvest fields was attracted to Helen and, after dating her several times, one night raped her behind Grandma's barn. It was not a violent act. He wanted her. She really didn't mind if he had her, but she didn't think they should. She struggled hard for a few minutes and then let the boy have his way. Nothing much happened that she didn't expect. Farm girls learn early that babies aren't brought by storks.

Much to the boy's surprise Helen made another date with him. They met behind the barn each night until the harvest ended. Not once did she enjoy sex. She did it for security, to overcome loneliness. She liked having a boy friend.

This sort of thing is hard to hush up in small towns and she got a reputation for being tough and wild. This clouded the fact that she had always been a hardworking, responsible girl.

After graduation from high school she went to Los Angeles to live with an aunt. The woman once had aspirations to be an actress and she encouraged Helen, with her good looks and healthy figure, to give it a try. Helen took acting classes during the day and worked nights as a carhop. Six months later she met at the school a handsome actor named Gary Sanders. As an actor, he had his looks as his talent. But Helen adored him. She fell in love and enjoyed sex for the only time in her life.

She moved in with the actor and to push his career she sacrificed her own. She took a day job filling medicine bottles at Doctor's Prescriptions.

A short while later she married Sanders and six months thereafter had his baby. He was having no success as an actor so she went back to Doctor's Prescriptions soon after the child, a boy, was born.

One day, about a year later, she returned home from work to discover that Sanders had run off with their teenage baby-sitter. They had taken her son with them. She never saw them again. Stunned, she stayed in her apartment for days, not going out, sleeping very little and eating not at all.

Helen did not mind so much losing the baby, but it almost killed her to lose her husband. Indeed, she considered suicide. She might have tried it had not a girl who worked with her at the lab grown worried by her absence and stopped by to see her. The girl took Helen in to live with her and explained to the supervisor at work what had happened, and Helen got back her job.

The news of her tragedy spread quickly around the plant. A month later Helen was called to the office of Robert Hencill, Sr., the president of the company. He explained that several months earlier his wife had died giving birth to their first child. He was looking for a nurse-housekeeper. Would Mrs. Sanders be interested?

She was, and for the third time in her life someone took her in.

Within six months Hencill, Sr., was sleeping with her, even though he was twenty years older than she.

She never *lived* with him. He was too old-fashioned for that. And for her part, she had had enough of close relationships with men. She had been knocked around enough trying unsuccessfully to get emotional security, now she concentrated on financial security. She had her own small apartment over the coach house. Later she had the entire building remodeled.

They went their own ways. His way was mostly work. He had just founded the company a few years before and devoted most of his time to making it prosper.

Her way was taking care of the house. For a girl raised on a Minnesota farm, taking care of Hencill, Sr., his son, and their home was an easy job.

Hencill, Sr., was a tiny man who worked too hard and had little time for her and even less for his son. She sometimes felt sorry for the boy. She didn't dislike him, she just had no deep feeling for him. Nor had she had for her own child. She just wasn't the motherly type.

She was considerate to the boy, but she had no affection for him. It seemed that the only one who wanted the boy was his mother, and she had died a few minutes after he was born.

As Mrs. Sanders grew older, her drive for financial security became almost psychopathic. She made sure Hencill, Sr., took care of her in his will. She pressed him so relentlessly that they had one of their rare fights. He said she was "ghoulish, hard and unfeeling." She agreed that she was hard. She'd had a hard life.

She won her demands: rent-free use of the coach house for her lifetime, and an annuity providing a twenty-five-thousand-dollar-a-year income, with cost-of-living increases. Hencill, Sr., made one stipulation to which she had agreed, but which now had come back to haunt her. He wanted the stock for her annuity left under his son's control. This was for voting purposes.

Up until this year there had been no problems. But when Hencill's own money had run out, he invaded Mrs. Sanders's trust without her authority. He used the money to cover lost bets and to make new ones. It was a trust without accounting and soon there was nothing to account anyhow.

It was because her very way of life was at stake that she agreed to help in the mad plan to fix the World Series. She was fifty-three years old and had lived more than half her life in the coach house. It was her home. And she was willing to do a great deal to save it, and her annuity, which she had justly earned.

The kidnapping itself did not bother her. She had survived one herself when her husband stole her child. She had survived an alcoholic father, the early death of her beloved mother, and rape.

She would survive this as well. But her trust in Robert was gone forever. She didn't want just to live rent-free anymore in the coach house. Just as she had with his father, she drove a hard bargain with him. She wanted to own the coach house and made him agree to deed it over to her and to give her fifty thousand dollars of his winnings as the price for her participation. Finally, she made him agree to relinquish control of the stock in her annuity.

Even after he agreed to all that, she didn't feel secure. She would be exposed to a kidnapping charge; she would be seen by Chad's family, who would never forget her face, her voice. She mused on how soft men were. When Hencill explained his desperate plan, he had emphasized, fearing her reaction, that there would be no need to harm any of the Chads. She wasn't so sure, but that didn't worry her. The Chads' future would be under her control. What did worry her was that her future really wasn't in Robert's hands, but in Roosevelt Chad's. And she was not sure the ball player would lose the Series. Or even could.

8.

In Chicago, at the end of six innings, the Cubs led the Dodgers two to zip. But Chad knew his team was going to win. He didn't know how, or who was going to do what. He knew only that the Dodgers were going to win.

It had been a fast game. The Cubs had gotten their two runs on an error and a homer. Otherwise, the game had sped by.

The Dodgers didn't score in the seventh and neither did the Cubs. In the eighth the Dodgers' leadoff man got on, and Chad felt this would be it. The next two men were out, and Chad came to bat. He thought he might hit one out. No one was more surprised than he when, on a one-ball, two-strike count, he swung at a hanging curve ball . . . and missed. He was out and the side was retired.

In the ninth the Dodgers' leadoff man walked, the next man singled, the third batter homered, and that was it.

In the bottom of the ninth the Cubs went down in order. The Dodgers were the National League champions.

The team was more interested in getting back to Los Angeles than in celebrating a victory that none of them had doubted would be theirs. The press, too, was unexcited, and the postgame interviews were quickly over.

On the flight back to Los Angeles, the pilot announced that the Angels had defeated the Senators in the third game of that playoff.

The Dodger plane landed at Los Angeles International at 12:30

A.M. Several hundred fans showed up to cheer, and Chad was called upon to say a few words.

At a quarter of two, Roosevelt Chad pulled in his driveway. He parked his Volkswagen in the garage and entered the house through the back door.

He found the kidnap note when he came into the kitchen. It was on the breakfast table, a plain piece of white paper with a typed message.

Mr. Chad,
 Your children and mother are unharmed. If you are the intelligent and sensible man the press describes you to be, your family will be returned to you. UNDER NO CIRCUMSTANCES contact anyone.

The note was unsigned. Chad knew at once that it was no hoax. However, the evilness of the act made his mind reject the truth.

"Camilla! Billy!" He dropped the note on the table and ran from the kitchen, up the stairs to the two bedrooms his children occupied at the rear of the house. Camilla's room was neat, orderly . . . and empty. Billy's room, the room of a boy, slightly disorderly in spite of his grandmother's care, was also empty.

Chad turned and ran down the corridor to his mother's room. It was closed. He rapped on the door. "Mother!" His voice broke. "Mother!"

He pushed open the door and went into the empty room. His face twisted as he fought back the tears. The pain was in his throat, at the pit of it, in the hollow. He felt the tears force through his eyes. He dropped to his knees and pressed his head onto his mother's pillow and wept.

He stayed a long time kneeling on the floor, his head buried in the pillow, his tears dampening it. He did not know how long he was there before he heard the telephone ring. He did not run to answer. He knew who it was, and he knew the phone would ring until he answered it.

He got slowly to his feet, watching the telephone, listening to it ring time after time. He picked it up and carried it to his mother's bed and sat down. He lifted the receiver and put it to his ear. His body shuddered and the sob, which sometimes comes after the weeping has stopped, caught momentarily in his throat. "Please, give me back my family," he said quietly.

There was a pause and through the receiver he heard a gasp of surprise. After the pause a voice said, "I want you to listen very closely . . ."

"How much do you want?" Chad cut him off.

"No money," the voice said. "I don't want money. I'm making a bet, a very big bet on the Series."

"I can't do that," Chad whispered, understanding immediately. "Look, I can raise a half-million dollars. Cash. I can get it for you as soon as the banks open."

"Forget money," the voice said. "Not for a million dollars. Lose the Series and you get your family back."

"I can't. What you want is impossible."

The voice on the phone told him it was not. In a rushed, anxious tone the voice told him how it was possible to lose a World Series.

Chad did not know that what he was hearing was the repetition of a theory dreamed up by a wizened old man in a Las Vegas betting parlor. But he knew that what he heard had some sense to it. He recognized the logic in the argument of dropped fly balls, booted double plays, men picked off base, and offensive failures in crucial situations. He didn't think it had ever been done, but he would have to admit that it could be done. With a little luck and good timing, what the voice told him to do was possible. But he didn't think it was possible for him to do it.

"I can't throw a baseball game," Chad said tonelessly. The enormity of the act weighed him down.

"You may not have to," said the voice encouragingly. "I think Washington is going to be your opponent and they're not without chances to beat you fair and square."

Chad wanted to say that he wouldn't throw a game. He wanted to say many other things. He wanted to shout his rage at the man. He knew that wouldn't help his family. And he didn't want further to upset the man, who he suspected was having trouble with his own fears and nervousness. So he said, "I'll think about it."

"Good, good." The voice relaxed. "I'm not a monster. But I'm desperate for money." The voice stopped suddenly, and Chad suspected the man had said more than he wanted. "I'm not a monster," the voice said again. "Your family is unharmed. I'll prove it."

And then Chad's mother was on the phone. "Are you all right, Roosevelt?" Her voice was strong and confident.

He took a deep breath. The tension began to flow from him. He almost wanted to laugh. How like his mother, the hostage of a kidnapper, to be concerned about him rather than herself.

"Mother, Mother, Mother," he said, shaking his head, letting himself laugh now with the joy of hearing her voice. "Oh, Mother, I love you and I am all right."

"Don't be frightened for us, Roosevelt. They didn't hurt us."

The kidnapper's voice was back on the line. He understood that Chad was frightened for his family. Well, he had his fears as well. His voice was tense again. He talked about the police finding out and the press and the Mafia finding out from the police and the gamblers refusing to take bets on the Series. "God knows I don't want to kill your family," the voice was saying, "but if this gets out you'll never see them again."

The line went dead. Chad shook with fear.

For a moment he remained on his mother's bed. When he heard the hallway clock chime two-thirty he got up and went downstairs to the study. From a writing desk he took pen and paper and began writing down everything he could remember from the telephone conversation.

It was nearly 3 A.M. when he finished the notes. He had been home little more than an hour, yet it seemed he had been there the whole night.

He had decided to call John Evans, the director of the FBI. He once had been placed next to Evans at a White House sports award dinner hosted by the President. Chad knew that he needed help and the FBI seemed the logical choice. He felt he could telephone

John Evans with the assurance that his call wouldn't put the kidnapping on the front page of every paper in the country. He had to have help. He might never hear again from the kidnapper. Why should the man call again? He had made his demand. Lose the World Series, or else. His family safely returned in exchange for losing.

Helplessness weakened Chad. Maybe the kidnapper had left a clue. You just couldn't kidnap three persons and not leave a clue. There was always a clue. At least in the television police series. He placed a call to John Evans. It was 3 A.M. Pacific Standard Time, 6 A.M. on the East Coast.

He identified himself to an FBI operator and requested to speak to John Evans. The operator gave no hint that she recognized the name Roosevelt Chad. She put him on hold while she transferred the call to a duty officer.

The duty officer was young and professional. He knew who Chad was but wanted to verify that he really was speaking to the Dodger shortstop. Chad hung up and waited for the duty officer to get his unlisted number from telephone company records and to call him back.

Once Chad's identity was proved, the duty officer put him on hold while he telephoned the director. A moment later Chad was speaking to John Evans.

WEDNESDAY
Three Days before the World Series

Just how much money is wagered yearly [on sporting events] is difficult to determine. Informed sources estimate as much as $500 billion, although a more reasonable figure of approximately $50 billion is accepted.

— *The Los Angeles Times,* February 9, 1978

9.

John Evans had been appointed interim director of the FBI after what the press called the Scandals of 23, which was the trial of twenty-three special agents on charges ranging from breaking and entering to misappropriation of government property.

Evans's appointment was temporary because the Congress was working on an FBI charter to establish once and for all boundaries of the Bureau.

Some editorial writers likened the appointment of John Evans to the elevation of Gerald Ford to the presidency. Both men found themselves in jobs they had never sought and probably in their wildest dreams had never lusted after. A further parallel could be made, and some editorial writers did so, that both men were selected because of their acceptability to many diverse factions.

There were those who doubted Evans's intellectual qualities for the job. He was not an abstract thinker. He was a checker, not a chess, player. His previous job as chief of recruiting required that he be a man of reasonable insight into other men's motivations, and that he have an abundance of charm and persuasion. He had been lifelong in the Bureau and knew it well. He had done nothing brilliant, but also he had offended no one. He was a mediocrity, but there are times when a quiet absence of talent is preferable to unsettling brilliance. Until the Chad kidnapping came along, it could be said that Evans was the right man at the right time. He wanted a smooth, short directorship. At the end, there would be a ceremony in the Rose Garden and a letter of commendation, perhaps even a plaque from the hands of the President himself.

In his term of office John Evans wanted no Hearsts or Hoffas. He wanted no PLO, SLA, or IRA. The call from Roosevelt Chad absolutely stunned him. Under no circumstances was the kidnapping to find its way into the press. If that happened, and the Chad family later were found dead, the responsibility would fall upon him. He did not want that stigma to carry into retirement.

He debated whether to contact his chief of the Missing Persons Section or Al Frazzini, the chief of the Organized Crime Section. He decided on the latter.

The two met in Evans's office at eight o'clock. Frazzini made notes as the FBI chief played a recording of his call from the baseball player. When it was over he switched off the tape and looked expectantly at Frazzini.

Frazzini nodded his head approvingly. "Chad seemed to handle it pretty well."

"I met him at the President's sports award dinner," Evans said. "He's a very bright guy."

"Well," Frazzini said, "they couldn't have gotten a better player. He can do it all, which means he can lose a game for you a dozen ways."

Frazzini was short, powerfully built, with thick black eyebrows and a balding head. Evans remembered that Frazzini had been a varsity baseball player at the University of Rhode Island. "Would it be advisable to call in the baseball commissioner?" Evans asked.

"Nah," Frazzini scoffed. "You heard Chad. He said he's not throwing any games and that if he thinks he can't perform one hundred percent, he'll take himself out of the lineup. We contact the commissioner, he'll pull Chad out of the lineup right now. It'll be the news story of the year. It could cause the family to be killed and the Series disrupted."

"We don't want that," Evans commented nervously.

"Those guys play under pressure all the time," Frazzini said confidently. "They're pros. They walk on the field, they turn off the world. Their parents die or the wife runs off with a rock musician, they go out there and play like champions. These guys have an instinct for handling pressure that normal people don't have."

"You think one ball player could actually throw a Series, Al, so that no one would know about it?"

"Certainly. He'd need a lot of luck, but it could be done. I'll give you a typical case. Remember the Series the Dodgers lost to the Yankees after taking the first two games? In the third game it seemed every time you looked at the TV the Dodgers had two or three men on base. They should have won by six runs. But they lost. Why? Because Graig Nettles, the Yankee third baseman, made a couple of sensational plays which turned the game around and, as it turned out, the Series.

"The plays he made were so difficult that if he hadn't made them, not one sports writer would have criticized him. So there you are, John; if you were a gambler and had your man playing third base in that situation, you'd have won. And not a soul would have been the wiser."

"A situation like that is unusual, though," Evans pointed out.

"Of course. That's why I said the player would need luck. The average Series game doesn't provide such a good opportunity. I mean, after a Series is over it's easy to go back and say such-and-such a play was the turning point. But that's damn hard to do when the Series is in progress."

Evans pulled a pipe and tobacco from a drawer.

Frazzini twisted his face in thought. "I'll tell you what one player can do in any circumstances, John. He can change the odds. That's why gamblers are always trying to get information about injuries to pro athletes. A quarterback has a fractured finger, a tennis player has a bruised leg, a shortstop has a sore elbow. The gambler's dream is to have this information on a key player and for the bookie not to have it. That's what's happening in this case. The Dodgers are going to be favored to beat either the Angels or the Senators. But if you're a gambler and you compromise Rosie Chad, the odds change drastically."

Evans stared at his desk top for a moment before posing another question. "Wouldn't it be easier for a pitcher to throw a game than an infielder?"

"Nah." Frazzini rejected the idea. "That's barroom talk, John, that the pitcher can walk a guy or groove a pitch, and lose a game. Jesus Christ! Even when they groove pitches for pregame homerun hitting contests most of the balls don't go out. Besides, you walk a guy, groove a pitch, some managers jerk you fast. If you're going to fix the Series with one man, you got to have that man in there for every inning of every game. And that's Rosie Chad. They got the right man."

Evans considered this and nodded his head. "Well, back to the problem of who did it." He began packing tobacco in his pipe.

"Who ever it was did it right. Right ball player, right plan. One phone call. Lose the Series, or else. That's all. No ransom. No drop point. No pickup. No chance to plant marked money. Nothing to trace. No more contact promised. Just hello and good-bye."

"They still have to bet the money."

Frazzini looked at his notepad. "Did Chad say how much?"

"He said they turned down a half-million ransom."

Frazzini found the notation on his pad. "Right. Well, why not, if you're smart enough to think that you can fix a World Series, you ought to be smart enough to make a killing from it."

"How are they going to get that much money down, Al?"

"Not in one bet, that's for sure. They're going to have to spread it around."

"The logistics seem staggering," Evans said, and lit his pipe.

"It won't be easy," Frazzini agreed. "But if they're real gamblers they should know how to do it. You'd have to believe they got that part figured out." Frazzini laughed wryly. "They better have it figured out, because if the Mafia catches them tampering with World

Series betting, they're gonna be much worse off than if we catch them."

"You mean if we catch them, they go to jail, if the mob catches them, they go to the cemetery."

The two men smiled. Frazzini stretched his short legs in front of him. "But a betting list would sure help," he allowed. "If you had a list of every bet, say, over twenty-five thousand dollars, somewhere on that list you might find your kidnappers."

Evans blew out a cloud of pipe smoke. "Is your pipeline into the Mafia good enough to get that kind of list, Al?"

Frazzini sprang nervously to his feet. His jaws twisted and a light went on behind his eyes. His lips formed in a mischievous smile. "Nah. Let's just call the Mafia and ask them for their betting list."

Evans's face reflected uncertainty over what Frazzini meant.

"I mean it, John. And they'd give it to us, too. You just said why. They don't like to be cheated. So, instead of me making concealed inquiries to unreliable sources, why don't I call up Ignazio Apicelli? He gets cooperation from every family in the country. They all trust him."

"And what are you going to say?" Evans asked doubtfully.

Frazzini laughed. "I say, 'Iggie, you dirty crook you, for a couple weeks we're going to work together. Some son of a bitch kidnapped Rosie Chad's family and is putting the muscle on him to throw the World Series. He's got sixty billion lire bet on it, Iggie. That's about a million bucks American. If we let him get away with it, he'll do it again. Next time maybe in the Super Bowl. Know what that means, Iggie? Means he's got his hand in your pocket. Means he's got the combination to your safe. Makes you want to get him, doesn't it, Iggie, pour concrete all over him, send him to the ol' swimmin' hole. We want him too, Iggie. He's violated a federal statute. You won't believe this, Iggie, but kidnapping is against the law. So let's join forces and get these sons of bitches.' "

Evans looked closely at Frazzini. "You really think they'd go along with it?"

"It wouldn't be the first time we did each other a favor." Frazzini sat back down. "But it will have to be done fast. I can telephone him this morning and tell him we'll make a deal. He appoints a representative and we'll appoint one. The two run the case together."

Evans swiveled his chair and looked out the window of his fourth-floor suite. On Pennsylvania Avenue the morning traffic moved swiftly. An airliner with landing gear lowered crossed Evans's view from left to right, gliding downward to National Airport. The muffled sound of jet engines came a few seconds later. Evans sucked on his pipe. The tobacco had burned out. He swiveled around to face Frazzini. "You're right, Al."

Frazzini got up. "So, who are you going to appoint?"

"Tom Jensen."

Frazzini's eyes grew large. He let out a long, low whistle. "Well," Frazzini sighed, lifting his shoulders, "if my family was kidnapped and I had a choice of Sherlock Holmes, Dick Tracy, Travis McGee, or Tom Jensen to run the case, I'd goddam sure pick Jensen."

"I can't name him to be in charge administratively, Al. That's going too far out on the limb. So your name will head the operation and appear on the paperwork."

Frazzini nodded in both understanding and assent.

"But Jensen will run the case," Evans concluded.

Frazzini laughed sardonically. "And that he will, John. That he will."

People meeting Tom Jensen for the first time were surprised to learn that he was in his mid-fifties. It wasn't so much that he didn't look it, but that he looked so very good. By even the most optimistic measure a lifespan of fifty-plus qualifies a man for middle age, a time of declining energies, however so slight. Tom Jensen looked too vital to be in decline. True, his brown hair, cut unfashionably short in the style of the forties, was turning gray, and the lines around his eyes had grown deeper. But his powerful body still moved with the agility of a much younger man. He was over six feet tall, weighed nearly two hundred pounds, and yet he moved with the grace and coordination of a jockey. He had a wide, strong mouth and a firm chin. His features were rugged and did not lend themselves to business suits and sports jackets. He looked as if he should be on the cover of *The American Hunter.*

As his name was being mentioned in John Evans's office, Tom Jensen sat in the kitchen of his home in suburban Washington. Propped before him on the breakfast table was the sports section of the *Washington Post.* As he sipped coffee he read an account of the Dodgers' winning the playoffs from the Cubs and the Angels' winning their first game against the Senators.

With another part of his attention he listened to Judy Channell, a nurse who occasionally spent a night with him, talk on the telephone to one of her girl friends. She had been on the phone for an hour trying to switch shifts.

In bed the night before she had thought it a good idea if in the morning she packed a picnic lunch and the two of them spent the day in the fall countryside. She wanted to picnic in a meadow and make love by a stream. The only problem: she was scheduled to work at noon. Now she was trying to get out of it. Unsuccessfully, it seemed.

That suited Jensen. He hadn't had much enthusiasm for a picnic.

"Yes," Judy said into the phone. Jensen looked up. Judy was a dark-haired, handsome girl. She tossed her head and made a face at the receiver.

"Thanks," she said in the tone of one who has nothing to be thankful for. She dropped the receiver on the cradle. "Last month I worked for her, this month she won't work for me. The picnic is off."

"Win a few, lose a few," Jensen philosophized.

"Don't be so philosophic about it," Judy pouted. "I don't think you really wanted to picnic anyhow."

Jensen gave her an A-plus for good instincts and read on about the upcoming World Series. Judy turned and went to the bedroom to collect her overnight bag.

The phone rang and Jensen answered it. There was a pause and for a moment he thought it might be one of Judy's girl friends calling back. Then a voice came on the phone. It was John Evans. He came quickly to the point.

"I want to see you as soon as possible, Tom."

"Is an hour soon enough?"

"Fine."

The line clicked dead and ended the first conversation between the two FBI men in almost a year.

Tom Jensen had been in the FBI almost thirty years. He had graduated from a small Nebraska high school in 1942. As he spoke fluent Danish and still had relatives in that country, he was recruited into the OSS. He had been used in Nazi-occupied Denmark and Norway. He finished the war a captain.

His service in the OSS gave him a taste for undercover work. He gave up his plans to study animal husbandry and instead used the G.I. bill to study law at Georgetown University. He had decided to make a career of the FBI.

In 1950 the Bureau had hired him as a clerk and when he got his law degree he became an agent. He was used as a troubleshooter, a roving agent to assist on tough cases. He quickly got a reputation as a superagent. J. Edgar Hoover marked him as a comer.

The two words most often used about Jensen were *respect* and *fear.* His knowledge and expertise were respected throughout the Bureau. He was totally dedicated, hard, and cold sometimes to the point of ruthlessness.

As J. Edgar Hoover grew older, there had been speculation within the Bureau as to who would succeed him. Everyone assumed one of his old cronies would get a temporary appointment. But in six months or a year a younger man would be moved in. No name was mentioned more often than Tom Jensen.

When the Watergate dam burst, Jensen lost forever any chance of the FBI directorship. It was rumored that he had placed illegal wiretaps and conducted illegal break-ins. Nothing was proved. Jensen was too good to get caught out on a limb like the Plumbers.

Jensen did what he had to do and left no evidence that he had done it. Jaworski's investigators could question Jensen's veracity, doubt his innocence, suspect his guilt . . . but they couldn't prove anything.

They didn't have to. The rumors about Jensen were enough to erase his chances to be the director of the FBI. One of the FBI post-Watergate problems was what to do with Tom Jensen. He wouldn't retire, and there were no grounds to fire him. Finally an aide to Clarence Kelley had the bright idea to assign Jensen to a minor nonsensitive post reviewing overseas operations. The office was in the State Department Building, therefore moving Jensen physically as well as administratively out of the J. Edgar Hoover Building.

After taking over the directorship, Evans had telephoned. The two had talked about the "old days" and at the end of the conversation Evans had suggested they get together soon for lunch. They never had.

At the same time that Jensen was on his way to meet Evans, George Butts, a senior vice-president of a large Los Angeles bank, received a phone call from Robert Hencill, Jr. Hencill and Doctor's Prescriptions were very important customers, and the vice-president gave the call immediate attention. Besides, he had been a good friend of Hencill's father. Afterward he called his chief cashier. "Paul, do we have six thousand hundred-dollar bills in the house?"

"I doubt it, sir."

"Get them. I want them by two o'clock."

For a moment the vice-president reflected on the problems of American businessmen in South America. It was a goddam shame they had to pay off every goddam two-bit dictator.

Ignazio Apicelli was bird-watching near the village of Flanders on the south shore of Long Island Sound when an aide appeared to tell him a call had come for him. Apicelli did not have to ask if the call was important. Had it not been, the aide would never have disturbed him.

The two drove to a roadside telephone booth and Apicelli telephoned the number in Washington. He listened carefully as Frazzini told him of the kidnapping. Apicelli immediately grasped the importance of the crime and the genius of Frazzini's solution. He concurred in the plan.

Jensen used the basement entrance to the J. Edgar Hoover Building. There were uniformed guards in the basement and a private elevator to the director's suite. The elevator was monitored by closed-circuit television.

Jensen walked from the car into a long, narrow corridor. At the end was a uniformed guard standing behind a chest-high desk. When he spotted Jensen he picked up a telephone and dialed a three-digit number. A moment later he spoke a few words into the receiver and hung up. As Jensen approached, the guard nodded at him. "You may go right in, Mr. Jensen."

The guard pushed a button and opened the door and Jensen walked into the office that once he had thought would be his.

Evans stood at his desk. He had forgotten how physically imposing Jensen was. How the man seemed to generate power. He exuded competence and confidence. Just seeing him made Evans feel better about the Chad case.

"Hello, Tom," he said in a hearty voice and stretched out a hand to be shaken.

Jensen crossed the room in long, light strides. "How are you doing, John."

The two shook hands. Evans nodded at the coffee service. "You got here just in time for the fresh pot."

Evans poured the coffee while Jensen sought a bottle of cognac from the cupboard. "My European taste," he explained.

"Bourbon for me," Evans said.

Jensen reached again into the cupboard.

"How's your farm in Denmark?" Evans asked. He knew Jensen was retiring there.

"Waiting for me," Jensen answered.

"Well, it won't be long now," Evans commented.

"A few weeks," Jensen answered. He sloshed some cognac into one of the cups, the bourbon into the other. The men picked up the cups.

"Okay, Tom, here's to your retirement and for old times' sake." Immediately he regretted "old times' sake" as he saw a flash of amusement appear in Jensen's eyes.

The latter sipped from the cup and then asked laconically, "What is it you want me to do for old times' sake, John?"

Evans smiled guiltily. "I want you to lead a kidnapping investigation, Tom."

Jensen shook his head. "Not me, John. I said no on Jimmy Hoffa, I said no on Patty Hearst, and I say no on this one, whoever it is."

Evans did not know Jensen had turned down the two cases. He pressed on. "It's the children and mother of Roosevelt Chad. It'll be a helluva case. The kidnapper is asking him to throw the World Series."

"Sorry," Jensen apologized. "Not me."

It had never occurred to Evans that Jensen would turn down the case. He poured some more bourbon into his coffee and went back to his desk. "Sit down, Tom." He motioned to the couch.

"I don't want to take up your time, John."

"You're not. Now sit down for a moment and let's talk about this."

"In about three weeks I retire, John. I don't need the headaches."

"Do you need fifty thousand dollars, Tom?"

Jensen looked into Evans's face before pouring himself another cognac and taking a seat on the couch. "Well," Jensen drawled, "I got a farm waiting for cows."

"I don't know cattle prices in Denmark, Tom, but fifty thousand dollars will buy a lot of heifers in this country."

Jensen was looking at him again. "Where are you going to get the money, John? Out of whose budget?"

"You worry about the case, I'll worry about the money."

"If I take it."

Evans thought now that he would. At first Jensen had said *no*, now he said *if*. There was a condition. Another one. He waited for Jensen to give it to him. It came directly.

"All right, John. But I want to cover myself. Don't take it personally. You know that I always cover myself. I want it on paper."

Evans picked up a pen from his desk. "What do you want?"

"Write this," Jensen said. " 'I, John Evans, promise to pay Special Agent Thomas T. Jensen, upon the completion of his investigation into the Roosevelt Chad kidnapping case, the sum of fifty thousand dollars.' Date it and sign it."

Evans hesitated and then said, "I'm going to add that you get the money after the successful completion of the case, Tom. I'm not paying you to take the case. I'm paying you to crack it." He took a sip of bourbon-laced coffee. "I want to cover myself, too."

Jensen nodded. "Fair enough."

Evans put down his cup, added his qualification to the contract, and signed it.

Jensen got up and walked to the desk. He took a look at what Evans had just written and signed. "Okay, John, you got a deal. Fill me in."

10.

Mrs. Chad woke up. Consciousness came to her slowly, like a camera being brought into focus. There was a pain in the back of her neck, like one she once had experienced after being sick and taking large doses of medication. Her eyes fluttered. For a moment she thought she was in a hospital. The room was bright. Around her bed was a white-curtained screen. She was on her back, her arms over the side of the cot. Her arms ached and she tried to move them. Something was tied to her wrists, holding her arms down. It was then that she remembered they had been kidnapped.

It began to come back to her. The orange juice that had been drugged. Awakening in the middle of the night in a strange room. Perhaps this room. She looked about her. She couldn't tell if it was the same room.

When she had awakened the first time it was dark and only a single lamp was burning. The children had not been with her and she was sick with fear. The fear had roused her quickly and made her alert. There had been two persons. She knew from their voices they were the ones who had pretended to take the pictures.

And then, miracle of miracles, she had been able to speak to Roosevelt. Only a few words, but it had given her courage and strength. Roosevelt, too; she knew from his voice.

Afterward the man had told her why she and the children had been kidnapped and that their captivity would last the duration of the World Series.

This had put her in despair. She had hoped they had been taken for ransom, that it soon would be paid, and they would be free. She had not counted on a week or ten days.

She had asked to see the children. The woman told her the children were unharmed and that she could see them the next time she woke up.

She hadn't understood what was meant by the "next time she woke up." The man explained that they would be kept drugged. There would be a three-hour waking period each day. However, she would not be awake at the same time as the children.

She understood without his telling her that this was to keep her from trying to escape. She would never leave the children.

She had been frightened about the drugs, and he explained them to her. Unlike the potion mixed in the orange juice, a new drug would be used. It would be injected.

Because they would spend so much time asleep, which would retard their digestive processes, they were to be fed a special diet of baby food complemented by honey, bananas, and soups. Exercise in the form of walking about the room for thirty minutes each waking period would be necessary. The man nodded at the woman. She would assist them.

Finally, the man assured her the drugs would not harm them. Within twenty-four hours after their release they would be almost back to normal.

The man had injected something into her arm then, and the last thing Mrs. Chad remembered was staring at the gun stuck into his waistband. In her sleep she dreamed that the woman had fired the gun.

Now a face covered by an orange ski mask appeared above her, from over the hospital screen. "Are you awake?" a female voice asked.

Mrs. Chad recognized the voice from the night before. It was the woman who called herself Mrs. Norton.

Mrs. Chad nodded. "Yes. Where are the children?"

The woman nodded past the screen. "Next to you."

She came around the screen. She was wearing a black pantsuit. "I'm going to let you get up," the woman said. "All the doors are locked. The windows are covered. Don't try to get away." The friendly manner of Mrs. Norton was gone. Now the woman sounded threatening and dangerous. In the woman's jacket pocket Mrs. Chad saw the outline of a pistol.

"I would never leave the children," Mrs. Chad said.

The woman bent down to the bed, and in a moment Mrs. Chad felt one arm free. The woman went around the cot and freed the other arm. She pointed to a door behind the screen. "There is the bathroom. You'll find nightclothes there. Change out of your street clothing," she ordered.

Mrs. Chad did as she was told. When she came back into the room she wore blue pajamas and a gray flannel robe. She looked around the room. It was long and spacious. At one end was a fireplace. At the other end, where she stood, was a kitchen and next to it the bath. She saw two doors and guessed they led outside or upstairs, or both.

The woman rose up from behind the hospital screen. "Come here and you can see the children." Her manner was abrupt.

Mrs. Chad looked down at them. They were asleep. Their faces looked peaceful. "Just before I put you back to sleep, I'm going to give you a chance to talk to them for a minute," the woman said. "It will be your last chance until you are released."

Mrs. Chad felt heartsick at that.

The woman continued. "I want you to tell them to mind me." Her voice, already hard, took on a menacing tone. "I will tell you right now that I will tolerate no trouble from either you or the children. If it was up to me . . ." The woman didn't finish.

Fear and panic struck at Mrs. Chad. The night before the man had sounded reassuring. But this woman had a cruelty that frightened Mrs. Chad. She wondered if the man approved.

"If the children give me trouble," the woman went on, "I'll change the drugs. And the new ones won't be so gentle on you. You won't wake up quite as quickly after it's all over. And if your son doesn't cooperate . . ." Again the woman's voice trailed off, and Mrs. Chad felt what was unsaid was more terrifying than anything that could have been said.

"You want him to lose a ball game?"

"Yes."

Mrs. Chad shook her head. "I don't know if he will." She shook her head again. "And I'm sure Roosevelt doesn't know either."

"He is going to lose," the woman retorted angrily. "You and the children are going to tell him so."

Mrs. Chad's spirits rose at the thought of talking to her son. "When will we talk to him?" she asked.

"You won't talk to him personally. You're going to make recordings. You are going to tell him to lose. If you don't cooperate, I'll send him a message. I'll tell him I have given his children a drug that may permanently affect the brain. And I won't be lying to him either."

Jensen twisted his neck to look at the two photographs Frazzini had dropped on Evans's desk. The late afternoon sunlight slanted into the room and illuminated the desk top. Jensen leaned forward and put both hands palms down on the desk and looked at the photos. One was a profile shot; the other showed the full face. They were of the man the Mafia had picked to work with Jensen. The photos showed him to be a handsome man of sixty. He had a full head of curly gray hair. He wore fashionable wire-framed spectacles. The profile showed a strong, blunt chin. The head-on shot showed full lips turned upward at the ends. The subject apparently had enjoyed being photographed for what obviously were police mug shots. His fiery black eyes were amused. Printed on both shots was his name, MICHAEL PATRICK MCGARRITY.

"Know him?" Frazzini asked. "I mean personally." He knew Jensen was quite familiar with many important Mafia characters.

Jensen shook his head. "I remember him as a lawyer and accountant."

"He's retired now."

"Why did they bring him out of retirement?"

Frazzini moved away from the desk and took a seat on the couch. "They had to send someone who knows what's going on."

"They've got a lot of people who know what's going on."

"He's retired and lost touch with their day-to-day operation," Frazzini explained. "He's safe."

Jensen snorted. "What do they think we're going to do, torture him for information?"

"Nah. The normal Mafia character is clanny and secretive, hell to work with. I've met McGarrity. He's a poor boy who went to Yale. He's a good mixer. A very social animal. You're going to have to spend a lot of time with him."

"Okay," Jensen said. "Now what's with Chad?"

Evans took the pipe from his mouth. "He's standing by, Tom. I told him not to bother anything in the house. He's waiting for instructions."

Jensen thought a moment. "Tell him to spend the night in a motel. That'll get him out of the house and keep him from tripping over any evidence."

"He said he's been careful."

"Good. I'll do a crime-scene investigation when I get there. Have him tell the neighbors the family has left town to escape the World Series excitement."

"Why not just say they've gone to Missouri?" Evans put in. "That's where they're from. Tell the neighbors they've gone down there to escape the press."

"Get the press in it," Frazzini said. "You can blame them and everyone will believe you."

Jensen overruled the two. "Just say out of town. That doesn't give them a fixed address where the story can be checked.

"And another thing, for the time being it's not necessary for anyone else in the Bureau to know any part of this. There damn sure will be no leaks from the Mafia. I don't want any from our side." He looked at Evans and Frazzini. "This is our secret."

"This secrecy bothers me some," Evans said. "I still wonder if we shouldn't bring the baseball commissioner in on this. What if Chad actually tried to lose the Series! The blame would be on us."

"I'm not worried about that, John," Frazzini argued. "Chad has been very open with us."

Evans looked inquiringly at Jensen. "What do you think, Tom?"

"You called me, John, I didn't call you. And before you called me you brought in the Mafia." He turned to Frazzini. "I congratulate you, Al. In my expert opinion you came up with what may be the only way to crack this. The problem is, you can't turn back now. If we solve this no one will blame the FBI for working with organized crime figures. But if something goes wrong, you will be pretty goddamned glad, John, for the secrecy. And I'm telling you it's too late now not to be secret."

Evans nodded his head slowly.

"But if it's any consolation, John," Jensen went on, "I think the kidnapper is an amateur. I think he can be caught."

"Okay, Tom," Evans said, drawing in his breath. "I guess you've said all there is to say." He looked at his watch. "McGarrity will be coming down from New York on the eight o'clock shuttle. I've made arrangements for you to meet him at a motel."

Jensen looked at both men. "One more thing. You know what

will happen to our kidnappers if Mr. McGarrity and his *family* find them before we do?"

"We've discussed that, Tom," Frazzini replied.

"I like to think we're a more efficient organization than they are," Evans said wryly.

On the West Coast it was nearly three o'clock in the afternoon. Hencill parked his black Lincoln Mark IV in the bank parking lot. From the back seat he took a large brown leather suitcase and carried it lightly into the bank.

Twenty minutes later, suitcase still in hand, he left the bank. Twice on the walk back to his car he shifted the suitcase from one hand to the other. In it was six hundred thousand dollars in hundred-dollar bills.

Across the city Billy and Camilla had finished their exercise period and were preparing to eat. The usual tireless energy of childhood was still obvious. Billy looked hungrily at a bunch of bananas on the counter and then distastefully at the dishes of baby food in front of him. "I didn't even like this stuff when I was a baby," he told his sister.

"Shush," she whispered, and glanced anxiously toward the woman.

Billy ignored his sister's warning. "Hey!" he called out. "I don't like apricot baby food."

The woman looked measuredly at him. "What would you prefer instead?"

"A cheeseburger," Billy replied. "And toast the bun."

His sister buried her face in her hands to hide her giggling.

A moment later she was in tears.

The woman's reaction to Billy's remark was immediate. She sprang from her chair, dumping the newspaper she had been holding onto the floor. In long, pounding strides she came toward the children. Billy watched her apprehensively, holding a spoon in his left hand, the jar of baby food before him on the tray.

In one quick motion the woman knocked the metal tray and the jar onto the floor. The jar broke and the tray bounced loudly on the tile floor.

The room was silent.

The woman bent over the boy. "Before you leave here, you'll be begging me for baby food."

At 8 P.M. Eastern Daylight Saving Time, an Eastern Airlines shuttle flight from New York landed at National Airport in Washington. Aboard the plane was Michael Patrick McGarrity. He felt he had been sent to Washington as an ambassador of sorts and had dressed himself for the occasion. He looked elegant in a three-piece black needle-striped suit. He wore a silver gray tie, and from his pocket protruded a blue, gray, and red silk foulard handkerchief. He wore black patent leather shoes. He carried a charcoal gray suede briefcase. He walked with a step that disguised his sixty years. His eyes sought any beautiful women in view and the look he gave them was younger even than his step. Many returned his look, and not just with friendly interest. He was a very good-looking man.

At the baggage counter he collected two matched suede suitcases. He gave a porter five dollars to carry them to the taxi line. "To the Airflite Motel," he told the driver.

At the motel the driver pulled off the street and steered toward the lobby entrance. "Around to the back," McGarrity told him. "Room forty-nine."

The driver pulled in a parking space in front of the room. "Don't bother with the luggage," McGarrity told him, and handed a ten-dollar bill over the seat.

He got out, set his suitcases on the sidewalk, and waited till the driver had pulled away before he went to the door and rapped twice.

Through the door he heard a television program. The volume was immediately turned down and a moment later the door opened.

There was a second of hesitation, an awkward pause, before the two men grinned at each other.

"Well, Mr. Jensen, over the years I've heard so much about you from the media that it's a great pleasure to meet you at last." McGarrity smiled broadly.

"Well, Mr. McGarrity, over the years I've heard so much about you from our Organized Crime Section that it's a great pleasure to meet *you* at last."

McGarrity broke into laughter and the two men shook hands. Jensen stepped aside to permit McGarrity to enter. "Would you like a drink?" he asked, after McGarrity put down his suitcases.

"What are you having?"

"Cognac."

"Cordon Bleu?"

"Not on my pay. How about Remy Martin?"

"It'll do," McGarrity said, the broad grin still on his face.

From a serving tray on the dresser Jensen took two plastic glasses sealed in paper. He broke the paper and poured three fingers of cognac into the glasses and handed one to McGarrity. "Here's to our success," Jensen proposed.

"Hear, hear," McGarrity agreed, and took a long drink of brandy.

The two men sat down, Jensen in a straight-backed chair. McGarrity took a seat on the couch. "I would like to make what we trial lawyers call an opening statement," he said.

"Do it," Jensen told him.

"I have been instructed by Signor Apicelli to assist you in any way that will not compromise us. I assume you'll work the same way."

"That's correct," Jensen admitted. "And if I may interrupt your opening statement, who will determine for you what is compromising and what is not? Will it be necessary for you to consult Signor Apicelli?"

"I think I can be the judge."

"The lawyer and the judge."

McGarrity laughed. "Yes. Isn't that an enviable position? There are certain conditions for our cooperation," he continued. "The first is that when, if ever, this crime becomes known to the public, we be given credit for our cooperation." Jensen was about to speak and McGarrity raised a hand.

"I know your director cannot go on television and thank our people. Nor do we want him to. That would be bad for our image as well as for yours. What we do want is for you to leak to the press that we have assisted you. Later I will tell you which aspects you may leak and which must be kept silent.

"After the leak, we of course expect you to deny our cooperation. But not too vigorously, please. Perhaps a 'no comment' would be preferable to a flat denial. Well, anyhow, your people will know how to handle it. But *this* is very important for our image. Go in any bar and you'll always hear some loudmouth shouting that one or another sports contest has been fixed by the Mafia. Absurd, of course. It would be anathema to us. We make money not by betting, but by booking bets. Anything that frightens off bettors is bad for our business. If the kidnapping is made public, please look out for our image. We operate on the up and up."

Jensen let the last remark pass. "There are no other conditions?" he asked.

"I'm certain there will be. I'll point them out as we move along. What do you want first?"

"I want two two lists of names. The first list should include the names of each of your clients who has wagered at least twenty-five thousand dollars on the Series."

"And the second list?"

"The losers. Clients who have had recent heavy losses. Big losers who might be in hock to you. Losers who may have become desperate."

"And what will you do with these lists?"

"We have quite an extensive system of files on some of our citizens." Jensen could not help but grin.

McGarrity grinned back. "How extensive?"

"Do you really want to know?" Jensen was amused.

"Yes. I love secrets."

"We have dossiers on seventeen million U.S. citizens and card files on about fifty-five million more."

McGarrity's eyes opened wide. His lips formed in a soundless whistle. "That *is* extensive. You have a dossier on me, of course."

"Of course."

"Have you read it?"

"Yes."

"What does it say? Don't tell me. I'll bet it's nasty. Is it nasty?"

"I wouldn't call it nasty. I'd characterize it as unflattering."

"I want to read it. Could you get it for me?"

"I can arrange it."

"Good. From our files I'll get the one on you." Jensen's face showed surprise, and McGarrity broke into laughter. "Did you think we keep no dossiers on our, our . . . opponents?"

"It never occurred to me."

"We do. I read yours just before leaving New York."

"Would you say it was unflattering?"

"No. I would call it nasty."

Jensen got to his feet. "On that note perhaps we should have some more cognac."

"I don't mind at all," McGarrity said. He was enjoying himself immensely.

Jensen fetched the cognac bottle from the dresser and poured some in each of their plastic glasses. "The next time maybe we could go fifty-fifty," McGarrity suggested, "and buy a bottle of Cordon Bleu."

"Why not?" Jensen assented.

"Now," McGarrity said, returning to the subject. "On these lists. What will you do with them?"

"The names on the seventeen million dossiers and fifty-five million index cards we have stored in a computer. The computer is tied in with two hundred forty other federal, state, and local computers. That makes it possible to collect, very rapidly, any and all information available on an individual. The names you give us we'll feed into the computer, which will give us a printout indicating if the person has a file in any of the other computers. As an example, if one of the bettors is, say, in income tax trouble, we'll take a closer look at him."

"At this point I must impose another condition, and it has two parts."

Jensen waited.

"First, it would be disastrous to us if our clients knew we had furnished their names to the FBI."

Jensen nodded. "That's understandable. It will not be part of any leak we may eventually make to the press."

McGarrity frowned. "A question arises. How many of your people know of our meeting? Know about the kidnapping?"

"Myself, Frazzini, and Evans."

McGarrity got up. He tried to pace, but the cheap motel room did not offer the area necessary for a good pace.

Jensen saw that McGarrity was deep in thought and did not interrupt him. The elegantly dressed Irishman picked up the cognac bottle and looked quickly at Jensen, who nodded. McGarrity poured both the plastic glasses half full. "Do you trust Evans?" he asked. "I mean absolutely."

Jensen looked into McGarrity's face, and for a moment the men's eyes were locked. "No," Jensen said at last.

McGarrity nodded every so slightly. "Mr. Jensen, you and I are going to be good friends."

"I want us to be," Jensen replied. "Now, what is the second part of your condition?"

"That you alone see the lists. That you alone process them."

"How long will the lists be?"

"Do you want nationwide lists?"

"Yes. With particular speed and accuracy on the West Coast. And I'd like that one first."

"That'll be no problem. I can have one for you in twenty-four hours."

Jensen's face reflected surprise.

"We have our own computers," McGarrity explained. Both men smiled.

"How many names do you anticipate?"

"Bets over twenty-five thousand dollars?"

"Yes."

McGarrity wrinkled his face in thought. "Between three and four hundred."

Again Jensen showed surprise.

"It's a rich country," McGarrity allowed.

"To get on your side of the fence for a moment," Jensen said, "how many in your organization know of our meeting and the kidnapping? It's most critical that we keep the crime from the press."

"Two. Myself and Signor Apicelli." McGarrity smiled ironically. "And Apicelli I trust absolutely."

"What about the bookmakers? Won't they ask why you want the lists?"

"Bookmakers won't enter into it. I'll get the betting lists from the computers. I'll get only the Losers List from the bookies. Apicelli can arrange everything."

Jensen nodded appreciatively. "What can you do in Vegas? We can't overlook the possibility that some of the money will be bet legally."

"How much are they betting?"

"We don't know. But from what they told Chad, they're hoping to get back more than a million dollars."

"They must be counting on Washington to win the playoffs," McGarrity mused. "The Senators would go into the Series a heavy underdog. For sure, as much as nine to five. Quite possibly two to one."

"So we're talking about more than a half-million dollars in bets," Jensen reckoned.

"They couldn't get that much down in Las Vegas," McGarrity said, "without raising suspicion. They'll have to go through us. At least for a good chunk of it."

"Can you get a list from Vegas?"

McGarrity shrugged. "A very partial one. You know we have our interests there, but Las Vegas has many book parlors and hand books where the money could be spread. I can get a Vegas list if you want one. And I suggest we drop the ante from twenty-five thousand to five thousand dollars."

"That would be a long list, wouldn't it?"

"Probably. From Las Vegas we're talking about a thousand names."

"Then I'm going to need help running them through the computer."

"Could I do it?"

Jensen laughed. "The pay isn't much."

"When you're retired every little bit helps."

McGarrity picked up the cognac bottle. "We're making a nice dent in it. Where did you develop a taste for cognac?"

Jensen gave the Mafia lawyer a three-minute rundown on his wartime service in the OSS.

"That information on you we don't have." McGarrity smiled.

"I'm retiring to Denmark," Jensen said. "I've bought a farm there."

McGarrity raised an eyebrow. "Really. I'm retiring to Ireland. Ballina. Do you know it?"

Jensen shook his head.

"In the northwest. Nothing there. Peace and quiet. Of course I'll have a flat in Dublin. One eventually gets enough of peace and quiet."

"You dabble in the IRA."

"Your dossier on me *is* a good one. Yes, I do. But not with the Provisionals. I'm a patriot, not a communist."

"Well, if ever you make it to Denmark, stop by for an aquavit."

"And you're invited for a Paddy should you visit Ireland."

They drank a cognac to that.

"We haven't talked about the most important lists." Jensen resumed their discussion. "The losers."

"You think the kidnappers might be losers?" Without waiting for Jensen to answer, McGarrity said, "I agree."

"How long a list are we talking about this time?"

"I don't know. I should think it wouldn't be more than a couple dozen names."

"I hope not. I plan to look exceptionally closely at them."

"It would be the proper thing to do."

"How much total action does your organization get on the Series, nationwide?"

"It depends on the teams and how soon the playoffs are over. Today is Wednesday, and Washington and California are still playing. If Washington doesn't win tonight, the playoffs won't be settled until tomorrow, and that leaves only one day, Friday, for the bettors to get in action. That's bad for business."

"Each year you must pull for three-game sweeps of the playoffs."

"That and popular teams to win them. You get the Dodgers and the Yankees and the action is thirty to forty percent greater than with provincial nines like Cleveland and San Diego. Who cares about them?"

"Clevelandites and San Diegans."

"And who cares about them?"

"You have a point."

"With the Dodgers and Washington or California, how much will the handle be?"

"Better with Washington. But still less than a billion. Maybe nine hundred million dollars."

"Jesus Christ!" Jensen exclaimed. "That's way above our estimates."

"Inflation," McGarrity explained. "And, as I said earlier, it's a rich country."

The telephone rang and Jensen answered. "I'll be right there," he told the caller. He hung up. "Our taxi is here to drive us to the terminal. We're booked on an eleven o'clock flight to Los Angeles."

Jensen took a suit bag and a much-used military valpack from the closet. McGarrity picked up his suitcases and followed Jensen from the room.

As the taxi pulled onto the street a crowd of cheering persons burst from a bar. Moments later a series of explosions could be heard in the sky. Tracerlike lights shot into the sky and exploded into streamers, cartwheels, and starbursts.

"The Washingtonians are celebrating," said McGarrity.

"I think the Senators just made it to the World Series," the driver said.

"Well, now the bettors can begin getting their money down." McGarrity added.

At the same moment that Jensen and McGarrity were boarding a plane for Los Angeles, Hencill was seeing Ilka off at Los Angeles International. He had made the necessary phone calls. Bookies in each of the four cities were expecting Ilka to make the bet. Ostensibly, he was to be out of the country on business. He experienced no difficulties. Bookies were interested only in the cash. Who delivered it did not concern them.

After Ilka got her boarding pass they went to the bar for a drink. Normally Ilka's entrance anywhere caused a turning of heads. Tonight it didn't. Her blond hair was covered with a wig of mousy brown curls. Her slim figure was undetectable under a sloppy pantsuit.

She did not like this, but she understood Robert's concern about undue attention. Still, she had packed another outfit that she would wear when she delivered the money to Nashville. She was not going to look like a dumpy American woman when she met Saccente.

Hencill looked down at the model's bag at her feet. In a false bottom were four envelopes containing the money she was to bet. There was two hundred thousand dollars in all. "Be careful of that," he cautioned.

"To take it, someone will have to kill me," Ilka answered.

Hencill had no doubt that she was serious.

THURSDAY
Two Days before the World Series

BOSTON (UPI) — State police this week made simultaneous raids on 23 locations in the Greater Boston area, cracking what was called "the largest illegal sports gambling syndicate in New England." . . . The majority of the locations were apartments utilized as so-called offices and handled . . . about $800,000 per day, or about $250 million annually.

11.

Jensen's first task Thursday morning was to establish in Chad's neighborhood a fake identity for himself as a county detective investigating a burglary. This would give him an excuse to question neighbors about what they might have seen on the day of the kidnapping, and it also would give him a reason to be in Chad's house. The crime-scene investigation would entail not only going over the interior, but also a walk over the area around the house. If he didn't first establish an identity, he took the chance that a neighbor, suspicious of his intentions, might call the local police. That would bring an element to the kidnapping that he absolutely did not want.

He had arrived in Los Angeles shortly before 1 A.M. It had been a pleasant flight. McGarrity was a good travel companion. They had had the first-class compartment almost entirely to themselves on the night flight. They had eaten a good dinner and drunk champagne and cognac and exchanged stories. When the stewardesses had finished their work, three of them had gathered around and the group joked and talked until the flight was forty-five minutes out of Los Angeles. One of the girls, a small blonde named Shirley, had slipped her phone number to Jensen. McGarrity also had scored. Jensen had watched with the professional respect of an experienced bachelor as the handsome and suave lawyer picked up Shirley's roommate, an Alabama girl named Linda who was three decades his junior.

Jensen had reserved a room at a Ramada Inn near Dodger Stadium. McGarrity had taken a suite at the Century Plaza. They had already discussed their arrangements, so after they landed it was not necessary to do more than shake hands.

At eight o'clock in the morning Jensen found himself on the street where Chad lived. He had been to two houses with little result. At least he was establishing his fake identity. As he walked through the neighborhood he felt eyes on the back of his neck. He could imagine the telephone calls being exchanged in the neighborhood. There had been a burglary at Roosevelt Chad's house, the neighbors would tell one another. A county detective was investigating the burglary right now. What was the world coming to!

Jensen spent two hours knocking on doors and talking to people, mostly women. He learned only that a green van occupied by a man and a woman had been seen at the Chad house on the afternoon of the day of the burglary. One of the neighbors thought the van was making a delivery from a hardware store. If that were true, why was a woman riding with the driver?

No one could give a description of the couple in the van. No one remembered any part of the license number. When Jensen was satisfied that there was no more information to be had, he went to Chad's house and let himself in. It was shortly before lunchtime.

Hencill lunched at Carmichael's office. The bookie sent out for two pizzas and they drank beer and talked while a clerk counted the stack of hundred-dollar bills. "You really like the Senators that much?" Carmichael said.

"Who's the best baseball handicapper you know?" Hencill asked.

Carmichael nodded his head respectfully. "You are, kid. You stick to baseball, you'd put me out of business."

The clerk stuck his head in the door. "Two hundred thousand. Right on the button."

After Hencill had gone, Carmichael said to the clerk, "I don't know how he does it. He musta dropped a million bucks already this year."

"I'll tell you how he does it," the clerk snorted. "When was the last time you bought a prescription?"

Roosevelt Chad sat on a stool in front of his locker in the Dodger clubhouse and slipped on his baseball spikes.

He felt strange. He'd begun to feel strange as he pulled on his uniform. Reporters had asked him innumerable times what his greatest thrill in baseball was. Usually he lumped them together.

There was his unanimous selection as Most Valuable Player, winning a World Series with a grand-slam homer in the ninth inning of the seventh game, breaking Pete Rose's consecutive hitting streak . . . all were big thrills. But he never had revealed his greatest thrill. No one would believe it. Maybe another baseball player, though not too many of them would, either.

His greatest thrill as a major-league baseball player was simply being a major leaguer. This thrill manifested itself each time he walked into a clubhouse and put on his uniform.

Chad loved being a big leaguer. He often told himself that when he lost this thrill, this love, he had better think about retiring. Today was the first day he had entered the clubhouse since his family was kidnapped. And when he had put on his uniform, the thrill was missing.

On the field he took a short jog and did some light exercises to loosen up. When practice began he found himself thinking of the kidnapper's theories on how to lose a game, and he watched teammates make plays, closely observing their actions. He watched the second baseman play a batter, move with the pitch, react when the ball was hit, field, and throw to first base. Chad tried to separate what was conscious from unconscious in a play. What was instinctive, what was brain controlled.

His problem was, as he thought about it, that all his life he had been practicing to make the two work as one, to make all the movements in a play seem as one instinct. His success in this attempt was reflected in his standing as a player.

Now it was his turn to field a ball. He waited for a coach to hit to his position. After the ball was hit, and he made the play, he found he couldn't separate his movements. He couldn't draw a line. He couldn't remember telling his legs to race to the right, his body to bend, his left arm to cross and reach down for the ball, his right arm to throw it. If his brain had issued these commands, he wasn't aware of it. It was all done instinctively. And if that were so, then there went the kidnapper's theory. How could a player intentionally throw a game, at least without drawing suspicion?

But there was another factor. Pressure. It was easy to stand on a practice field and field balls hit by a coach. The pressure would come in a game. The pressure would come on a pressure play in a pressure game in a stadium with fifty thousand persons shouting at him. That's when the kidnapper's theory on losing a game on a defensive play would be proved or disproved.

Hitting was a different matter. It was less instinctive, more conscious.

Waiting his turn at the batting cage he watched Boyd Simpson, the Dodgers' first baseman, take his cuts. It took less than a second for a pitched ball to reach the strike zone and for Simpson to react. But in that time a complicated series of events took place. Chad mentally put himself in the batter's box and went over each step.

He was a switch-hitter, this time batting right-handed. He dug in, putting his weight on his right leg anchored deep in the batter's box. While waiting for the pitch, he swung the bat to keep himself loose. His mental concentration was building. His fingers squeezed and loosened on the bat, he wiggled his shoulders, hulaed his hips. Loose physically, tight mentally. Maximum calm, maximum concentration. When the pitcher began his motion, Chad shut out the world. He heard neither the crowd roar, nor the voice of a kibitzing catcher.

His eyes were honed to the pitcher's throwing arm. He catalogued pitchers, and experience often told him the type of pitch he would get by the point where the ball was released. Also, the sooner he picked up the release of the ball, the more time he would have to judge it.

Now the pitcher released the ball. He had from two- to three-fifths of a second to swing or take. If a player decided not to swing he could simply be called out on strikes, possibly losing a game.

But a real hitter couldn't do that. People didn't expect Roosevelt Chad to stand, bat on his shoulder, and watch pitches sail by. He struck out rarely, and when he did it was almost always swinging.

The swing was the key. He placed himself mentally back at the plate. He had picked up the flight of the ball. It was a pitch he wanted. He strode forward, the weight coming off his rear leg. He kept his head steady as his forward shoulder drove into the pitch. At this point his entire body was in movement. His hips pivoted, the weight transferred to his front foot, the bat moved smoothly downward in a wide arc. He used the power from his shoulders, arms, and wrists and whipped the bat into the ball. When contact was made, his wrists rolled over, permitting him to keep both hands on the bat while he followed through.

Why was he one of the game's best all-time hitters? Reporters had asked him a thousand times. There was a combination of reasons, "blessings" Chad called them. He had strong shoulders, arms, and wrists. He had unusual hand–eye coordination, which permitted him to wait until the last possible moment to swing. He had incredibly fast reflexes. And he had a perfect swing.

The latter was not a blessing, but a goal attained through thousands of hours of practice. He had spend a lifetime finding a groove. Could he for one time at the plate lift the bat out of the groove? If he could handle a bat to hit to the opposite field, to hit behind and in front of a runner, to find the gap in the outfield, could he also use the bat to make an unsuspicious out?

Boyd Simpson moved out of the batting cage. It was Chad's turn.

He slipped the weighted ring off the bat and tossed it toward the dugout. He picked up the resin bag one more time to give friction to his hands, to keep the bat handle from sliding. His bat was a light one with a slight taper. It weighed thirty-two ounces, two pounds, which was light for a man of Chad's strength. But it enhanced even more his God-given quickness.

Shaking himself like a wet dog, he stepped into the batter's box. "All right, Rosie baby," the batting practice pitcher called out. "It's the seventh game of the Series, bottom of the ninth, we're behind one run, two outs, a man on first, you're at bat, two strikes, I'm Dizzy Dean, see if you can hit me."

"All right, Dizz baby," Chad called back, "just try to throw one by me."

The batting practice pitcher laughed, then his face took on a mock-serious look as he continued the put-on. He looked at an imaginary runner on first, faked a throw, stared evilly at Chad, went into his motion, reared back, kicking his left leg high into the air, and threw.

Reacting with the speed of a gunfighter, Chad unholstered his bat and pulled the trigger. The weapon hit the ball squarely, propelling it with missilelike velocity over the infield, over the outfield, over the fence, and high over the stands.

Players, sportswriters, grounds keepers watched it go and then joined the pitcher in looking with awe at Chad.

When the ball disappeared from sight the pitcher turned to Chad. "Christ, Rosie! You just won the World Series."

Chad looked away. He hadn't planned to. He had tried to fly out deep to center.

He stepped back in the box.

He was in a hurry to finish practice, which made it hard for him to concentrate.

After he took his cuts he walked rapidly to the dugout. The Dodger manager stood on the top step. "What the program, Skipper?" Chad called to him.

"That's it, Rosie. No practice tomorrow." The manager slapped him on the rump as he walked by. "Relax. Take the kids to Disneyland."

"Can't do it, Skip. School day."

"Didn't you ever play hookey?"

"Too many times, Skip. That's how I ended up a ball player."

A group around the dugout laughed.

Chad hurried through the shower, dressed, and spent a precious five minutes with a UPI sportswriter. The minutes were precious because he was in a great hurry.

In the parking lot he was delayed again. A group of kids stormed him, and he hurriedly scribbled his name a dozen times. Normally he had great patience with this duty. He remembered childhood weekend trips from St. Joseph to Kansas City and waiting for ball players to sign autographs. "Sorry, kids," he apologized. "That's all I've got time for today."

He trotted to his Volkswagen Rabbit, once more signed his name for a persistent boy, and drove off. He headed for the nearby Ramada Inn, where an FBI man from Washington was waiting for him.

Jensen sipped coffee and read his notes while he waited for Chad. The FBI man did not play the role of pastor to the families of kidnap victims. He was not sympathetic and comforting. Dealing with kidnappers is a tough, dirty business, and Jensen wanted his clients to be aware of the truth. The truth made them receptive to orders, and if they did what he told them to do, he more often than not could get the victim returned in mint condition. A bit undernourished perhaps, and certainly half frightened to death.

Kidnappers could be manipulated. You must never lose sight of the fact that they committed the crime because they were desperate for something or needed or wanted something very badly from the victim. If you used this as leverage and got the confidence of the kidnapper, you could manipulate him.

Jensen knew how to manipulate a kidnapper, but he could not do it himself. He could not furnish what the kidnapper demanded. Or even promise to. Only Chad could do that, could manipulate the kidnapper. Chad was the one who would have to do it, and he would have to learn fast how to do it. He would learn it fastest if Jensen remained coolly impersonal.

Jensen only hoped that the ball player would not lose heart and attempt to negotiate on his own with the kidnappers. That was

Jensen's fear. It was the reason why he never told a ransom payer any more than he needed to know. You never knew when one would lose heart and go over to the other side and try on his own to get the victim back.

When Chad arrived, the social amenities were brief. Jensen waved toward a coffee table that sat between a couch and two chairs. On the table was a metal insulated coffeepot and cups and saucers. "Sit down." Jensen said. It was more of an order than an invitation.

Chad sat down in one of the chairs. Jensen seated himself on the couch. "The crime-scene investigation of your house has so far produced no leads and the interrogation of your neighbors was equally unproductive. So we're at a standstill until the kidnapper telephones again." Jensen spoke matter-of-factly, as if he were a postal clerk telling a customer a package hadn't arrived.

Jensen's apparent lack of sympathy or concern awakened a hostility in Chad. Besides, he had come to the motel with great expectations and this news smashed them. He struck back. "He didn't say anything about calling back. Why should he? He has my family; I know his terms. I don't think he'll call back again," Chad said with finality.

Jenson didn't consider Chad's argument. "He'll call again," he said in the tone of a judge overruling a backward lawyer. "Depending on how the Series goes, he may call a bunch of times."

"He'll be out of luck if he calls me at home," Chad said, sulking. "I'll be in Washington most of next week."

"He'll get hold of you."

"How do you know? You just told me you have no information on him. He sounds like he's smarter than . . ." Chad stopped.

"Well," Jensen said patiently, "he will call again, and what we have to figure out is what you're going to say."

"That will depend on what he wants." Chad knew that he was pouting.

"He's already told you that," Jensen said. "Now he'll want reassurance that he's going to get it."

Chad's head snapped up. Indignation showed on his face. He

stared at Jensen. "I told your *boss*," he said finally, emphasizing *boss*, "that I was not throwing any games. That I would give one hundred percent all the way. That if the time came I couldn't, I'd take myself out of the lineup. That I'd pay a ransom. But that I'm not throwing any games. And if you'd have done your homework, Mr. Jensen, you'd have known this isn't the first time I, or other ball players, have been threatened. Seriously threatened."

"This is the first time there's been a kidnapping."

"Granted. But three years ago, after the fourth game of the World Series, someone fired two rifle shots through my front window . . ."

"And the next day you hit two home runs to win the game and give the Dodgers a lead of three games to two," Jensen finished.

"All right. Then you do know there have been some hairy situations that were kept from the press."

"Mr. Chad, the FBI is not asking you to cooperate with the kidnapper and lose the World Series. We're asking you to cooperate with us and tell the kidnapper you're going to lose."

The anger left Chad's face and was replaced with distaste. A mirthless laugh escaped his lips. "I'll try. I just hope I can control my temper and not shout at the guy."

"Go ahead and shout," Jensen said, "Scream, threaten, say anything you like. Just keep reassuring him that you're going to throw the Series. That's all he's interested in. If you shout, and you're convincing, he'll certainly understand that you have a right to be mad, and it'll give you credibility. All the assurance in the world is meaningless if he doesn't believe it. And promise him a ransom."

"I did that once. He said to forget it."

"Promise it again and if he says, 'Forget it,' ask him what happens if you should become injured and miss games and the Dodgers win the Series. Point out that reality to him and see what he says."

"I did miss two games in the Series against Kansas City."

"Remind him of that. He obviously knows the game well. So without making an issue of it, keep mentioning ransom. It'll take root in his mind and we can use it later if we can't beat him another way."

Chad liked it that Jensen had said "we." Suddenly he felt less alone. "What else should I say? Besides offering him a ransom."

"Buy a pocket notebook. As soon as the call is over, write down everything you can remember. Try forming a mental image of him. Age, physical description, psychological impressions. As much of a physical and mental picture as you can get."

"Maybe I can ask some questions. Subtly, I mean, so he doesn't get suspicious."

"Forget that. He became suspicious the moment the thought entered his mind to kidnap your family. Everything we do now is a maneuver to overcome his suspicion. We've got to make him trust you, to realize you're in this thing together."

"I don't follow that."

"He took your family to get you in his power."

"Right."

"Now he's bet a huge sum of money and he's in your power."

Comprehension appeared in Chad's eyes. "Because he needs me to win."

"Exactly. You two are partners."

Chad shook his head. "I never thought of it that way."

"Neither has he. You've got to point it out to him. And you must build up a relationship with him. He's got to trust you when you tell him you haven't called the police. He's got to trust that you are going to lose the Series. Or at least try."

"Okay. But a single player can't lose a game his teammates are winning ten to nothing. I think it's going to be a close Series. The Senators are the kind of team who give us trouble. But just what if we rolled over them, what then?"

"That's where the ransom comes in. Believe me, Mr. Chad, if the Dodgers win, and the guy is convinced that you did your part, he isn't going to turn down a half-million dollars. He'll take the ransom and give you back your family."

Chad leaned back on the couch and thought a moment. It made sense. Everything fit. He looked at Jensen. "But what's happening to my family all this time? How do we know he hasn't already . . . ?" He couldn't finish.

"Until he gets what he wants from you, your family is not in danger. He needs them. We will . . . you will make him need them. Ask for messages from your family. Demand to hear from them. If nothing else, he can make tape recordings. Use your leverage. He wants your assurances. Make him pay for them. It'll build up a give-and-take relationship and make him constantly aware that your family alive is an asset to him."

"When do they become a liability?"

"The moment he wins his bet or collects a ransom. That's why you've got to build a relationship with him, so that he'll keep his word."

For a moment Chad sat silently, thinking. Then he slammed his right fist into the palm of his left hand. "What if he doesn't call again? Just what if he doesn't?"

"He will," Jensen said. "I promise you he will. The first time Washington loses he'll be on the phone faster than a heartbroken teenager."

Chad shook his head.

"What?" Jensen asked.

Chad shook his head again. "It sounds like you're telling me you have no chance to find the kidnappers." He looked into Jensen's face. "Is that what all this means?"

"What it means is that my foremost concern is for the safety of your family," Jensen answered. "They are my first priority. Finding the kidnappers is secondary. What I've been telling you is that the ultimate success depends upon you. I promise the kidnapper will call you again. If he has a bad experience, he may not call after that. That's why I'm briefing you on what to say. We don't want him to have a bad experience. We want him to trust you, to call many times. Each time he calls we learn more about him. He may make an unconscious slip of the tongue that will help us identify him or will reveal the whereabouts of your family. Or we could get lucky and trace a call. So we're not without chances. But should all our chances fail, because of fate or just plain bad luck, you'll still get your family back because we have set him up. We've conned him."

Chad thought about that. "Okay."

The two men stood up. "Any questions?" Jensen wanted to know.

"No. I think I got everything. I offer him a ransom. I take notes. I analyze and draw a mental picture of him. I build up a relationship and get his trust. I set him up, maneuver, and con him."

"And you reassure him."

"Right," Chad agreed.

Jensen put out his right arm, and the two men shook hands.

"You're going to be all right," Jensen promised. He took a note pad from his coat pocket and tore a sheet from it. He wrote a number on it and handed it to Chad.

"This number in Washington is manned around the clock. You can call it collect. My code name is Manning. Yours is Schuyler. You can also call me here at the motel. Call any time. For any reason."

For the first time during the meeting Chad smiled. "Will you reassure me, Mr. Jensen?"

"Well, Mr. Chad, I won't con you."

Less than thirty miles away the ball player's children had finished their exercise period and were waiting at the kitchen table for food. Behind them the woman had taken two small cans of prepared food from a cupboard. She opened them, quickly warmed the contents, emptied them into two bowls and set both and a spoon in front of Camilla. The woman turned and walked back to the counter. Camilla began to eat hungrily.

Several minutes later Billy looked over his shoulder at the woman. She was seated on a stool, a cup of coffee in one hand, a cigarette in the other. She looked back at Billy. "Do you need something?" she asked.

"You forgot my food." His voice was hesitant.

"No, I didn't. You ordered a cheeseburger with a toasted bun. I don't have it."

Billy lowered his eyes. "I'll have some of that other stuff then."

"What other stuff?" The woman's voice was innocent.

Billy formed his lips to say baby food, but couldn't get it out. "What my sister is eating," he said at last.

"And what is she eating?"

Billy looked angrily at the woman. "You opened it, you oughta know."

Camilla shot a worried glance at her brother. Behind them a mirthless laugh came from the woman's lips. "You're a very smart little boy, you are," the woman said. "Yes. I know what your sister is eating. It's apricot baby food."

"Okay," Billy said. "I'll have some."

"Some what?" the woman persisted.

Billy ground his jaws together. "Some apricot baby food."

The woman got off the stool and walked past the table. "No," she said. "You don't like it. And I don't want a precious, smart little boy like you to eat anything you don't like."

"But I'm hungry," Billy protested.

The woman paused and looked at him, a cruel smile on her face. "And you're going to get hungrier," she said.

FRIDAY
One Day before the World Series

You can't sting the mob guys's bookies.
> — TONY CUILLA, a self-confessed fixer of horse races.
> A *Sports Illustrated* story, November 6, 1978

12.

Thursday afternoon Hencill had flown to Las Vegas to bet a hundred thousand dollars. He wanted to do it inconspicuously. He did not know what was going to happen in the next seven or eight days: if Washington would win the Series on their own, or if Chad would have to help them. Nor did he know if Chad, after his family was returned, would go to the police. Hencill supposed this would depend on the ball player's performance. He certainly wouldn't go to the police if he threw the Series. But Hencill had to consider that the story might come out. If it did, you could bet that the FBI would be making inquiries in Las Vegas, perhaps even subpoenaing betting lists. Hencill wanted no fingers pointed at him. If he went into a casino and bet one lump sum of a hundred thousand dollars, fingers *would* be pointed at him. But if he spread the money around in bets of five and ten thousand dollars he would remain anonymous. He couldn't be cautious or suspicious enough.

And he had to bet the money now. He had to get down every penny of the six hundred thousand dollars that he could. He couldn't bet more than two hundred thousand with Carmichael, and even that was pushing it. If ever the kidnapping became news, he didn't want the Mafia as well as the FBI after him.

He also had extended the limit of the bets in the four cities to which Ilka was taking money. He was betting ten thousand to fifteen thousand more with each bookie then he ever had before. They wouldn't care. But they could become suspicious.

The most disappointing factor was that even after the two hundred thousand dollars he bet with Carmichael, the same amount dropped off by Ilka, and the hundred thousand he was getting rid of in Vegas, he'd still have a hundred thousand left over. He'd have to bet it on one or more individual games and that was risky for two reasons. One, he might not know beforehand which game Chad would throw, if it did come down to that. Two, by betting an individual game he would get individual game odds, which were far less favorable than the Series odds of two to one. Most likely he'd get even money or a little bit more, and that with no guarantee he'd win. Well, he'd just have to wait and see and do the best he could.

He made three bets Thursday afternoon and then he checked into Caesar's. He ate a good dinner, caught a show, and played some blackjack. He won twelve hundred dollars. It was the first time in a long while that he'd won at that game and he hoped it was an omen.

Friday after lunch he began betting again. He'd make a bet, move around town for an hour or two, then make another. Sometimes he'd go back to the hotel and change clothes. He was taking no chances on later identification.

He wished he could telephone Ilka. It was poor planning on his part that he hadn't told her to call him at Caesar's. He wondered how she was doing.

Darkness was falling as the plane carrying Ilka from St. Louis landed at Nashville. It had been a long day for her. She had made bets in Chicago, Kansas City, and St. Louis. In St. Louis she had felt exhausted, sapped of energy by the incredible tension she had begun to feel at dawn when the overnight flight from Los Angeles approached Chicago.

But now, as a stewardess announced their imminent arrival in Nashville, Ilka felt refreshed. It struck her that Saccente might not be at the bookie parlor and this thought annoyed her. She quickly brushed it away. He would be there. He knew she was coming and she remembered the lust with which he had looked at her in Vegas.

In the motel room she turned on the bathwater and quickly stripped off the ugly pantsuit. From the model's handbag she took a pair of beige flair pants and a brown cashmere sweater. In the nude she exercised fifteen minutes. When she finished her body felt firm. She stepped into the bath.

A taxi dropped her in front of a lounge called the Chesterfield Club. On the same street were a half-dozen other bars and supper clubs.

Heads turned appreciatively as she entered. She used the code given to her by her husband and was led through the lounge to a back door, which opened into a corridor, which emptied into a large, well-furnished office. Except that it was occupied by older, rather crude-looking men, the office could have been an insurance agency. The men were busy on the telephones and referred repeatedly to lists of names chalked on a large board at the end of the room.

All the men looked up when she entered, though only one spoke to her. He was very courteous. Mr. Saccente would be with her in a minute. He waved her to a comfortable chair.

While she waited, the tension in her rose again. It was not one of fear, but a sexual tension. To Ilka, sex was not only something she liked, it was also a requirement. Her body needed and craved it as it needed sleep, food, and exercise. She looked nervously at her watch. It was seven-thirty. She had to catch a plane at midnight. She didn't want to have to hurry with Saccente.

A door opened and he appeared. Ilka stood up. With satisfaction she watched Saccente look approvingly at her. Although her cashmere sweater fitted skin-tight, she made a motion to smooth it, running her hands across her flat stomach.

"What a pleasure you are here," Saccente said. "Please come into my office."

Ilka took a deep breath, her breasts rising, and stepped forward. She handed him the package.

"Pete," he called to one of the men. "Take care of this, please."

"Yes, sir," said the man named Pete. He was the one who had greeted Ilka when she came in.

Saccente motioned for Ilka to enter the office. He followed her in and closed the door behind them. "Would you like a drink?" he asked.

"Yes, please. Champagne, if you have it."

"I have it."

He opened a bottle of Dom Perignon and poured two glasses full. "How nice it is that you are here," he told her and touched his glass to hers.

"For me, too," she said. "I'm sorry we didn't have a drink in Vegas."

They took another sip from their glasses and then a buzzer sounded in the room. "Excuse me," Saccente said, and walked to an intercom on his desk. He depressed a switch and spoke into the machine. "Yes," he said.

"Fifty thousand, sir," said a voice, which Ilka recognized as being that of the man named Pete.

"Thank you," Saccente said. He took a slip of paper from his desk and handed it to Ilka. "Your receipt," he told her. "You see, I've been waiting for you."

Ilka smiled. "For me or the money?" she teased.

"For you," answered Saccente. "Since Las Vegas."

Ilka put down her wineglass and walked to Saccente; she circled her arms around his waist and lifted her face to his. "Yes," she said. "And I have been waiting since Vegas, also."

He kissed her; she kissed him back. Then she reached up and pulled his tie loose and opened his shirt. He watched as she ran her hand across his chest. She liked the feel of the coarse hair and the heavy muscles of his chest. She sighed as his hands lifted her sweater and cupped her bare breasts. "I don't have much time," she whispered. "I have to . . ." She caught herself before she said "catch a plane at midnight." Instead she said, ". . . be home at midnight."

There was a couch to the side of the room and he took her there.

Later they sipped champagne. Saccente put on a robe, but Ilka prowled his office in the nude. He watched her, and once he said, "American women don't have bodies like yours."

"No, they don't," Ilka agreed.

The second time they made love long and luxuriously. They played with each other, delighting in watching each other's passion rise and fall. Finally, with time running short, Saccente acted out Ilka's fantasy and took her savagely.

He personally escorted her to the taxi. Before she got in he handed her the receipt for the bet. "Who picks up the money if Washington wins?" he asked her.

"I do."

He smiled. "Then I hope your husband wins."

"I am worth so much money!" Ilka was flattered.

"I don't expect this to end with the World Series," he said.

"No. Certainly not," Ilka lied. She kissed him hurriedly on the mouth and got into the taxi.

McGarrity was a civilized man who enjoyed the niceties of life, and it annoyed him that he first missed the cocktail hour and now was working into the dinner hour. It was past eight o'clock when he had finished collecting the names of the bettors, and his work was just beginning.

He left the office where the betting lists had been supplied and drove slowly down the street looking for a telephone booth. Two blocks away he found one near a closed service station.

He dialed a number in New York City, deposited the amount asked him by the operator, and waited. A moment later a deep male voice answered. It belonged to Ignazio Apicelli.

"This is Michael. I have the lists."

"You had no difficulties?"

"None. I'm on my way now to turn them over to Jensen."

"Have you gained his confidence?"

"He understands our position on the fix, that it is equally abhorrent to us. He is convinced we had nothing to do with it. He agreed to your conditions concerning our cooperation. I trust him. I'm certain he trusts me."

"Good. Trust is everything. He must believe we are doing our part."

"I'll keep you informed."

"A daily report is not necessary and is inconvenient for both of us. Call only when you have news."

Next McGarrity drove to a nearby post office. At eight-thirty the lobby was nearly deserted. Only a few stragglers collecting mail from their boxes. A secretary came in with a large handful of business envelopes.

McGarrity's destination was a public copying machine. It was at the far end of the lobby. He made a duplicate of the "Losers List" and placed it in his inside coat pocket. The original he placed in an envelope and wrote on the outside, JENSEN.

He used a public phone at the other end of the lobby to call the FBI man at his room in the Ramada Inn. "I'm on my way," he told him.

McGarrity parked his car in front of Jensen's room. Before he got out he took the duplicate losers list from his inside pocket and locked it in the glove compartment, which contained a packet of literature from the automobile rental company. From the back seat he took a package. He locked the car and went to Jensen's room.

"I have a surprise for you," McGarrity said after the men had shook hands, and handed Jensen the package.

While Jensen unwrapped it, McGarrity took from the bureau two glasses sealed in the customary motel style. "Real glass," he commented, holding the glasses up.

"I'm moving up," Jensen replied. From the wrapping paper of the package he pulled out a bottle of Cordon Bleu. "It'll go with the real glasses," he commented.

McGarrity chuckled. Jensen opened the bottle and poured the two glasses full. "Ah," Jensen said after taking a generous drink of the spirit. "This is the good life."

"It does make life rather a bit more livable, doesn't it," the lawyer agreed. From his inside pocket he took the envelope marked JENSEN and dropped it on the coffee table. "The lists," he said.

Jensen opened the envelope. "How many names?"

"Three hundred forty-seven big bettors. Twenty-two losers."

"Complete as of when?"

"An hour ago. And it includes the entire country."

Jensen's face showed respect. "How much money is represented?"

"I didn't total it," McGarrity told him. "I'd guess thirty or forty million dollars."

"In comparison, the money we're looking for seems a small amount."

"Not so small," McGarrity said. "Many men would kill for it."

Jensen looked up from the lists. "Someone in your organization, for example. Should you stumble onto the kidnappers before we do, it'd be an easy matter to have them shot and leave the money, so to speak, in the treasury."

"Yes, it would."

"But you wouldn't do that?" Jensen held his gaze on the Mafia lawyer.

McGarrity laughed. "Me! I should never do anything so stupid. To hell with the treasury. Personally, I'd wait until the kidnappers had the winnings in their pocket and then I'd shoot them."

"That's a helluva idea," Jensen said.

"Isn't it."

Jensen turned toward the bureau. "I also have a present to give. Two, as a matter of fact."

"It's like Christmas!" McGarrity exclaimed.

Jensen opened his briefcase and took out a large, thick folder. On it was printed MCGARRITY. He handed it to the lawyer. "Your FBI file," he said.

"Isn't that nice," smiled McGarrity, and pulled a smaller envelope from his side jacket pocket. "And here is our file on you."

"Ours is thicker," Jensen noted.

"Yours was prepared with taxpayers' money," McGarrity reminded him, "while we deal in private capital."

McGarrity opened the folder and thumbed through the papers. "Well, with all this reading material I'm sorry I didn't bring another bottle of cognac."

"That's your second present," Jensen said, and went to the dresser, opened a drawer, and pulled out a second bottle of Cordon Bleu.

"By Jove, we've got enough to make a night of it," McGarrity laughed.

"All we need is dancing girls."

"Shall I call Linda and Shirley?"

Jensen laughed. "Perhaps later. Let's get the work out of the way."

"Yes, you're right. Well, have a look at the lists. There are some very interesting names."

Jensen pulled the sheets out of the envelope and looked at the first page. "Good God! Look at this bet by a United States Senator." Jensen peered over the top of the sheet. "If he's got a hundred twenty-five thousand dollars to bet on the World Series, it makes you wonder if he returned the unused portion of the public funds given him for last year's presidential primary."

"No fair using the names for anything but kidnappers," McGarrity reminded. "But take a look at the fifth name."

Jensen cast his eyes down the list and then began laughing.

"Yes," McGarrity said. "Sheila Powell, Hollywood's most famous whore, likes the Senators for one hundred thousand dollars."

"But why the Senators?"

"Maybe one of the Dodgers turned her down."

"Or didn't pay her," Jensen added. He looked again at her name on the list. "How many men would that be at a hundred dollars a throw?"

"Off the top of the head, I'd reckon enough to staff two divisions of infantry and an artillery brigade."

Jensen continued through the list. "Now, this is interesting. A labor union has bet one million on the Senators, while an aircraft company president bet only seven hundred fifty thousand." He looked questioningly at McGarrity.

"Reassuring, isn't it," the lawyer said, "to know that labor makes larger bets than management. Makes one believe that so long as that continues, the country is safe from communism."

"But why would a labor union bet a million dollars on the World Series?"

"Knowing that particular union as I do," McGarrity said, "I'd guess their leaders have stolen from the pension fund and need to win the bet to replace the money."

"And if they lose?"

"They'll bet two million on the Super Bowl. And, if necessary, four million on the hockey playoffs. Sooner or later they'll win."

"A chance for everyone," Jensen philosophized. "That's what makes America great."

"More cognac?" McGarrity offered.

"Please. And what's the latest we can call the stewardesses?"

"My dear chap, stewardesses are always ready. By the nature of their profession their bodies know no time zones."

"Why don't we push ahead with our work and perhaps we can telephone them later."

"An absolutely splendid idea," McGarrity enthused. "And when at last we bring this kidnapper to justice, I'm going to shake his hand for bringing you and me together."

"Cheers to that," Jensen said, raising his glass.

2.
The World Series

SATURDAY
Game One

In 1919, professional gamblers bribed eight members of the Chicago White Sox to throw the World Series against the Cincinnati Reds. The men were paid a total of $100,000. Cincinnati won the nine-game Series five games to three.

13.

At 5 A.M., Jensen was awakened by the ringing of the telephone. He extended an unsteady hand to lift the receiver and knocked the lamp off the nightstand. He heard the bulb smash.

"Hello," he grumbled into the receiver. His head pounded. His mouth was dry.

"Good morning, sir," said the wake-up operator in a bright female voice. "It's five o'clock."

For a moment he thought it was Shirley, the blond stewardess in bed with him. Then he realized she couldn't at the same time be asleep beside him and talking on the telephone.

"Thank you," Jensen answered in a hoarse grumble, and hung up. He had to call Evans. He hated the goddam time difference between Los Angeles and Washington. So as not to step on broken glass he maneuvered himself over Shirley's body and off the other side of the bed. He moved his hand along the wall of the darkened room until he found a switch and turned on the overhead light.

On the coffee table was an empty cognac bottle and one three-quarters empty. He and McGarrity had drunk and talked until the stewardesses had shown up at midnight.

He stumbled into the bathroom and took a shower. He felt revived when he came out. He telephoned Evans.

"You're up early, Tom," Evans's voice came over the line.

"I got the lists late last night, John. It was either roust you out of bed or me get up at five o'clock."

"I appreciate the consideration."

"Don't. I flipped a coin and I lost."

"How's it going out there?"

"We'll see what I get out of the names."

"When are you coming back?"

"Immediately after Sunday's game."

"I'll have the computer reserved for you Monday morning."

Jensen hung up. He contemplated Shirley beside him. She was on her stomach. He put a hand on her curvaceous bottom and rubbed it. She stirred. "Is it time to fly again?" she said drowsily.

"Well, it's time again," Jensen said, "and you can call it anything you want."

At dawn Hencill landed his plane at Santa Monica airport. He was tired and happy. It was done. The money was bet. Another step was completed.

Ilka's Porsche was in the driveway, and he pulled in behind it. The door to the house was locked, and he rang the bell and then let himself in with his key. He opened the door and saw Ilka coming down the stairs. She stopped when she saw him. "You're back," she said unemotionally.

"Yes," he said. "And I'm hungry."

He walked toward her. In other days she would have kissed him. Now she turned and walked toward the kitchen. "I make you a breakfast," she said over her shoulder.

As Hencill ate he read the *Los Angeles Times* sports section. It was filled with World Series stories and statistics. He glanced at the box titled *About the World Series*.

ABOUT THE WORLD SERIES

RULES — First team to win four games wins Series.

TEAMS — Los Angeles Dodgers (National League) vs. Washington Senators (American League).

RECORD OF TEAMS — Dodgers won 107 games, lost 52 during regular season, won playoff from Chicago Cubs, three games to none. Senators won 87 games, lost 72 during regular season, won playoff from California Angels three games to one.

MANAGERS — Dodgers, Steve Walton; Senators, Paul Ryan.

BETTING ODDS — Dodgers favored to win Series, 2–1; Dodgers favored to win opening game, 9–5.

FIRST GAME — Today, 1 P.M. (P.D.T.), at Dodger Stadium, Los Angeles.

SECOND GAME — Tomorrow, at Los Angeles 1 P.M.

THIRD GAME — Tuesday, 8:15 P.M. at Robert F. Kennedy Stadium, Washington, D.C.

FOURTH GAME — Wednesday, 8:15 P.M., at Robert F. Kennedy Stadium, Washington, D.C.

FIFTH GAME (if necessary) — Thursday, 8:15 P.M., at Robert F. Kennedy Stadium.

SIXTH GAME (if necessary) — Saturday (Oct. 25), 1 P.M., Los Angeles.

SEVENTH GAME (if necessary) — Sunday (Oct. 26), 1 P.M., Los Angeles.

TODAY'S STARTING PITCHERS — Dodgers, Randy Gibson (26–8) and Senators, Don Huber (12–9)

RADIO AND TV — See Broadcast Box elsewhere on this page.

PROBABLE WEATHER — Temperature in the 80's. No chance of rain.

DODGER STADIUM TICKETS — Approximately 6,000 bleacher seats ($5 each) will go on sale at 9 A.M., each day. All other tickets have been sold.

Hencill closed the paper and went upstairs to take a shower. In five hours it all would begin.

On a mast high above Dodger Stadium the National League pennant fluttered in a playful breeze. Around the stadium the breeze rippled the World Series bunting draped over the box seats and behind home plate and along the foul lines.

The Washington Senators had filled the bases with one out. At shortstop Chad played back, hoping for the double-play. The pitcher got his sign, stretched, looked at the runner on third, kicked his left leg high in the air, and made the pitch.

The hitter slashed the ball toward the left side of the infield. It was the double-play ball Chad had hoped for. His instincts surged, pushing him to his right. His legs remained fixed to the ground. He heaved his body, but his legs wouldn't move. He watched the ball. Strangely, it moved in slow motion. Again he threw his body to the right. His legs refused to move. He let out a shout and woke up.

He looked at the electric clock on the nightstand. It was a few minutes before eight o'clock. He lay for a long time thinking of his family, and the World Series game that would begin at one o'clock.

There are credit bureaus that adhere to good business practices, and there are others that do not. Confidential Credit and Investigation Bureau belonged to the latter category. A credit check by Confidential Credit was not an investigation; it was an inquisition. A Confidential investigator would not hesitate to slip a hundred-dollar bill to an office manager, supply a woman to a minor executive, or blackmail a homosexual executive. Confidential was definitely a disreputable firm. It was also an extremely efficient one. The Mafia was a not-infrequent client.

The bureau was housed in a building that was run-down when Raymond Chandler was writing about Los Angeles. Weather and time had worked on the four-story brick pseudo-Gothic building to make it so ugly it was almost beautiful. Above the entrance was the name, Zelt Building. Zelt had been an obscure realtor who died in the late twenties. The name was above the entrance, a grimy glass door between gargoyles.

At midmorning, McGarrity parked his car a short distance from the Zelt Building and walked toward the entrance. Confidential Credit occupied three rooms on the top floor. There was the reception room and, behind it, two rooms side by side. The receptionist, a woman in her middle fifties, was running to fat and overly made up. McGarrity guessed she was an ex–chorus girl or a retired whore. His name meant nothing to her, but she sent him right in to see Leo Gotnich, the manager.

Gotnich was a small man in his late thirties who looked as if he were in his late forties. He had thinning hair, thick glasses, and a triple chin. He was the type to keep dirty pictures in his desk. Indeed, he was reading, as McGarrity entered, a novel titled *The Co-Ed Rapist*. He closed the book and slid it to the side of his desk. He did not get up. "Howarya," he said tonelessly.

McGarrity nodded at the book. "Thinking of going to college?"

The manager didn't react. He pushed his thick eyeglasses higher on his nose and rubbed a hand over his chin.

"I'm Michael McGarrity," the lawyer said.

"I know who you are," Gotnich said, and extended a plump hand.

"Good," McGarrity said. "That'll save us time."

From his inside suit coat pocket he took out three folded sheets of paper. On them were written the names, addresses, and telephone numbers of twenty-two so-called losers. He shoved them across the desk. "I want some telephone taps."

"No problem."

"It could become a problem if anyone finds out about it."

The manager grimaced with displeasure. "It's strictly between you and me, Mr. McGarrity. That's the only way we can stay in business. If you asked me to tap my own phone, I wouldn't even tell myself."

Gotnich bent forward and looked at the lists. "Do you want a tap only on the phone listed or on all the phones in a residence? Today a lot of parents give their kids a phone and then use it themselves to make calls they don't want anyone to hear." He looked up. "I mean, so long as you're after information you might as get it all. And the service costs only a hundred bucks more per phone."

McGarrity nodded assent. "Good."

Gotnich made a note on the first page of the lists. "A lot are out of state."

"Will that be a problem?"

"No. I just mention it so you know it'll cost more."

"That doesn't bother me."

"I didn't think it would."

"I want the taps collected each night around midnight and in my possession the next day. I'll be leaving Sunday night or Monday morning for Washington. I'll be there most of the week."

"That won't be easy," Gotnich said. "How many cities have we here?" He bent forward and ran his eyes quickly over the lists. "The best is that I arrange assembly points to the West, Midwest, and East."

"I don't care how you do it."

"You're right. That's my responsibility. I'll send them to you air express."

"No air express," McGarrity said. "They have to be hand-carried."

"That would be better," Gotnich agreed. "As long as you're going to this expense you might as well spend a little bit more and be sure of delivery. I mean, I guarantee the taps, not the air express."

"Let's go with the couriers," McGarrity told him.

"Okay," the manager said, "I'll start it moving." He picked up the phone and dialed a number.

For nearly two hours McGarrity listened to Gotnich phone instructions for wiretaps. When he was finished the man scribbled some figures on a pad and did some quick computations. "How about letting me have ten thousand up front. Not for me — it's that I got to pay my phone tappers in advance."

McGarrity took out his wallet. "I hope they are reliable."

For the first time the manager became animated. His face lighted. "They're the best," he boasted. "Cops. Every one of them. They got the best equipment, the best training. That's all we work with — cops. There's no one more efficient or honest than a crooked cop."

McGarrity stood up and dropped ten one-thousand-dollar bills on Gotnich's desk. "I'll be in touch," he said.

On the street he got into his rental car and headed for the freeway. He was going to watch the first World Series game with Jensen on the television set in Jensen's room.

He got caught in the traffic crush headed for Dodger Stadium. After inching by one exit he pulled off the freeway and wove his way over surface streets toward the Ramada Inn.

As he arrived at the stadium, Chad felt no pressure. In the excitement preceding the game he even was able momentarily to forget his family's plight.

The locker room was a cacophony of jokes, good-natured insults, wisecracks, and obscenities. Chad exchanged a story with the trainer. A batboy brought him a half-dozen balls to autograph. Danny Dougherty, the Dodgers public relations man, came by with a special request from a Japanese television network for an interview after the game. All this kept his mind off his family.

Chad's mother wished she could have watched the pregame show. Though the woman in the ski mask had lowered the sound, Mrs. Chad could make out the announcers as she walked about the room during her exercise period. The woman had turned the screen to the front of the room so she could watch the picture and at the same time look over the set, which gave her command of the room.

Mrs. Chad considered whether to ask permission to watch the first inning of the game. It would give her such a lift to see Roosevelt just once.

"That's enough exercising," the woman called out. "I put fresh sheets on your nightstand. When you change the linens you can eat."

The woman's voice was cold and dictatorial. Mrs. Chad couldn't get over how deceived she had been by the woman.

Mrs. Chad nodded and walked behind the hospital screen that stood by her steel cot. She heard the woman go into the kitchen.

When Mrs. Chad pulled off the pillowcase, a piece of paper fluttered to the floor. She stooped down and picked it up. There was childish writing on it and immediately she recognized Camilla's hand.

The note was a slip from a shopping reminder, the kind one finds hanging in a kitchen. The message on it woke her up more than a morning of exercise periods. Camilla had scrawled, "She won't feed Billy."

Without making up the cot Mrs. Chad came quickly from behind the screen. The woman looked up, startled.

"You're not giving my Billy anything to eat," Mrs. Chad said accusingly. Too late she realized the stupidity of her action caused by fear and anger.

The woman stormed toward her and snatched the paper from her hand. Quickly she glanced at it. "Your grandson is a smart aleck," she said.

"He's just a little boy," Mrs. Chad said, tears appearing in her eyes. "I don't know what he has done but he loves to be funny and make people laugh. He doesn't mean anything bad. Ever."

"He doesn't make me laugh," the woman snapped back.

"You have to feed him," Mrs. Chad said, anger overcoming her distress. She took a bold step toward the woman. In a second she was looking at a pistol held in the woman's right hand.

"I will use this," the woman warned. "And don't ever think that I won't. If it were up to me, the three of you would have disappeared a long time ago."

For a moment the two women stared at each other. Finally, the woman motioned toward the counter where she had been in the process of opening a jar of baby food. "If you want to eat, do so. If not, I'll put you back to sleep."

Mrs. Chad shook her head. "Give my food to Billy."

"Don't worry. He gets fed today."

"Do you promise?"

The woman pointed the gun directly at Mrs. Chad. "I think it is very important that the three of you learn as quickly as possible that I mean exactly what I say."

Silently Mrs. Chad sat down at the table and began to eat. She was not hungry, but she had to keep up her strength.

After she was finished she asked the woman, "When can we tape a message to Roosevelt?"

"Tomorrow," the woman answered.

Mrs. Chad did not ask to watch an inning of the ball game. She knew the request would be denied, but before the woman put the needle in her arm she asked again about Billy. "Remember, you promised to feed Billy," she said.

The woman snickered. "Don't worry." She plunged the needle into Mrs. Chad's arm. "Today I'll give him a double ration."

"That'll be good," Mrs. Chad said, immediately feeling the drowsiness attack her.

"Yes. He can have his sister's share. Little girls who are tattletales don't need to eat for a few days."

Mrs. Chad struggled to raise herself, but the drug had taken hold and she sank back on the cot.

It never rains in southern California in October. The sky over Dodger Stadium was deep blue. The sun was warm. The air was free of smog. It was the kind of day loved by the chamber of commerce and by realtors who sell property to easterners.

Ten minutes before game time the celebrities, whom Los Angeles papers called the "Hollywood Connection," were already in their seats. They represented television, movies, records and every phase of the entertainment industry.

Cary Grant was there, so was Alice Cooper, Redd Foxx, Gene Kelly, Toni Tenille, Walter Matthau, Doris Day, Harvey Korman, Roger Corman, Tom Jones, Jonathan Winters, Telly Savalas, Johnny Carson, Sue Raney, Pat Henry, Jerry Lewis, Mike Douglas, Don Rickles, Danny Kaye, Milton Berle, and a cast of fifty-five thousand less-famous fans.

The Dodger Blue broke from their dugout. The stadium exploded with a roar. A moment later the Wonderful Washies, as sportswriters were calling them, came onto the field.

The teams lined up along the foul lines. A Rolls-Royce came onto the field to carry Mr. Frank Sinatra to center field, where the Marine Corps band awaited to accompany him in the National Anthem.

The television cameras opened on Sinatra, then panned the crowd, moved down to the teams, paused for a moment on several superstars, then came back to Sinatra again for the final bars of the song.

A roar went up as the music ended.

Attention shifted to a box behind home plate, where the baseball commissioner stood with former Dodger pitching greats Sandy Koufax and Don Drysdale, who were going to throw out the first balls; one left-handed, the other right-handed.

The tension hit Chad when the umpire called, "Play ball." It slammed into his chest, squeezing it with viselike strength. He knelt to retie a shoelace. As he bent down his right knee buckled. His fingers shook so badly he could hardly tie the lace. He straightened up and the stadium swirled before him.

He was frightened, terrified. He fought back the panic building within him. Washington's leadoff batter came to the plate. He was Elmer Verban, their rookie All-Star second baseman. Scouting reports described Verban as a batter who slashed the ball and hit vicious line drives.

The first pitch to Verban sprang off his bat like a bullet emerging from a rifle barrel. The television cameras showed Chad taking three catlike steps to his left before diving and, with his body fully extended, making a sensational catch.

Hencill sat in his den, his face a mask of stone. He didn't care what Chad did in the first inning of the first game, he told himself. He hadn't bet on that. He had bet on the Series. It had a long time to run and he would save his excitement for later.

In the bottom of the first inning, with one man on, Roosevelt Chad hit a home run deep into the left field stands. The Dodgers led two to nothing.

Already in a bad mood because of the note the girl had written, Mrs. Sanders became absolutely furious when she saw the home run. She was sick of the entire family and it was only the first game of the Series.

She waited till the children finished their exercise period before confronting the girl about the note.

"I don't care," the girl said angrily. "You're going to make my brother sick. He's just a little boy and he needs to eat."

"He'll get plenty to eat today. He's going to get your share."

"I don't want it," the boy said.

His sister shushed him.

"And you're going back to bed right now," Mrs. Sanders told the little girl.

Tears sprang to Camilla's eyes. "But I want to stay with my brother. You said we can stay awake three hours."

Mrs. Sanders grasped Camilla's arm roughly where the drugs had been injected, and the girl gasped in pain.

"You write any more notes," Mrs. Sanders threatened, "and I'll put you to sleep so you won't wake up till Christmas."

In the bottom of the seventh inning Chad drove in another run with a single.

Washington won the game, four to three.

SUNDAY
Game Number Two

One of the White Sox players bribed by gamblers to throw the 1919 World Series, actually won two games single-handedly with his bat.

In the third game the player knocked in all the runs as his team won three to nothing.

The sixth game went into extra innings and the score was tied four each in the tenth when the player came to bat. He singled, driving in the winning run.

14.

At 7:30 A.M. Hencill came into the coach house. He brought with him a small tape recorder. It was a lightweight, simple piece of equipment, and he quickly demonstrated to Helen how it worked. Afterward, he rehearsed her a half-dozen times to make sure she understood exactly how to work the machine.

The first message would come from Mrs. Chad and he would take the cassette with him on the plane. Whatever the outcome of game number two, he planned to fly to Washington afterward. Monday he would contact the ball player. The message would prove the family was all right, and it would keep pressure on him. "Have his mother say they miss him, or something like that," Hencill suggested.

"Christ!" Mrs. Sanders said disgustedly. "You wouldn't know the family was kidnapped. You'd think they were visiting us while Chad is on a business trip."

"What do you suggest?" Hencill asked angrily.

"We kidnapped the family to force him to lose the World Series.

We won't do that by sending him 'having a wonderful time, wish you were here' messages. If you want to pressure him, play a tape of his children crying."

"That's out," Hencill said flatly. "We're not abusing the children." He looked suspiciously at Helen. "Are they all right? Are they eating properly?"

"They're getting fat," Mrs. Sanders said sarcastically.

"We're not going to hurt them," Hencill said again. "I won't have it."

"Then why did we bother to kidnap them? Why didn't we just send a threatening letter? If he doesn't believe his family is in danger, he's not going to help us."

That stopped Hencill momentarily. "When the time comes, we'll do something." He looked directly into her face. "But not until I say so."

"Christ!" Mrs. Sanders complained. "You aren't locked in this house taking care of them. I am."

The argument upset Hencill and he didn't eat the breakfast Mrs. Sanders had made him. Instead he drank several cups of coffee. Shortly before Mrs. Chad's waking period began, at nine o'clock, he left the coach house. He didn't want to see the family awake. Mrs. Sanders knew this and laughed as he scurried out.

He went to the plant, hoping to use the quiet Sunday morning to catch up on work. He would watch the game on the TV set in his office.

After he was gone Mrs. Sanders prepared herself for the distasteful task of baby-sitting the Chad family for the next six hours. The grandmother from nine to twelve, the children from twelve-thirty to three-thirty.

Mrs. Sanders liked living alone. The family set her on edge.

At eleven o'clock Sunday morning, the assistant city editor of the *Los Angeles Times* looked up from his desk and called out, "Davis!"

From a field of desks, most of which were unoccupied because it was early and it was Sunday, a young woman got to her feet and walked toward the editor.

"Davis, go out to Palm Acres, ring a few door bells on Rosie Chad's street, see if his neighbors are ignoring the game today, or throwing World Series parties. Do a piece on how a rich neighborhood reacts when one of its residents is a famous baseball player."

Amanda Davis was new at the *Times,* her first job, which was why she had drawn the early Sunday duty. "What if there's no reaction?" she asked.

"That's a story too," the editor told her.

"Want a picture?" She asked eagerly. She was a reporter-photographer.

The editor shrugged. How did he know if he wanted a picture? He didn't know what she would see. "Take a couple shots," he told her. "I'll look at them."

He handed her an assignment slip with Chad's address and a few minutes later she smiled and waved as she hurried from the city room.

She's already composing her acceptance speech for the Pulitzer Prize award, the editor thought. The assignment was a typical unimportant World Series story. The World Series was always media overkill.

In Beverly Hills Mrs. Sanders let Chad's mother tape the message before the pregame television show began.

"What should I say?" Mrs. Chad asked.

"Tell him to lose."

"I couldn't say that." Mrs. Chad shoook her head. She stared a moment at the woman. "You didn't feed Camilla yesterday."

"She gets fed today."

"Will you promise me?"

Mrs. Sanders turned angrily. "I told you yesterday — I mean what I say."

Mrs. Chad was silent for a moment. Then she asked, "May I tape a message to the children?"

"I don't see any good coming of that. I'm not here as a Western Union messenger."

"It would make them feel better," Mrs. Chad persisted.

"You're not here to feel good," Mrs. Sanders said. "You're here to get your son to lose the Series." She held the tape recorder close to Mrs. Chad's mouth. "When I count three, start talking. Keep the message short. Just three or four sentences. And don't waste your time complaining."

Hencill turned on the picture for the pregame show, but left off the sound as he continued working. Though the plant was in operation, the general offices were closed and he liked the feeling of aloneness. From his desk he looked out a picture window onto a lawn as carefully tended as a golf green. Beyond it was a row of bushes. The suite was a refuge. It occurred to him that he would not like to lose it. It further occurred to him that he had not thought of that consequence when he was gambling away his money.

He had been too upset with Mrs. Sanders to eat breakfast, and now he was getting hungry. As soon as the National Anthem had played, he turned up the sound on the TV. He settled back in his chair to watch the first inning. The leadoff batter was Verban, the Washington rookie sensation. He hit the first pitch for a home run. Hencill shouted happily and applauded as the rookie rounded the bases.

His good times were just beginning. The second pitch of the ball game suffered the same fate as the first. It was two to nothing, and Hencill felt famished.

The next two men walked, and the Dodgers changed pitchers. The new pitcher was greeted with the third home run of the inning, and Washington led five to nothing.

Hencill could wait no longer for food. He left his office and walked through the darkened general offices to the food automat in the lounge.

Jensen and McGarrity were watching the game in the stewardesses' apartment in Brentwood. Shirley was from Illinois and Linda from Alabama. Both had been married to pilots. Now they were content, for a while at least, to lead the single life. They had invited

Jensen and McGarrity for lunch and to watch the World Series game. The men had passed themselves off as businessmen from the East.

Shirley cooked (Lasagna Galesburg, McGarrity called it) while Linda baked homemade bread and made a special Alabama green salad (Salad Selma, McGarrity called it). The men had brought wine and cognac.

Before the game started, Shirley had organized a run pool for the four of them. She was a great game player. Fortunately, Jensen noted to himself, not when it came to her private life: she enjoyed sex immensely and was very aggressive about it.

Lunch was finished and they were drinking coffee and cognac when the Dodgers came to bat in the bottom of the fourth inning, trailing five to nothing. The first two men were out and then an error and a walk put two men on, with Roosevelt Chad coming to bat.

"I'd walk him," Shirley advised.

"I'd tempt him to swing at bad pitches," said her roommate.

"You'd tempt him all right," McGarrity commented.

Linda giggled and poked McGarrity in the ribs.

"I'd give him nothing to pull," Jensen said.

Shirley turned to McGarrity. "What would you do, Mike?"

"Hit him with a bean ball," McGarrity answered. "That way you might get him out for the whole Series."

Chad hit a one-and-one pitch for a home run. The Senators' lead was cut to five to three.

As Chad trotted around the bases, McGarrity turned to Jensen. "I know people who aren't going to be happy about that."

"The Dodgers are going to win the Series," Linda promised.

"I wouldn't bet on it," McGarrity warned.

"Why?" Shirley asked.

"I think it's fixed," McGarrity said.

"Phooey," Shirley said. The girls began laughing. Jensen and McGarrity joined them.

Hencill had some doubts that the Series was fixed. He had returned from the automat with a tray of enchiladas and burritos. He wolfed them down while enjoying the Senators' lead. When Chad hit the homer, Hencill felt the Mexican food start a revolution in his stomach.

He couldn't understand what was wrong with Chad.

Maybe the home run was an accident. Hencill was a successful baseball bettor because he was a keen student of the game. He had played himself and always had felt that only his size had kept him from great success. He understood the game. He understood concentration, instinct, and habit. He asked himself whether these ingredients had dominated when Chad hit the home run, or whether the ball player was determined to play the Series honestly, stringing him along in the meantime.

Hencill denied the last. You didn't string someone along who had life-and-death control over your family. This was only game number two. And the Dodgers had lost the first one. Christ! They were behind in this one. Why was he getting excited? When the time came, when the pressure was on Chad, the ball player would know what was at stake.

His mind accepted this reasoning. His stomach did not.

Amanda Davis got to Palm Acres an hour before game time. At the very first house, the one directly opposite the Chads', a World Series party was in progress. In a spacious yard the host monitored pregame activities on TV while he barbecued hamburgers for his guests, some of whom lived on the street, while some, he told Amanda, were from other areas of the city.

Amanda accepted a hamburger and sipped a beer as she wandered around talking to people. TV sets were on in the kitchen, the den, a basement game room, the living room, and even the bathrooms were furnished with small-screen portables. Amanda waited for game time to begin and then took several pictures of guests watching sets both inside and outside.

Then she moved on.

At the next house the residents were watching alone. They offered her a beer, she took a Coke, and talked to her hosts between plays. One very important piece of information came out of the visit. The people said a county detective had been in the neighborhood asking questions about a burglary which had taken place at Chad's house.

Like all good *Times* reporters, Amanda daily read the paper from cover to cover. She recalled no story about a burglary at the baseball star's home. And it certainly would have gotten some coverage, considering the timing, no matter how small the loss.

At the next house, where a small party was in progress, the hostess told her the same story about the county detective. Amanda did some interviews then watched an inning of the game. In the top of the fifth the Senators loaded the bases with no outs. The party became quiet while the guests watched the Dodgers use two pitchers to get out of the inning without Washington scoring.

In the bottom of the inning the Dodgers struck back, getting their first two men on with no outs. Before the inning was over the Dodger catcher doubled, driving both runners in. The score was tied at five all.

Mrs. Sanders monitored the game through the earphones of her portable radio. At the same time, she kept a close eye on the children. The note incident proved they couldn't be trusted.

The children were walking toward her now, on the downward leg of their promenade. She saw them whisper to each other and then the girl asked, "Would you please tell us, ma'am, the score of the ball game?"

Mrs. Sanders wasn't buying any of this "please" and "ma'am" crap. "No," she said. "I won't tell you the score."

"We'll find out everything when we get home," the boy consoled his sister.

"*If* you get home," Mrs. Sanders threatened.

The boy's face fell. The girl looked angrily at her. Mrs. Sanders smiled at them.

After the exercise period she fed them. It was the first time in three days that they both were fed. She left the radio next to the tape recorder on top of the TV and went to the kitchen. There she opened the jars of baby food and poured juice.

She looked around and saw the girl walking toward the TV. "Where do you think you're going?" she called out.

"Is that a tape recorder by the radio?" the girl asked.

"Yes. And stay away from it."

"Did Grandmother made a message for Daddy?"

"Yes. Now come back here."

The girl turned. "I'd like to send a message, too," she said.

"I bet you would." Mrs. Sanders was sarcastic.

The girl looked defiantly at her. The girl was trouble.

While the children ate, she tuned in the game. At the top of the eighth inning Washington scored twice and took a seven-to-five lead. Mrs. Sanders's spirits soared. If Washington won, and took a two-game lead home with them, they would have the Series in the bag.

She remembered Chad's fouth-inning home run and that soured her again. If he hadn't hit that, Washington would already have the game in the bag.

She put down the radio. It was chore time: the boy made the beds; the girl cleaned off the table.

After the girl finished her work she asked for permission to go to the bathroom. Mrs. Sanders assented. Robert had taken the lock off the door, and she had cleaned out the medicine cabinet, so there was no need to accompany the girl.

The accumulation of dishes from Mrs. Sanders's breakfast and the Chads' meals was in the sink, and she cleaned them off and put them in the dishwasher. She turned on the machine and moved from the counter. It occurred to her that the game must be over, or nearly over.

She looked for the radio. Where had she put it? She walked to the front of the room. She thought it was on the TV, but that turned out to be the tape recorder, which she picked up, ejecting the tape made by Mrs. Chad and putting in a new cassette. At that moment she heard a cry from the direction of the bathroom.

She half turned and the door burst open and the girl ran out screaming.

"Stop that!" Mrs. Sanders screamed back, not knowing what it was about, but frightened.

The girl was standing with the portable radio in her hand. "Daddy won!" she shouted. "He hit a home run and won the game. Daddy won!"

The boy came from behind the screen where he had been making up his cot. He ran laughing to his sister and threw his arms around her. The girl turned the volume of the radio up to its highest decibel and looked defiantly at Mrs. Sanders. The roar of the crowd and the announcer's voice filled the room.

"DODGERS WIN! DODGERS WIN! In the bottom of the ninth, two men out, two men on, two strikes on Rosie Chad, and he hit the next pitch out! DODGERS WIN! DODGERS WIN!"

Mrs. Sanders's head swirled. The defeat, the noise, the defiant child combined to blind her with rage. Still holding the tape recorder she ran toward the children.

"DODGERS WIN! DODGERS WIN!" The sound of victory filled the coach house.

Mrs. Sanders snatched the radio from the girl and flung it to the floor. The case popped open and a battery rolled out. The crowd's roar was gone. In a second motion, Mrs. Sanders slapped the child across her mouth. Immediately, a spot of blood appeared where the upper lip had been cut by a tooth. For a second the child continued her defiant stare and then she broke into tears.

"Do you want to send a message to your father?" Mrs. Sanders shouted at her. "Here!" She pushed the tape recorder close to the child's face. "Tell him anything you want. I swear to God he'll get the message. I promise you he'll hear it. He'll hear it if I have to call him up myself."

She slapped the crying child twice more. Beside her, the boy was also in tears.

"Talk!" Mrs. Sanders ordered. "Talk!" She ground the tape recorder into the child's face. "Talk!" she screamed.

"Oh, Daddy, Daddy," the girl wept, "please come and get us. She won't give us anything to eat. Oh, Daddy, I'm so afraid. I hate this mean woman."

Mrs. Sanders slapped the child again. The boy sprang at her, his fists clenched. "Stop hitting my sister, or I'll kill you!"

There was a bathroom and shower connected to Hencill's office. He had been in the room for five minutes, ever since he had watched Chad's game home run land in the right-field bleachers. He was on his knees throwing up in the toilet, filling it with undigested Mexican food. Keeping his head squarely over the bowl, he reached out with his right hand for the roll of toilet paper. He wiped his mouth and his left shirt sleeve where some of the vomit had spewed. Then he threw up again.

He waited five minutes, and when he was sure it was over, he got to his feet and turned to the sink. He splashed water on his face and soaked his left sleeve. He saw some vomit on his right shoe and used a wad of toilet paper to clean it off.

He got sick again on the way home. He pulled to the side of the freeway, opened the door on the passenger side, and threw up on the grass.

Mercifully, Ilka was not at home when he arrived. He was packing when the telephone rang. The call came from the coach house. It totally unnerved him.

"Chad won't win any more ball games," Helen said, her voice a sheet of ice. "I've taken care of that."

Hencill did not know what she meant, but he was frightened. He thought he was going to be sick again. It was a mistake to have involved Helen.

"Are you there?" she asked when he didn't reply.

"Yes."

"Did you hear me? We won't have any more problems with the ball player. I've fixed it."

He was afraid to ask, but he had to. "How did you fix it?"

"I sliced off his daughter's ear."

Men do not scream well, and Hencill did it more poorly than most. It was a frightening gargle, as if he had something caught in his throat and was trying to force it out.

He dropped the telephone receiver and ran from the room. He took the stairs two and three at a time. Near the bottom he missed a step and pitched forward. He covered his head with his hands and somersaulted once. He leaped to his feet, tore open the front door, and raced across the lawn, through Helen's flower garden.

The door of the coach house was locked. He pounded on it, beating it with his fists.

When Helen opened the door her face was alight with a triumphant smile. He pushed her aside and ran toward the hospital screens. He didn't know where the girl was. He knocked over the first screen. Mrs. Chad stared at him through one open, unconscious eye.

He turned and strode quickly to the next screen, which he kicked away from the bed. A sheet was pulled over the form of a child. He pulled it back. The boy lay asleep on his stomach.

The third screen was at the end of the room. He ran toward it, then slowed as he neared it. He was panting heavily. Sweat ran down his back and dripped from his face. He took a deep breath and looked behind the screen. A towel had been thrown over the girl's head. A groan escaped his lips. He stepped forward.

Gently he lifted the towel from the girl's head. He flinched momentarily as her head came into view. She was on her side. Her left ear was visible. It was unharmed. Cautiously he raised the girl's head. She moaned in her sleep. He turned her head slightly to look at the right side.

"JESUS CHRIST!" he screamed. He turned and ran toward Helen. "YOU'RE CRAZY. JESUS CHRIST! YOU'RE ABSOLUTELY CRAZY!"

Hencill grabbed her hair and snapped her head back. He slapped her hard, twice.

"YOU DIDN'T DO IT!" Hencill shouted. "YOU DIDN'T CUT OFF HER EAR!"

She shook her head. "No," she gasped.

"Then why did you tell me that? Why did you say such a horrible thing?"

"For months the Getty kidnappers got only conversation from the family. They got results damn fast when they mailed the boy's ear to his family." She grinned. "Look at the results I just got from you. Imagine how Chad would feel." She motioned at the tape recorder. "If you think it's going to do any good sending sweetheart messages to the ball player, then you're the crazy one."

It was Hencill's turn to become deadly serious. "If you harm one of those children, if you touch one of them without my say so, I swear to God I'll fix you like you fixed Ilka's dog."

Mrs. Sanders smiled at him. "You haven't got the guts," she said simply.

For a long moment the two stared at each other. The first to look away was Hencill.

"The children are in perfect condition," she said consolingly. "They haven't been touched."

Hencill turned away. He looked around the room, his eyes falling on the tape recorder. He retrieved it from the kitchen table. "I'll phone from Washington." His voice was cold and quiet. "I am going to call you just a few minutes before I call Chad so you'll have to operate quickly. I'll hold my cassette close to the receiver and on a count of five you start playing yours. That's how we'll transmit messages."

He handed her the tape recorder and left the coach house.

Mrs. Sanders watched him go. When he slammed the door behind him, she muttered, "Fool!"

It was nearly five o'clock when Amanda returned to the city room. She went directly to the assistant city editor and told him about the alleged burglary at Chad's house.

His face reflected puzzlement. "Call Schmidt and ask him to run it down," he told her.

Larry Schmidt was a veteran *Times* police reporter. Little happened in Los Angeles County that he didn't know about or couldn't find out about.

Amanda telephoned from her desk. She sensed Schmidt didn't have much patience with young reporters. "Did you work last week, Larry?" she asked, wondering if she shouldn't have called him Mr. Schmidt.

"Sure. Why?" He sounded annoyed.

"Was there a burglary at Roosevelt Chad's house?"

"I don't know. Was there one?"

She quickly told him about her experience in Chad's neighborhood.

"I'll get right back to you," he said, the annoyance gone.

Half an hour later he was on the phone. "I think I got it. I talked to the chief of detectives. He said this ploy is being used a lot nowadays by burglars. They go into a neighborhood, pass themselves off as law officers, then case the area. It's a perfect cover."

"You mean the detective was a burglar?"

"Maybe. Or a peddler of some kind. The county will run extra motor patrols through the area."

After Schmidt hung up Amanda reported her information to the assistant city editor. "Shall I tack it on the end of my neighborhood story?"

He thought a moment and then shook his head. "No. It's unimportant."

MONDAY
Travel Day

In the post–World War II era, more than half the Series have gone the full seven games.

The first World Series was played in 1903. Boston won the best-of-nine-game Series by beating Pittsburgh five games to three.

The first game was played in Boston. Cy Young was the losing pitcher.

At the end of seventy-five years of play, the American League had a Series edge of forty-five to thirty.

Each year half of the persons in the United States (110,000,000) watch some portion of the World Series on television. As many as eighty million persons may watch an individual game.

15.

Chad woke in his Washington hotel room at nine o'clock. Normally that would mean he had overslept, but not when he considered that his body was still on West Coast time, where it was 6 A.M.

He forwent his usual gymnastics, opened the window curtains, and looked out onto a fine fall day. He considered whether to breakfast in his room or go down to the hotel restaurant. He was a modest man, but he was a realist and knew that he was famous, that his public appearances always drew autograph seekers. On game days, when from the moment he woke he began psyching himself up to play, he avoided public contacts as best he could. Today he didn't want to be alone in his room. That would leave him brooding about his family, which wouldn't help them, or himself.

He'd been twice to Washington, and neither occasion afforded an opportunity to sightsee. His first trip to the capital was to the White House for the sports dinner, hosted by the President. He had flown in late one afternoon and departed the next morning. His travel arrangements had been similar when he had been honored at a dinner sponsored by the Washington Baseball Writers Association.

He left the room and went to the lobby, where he bought a paper before going into the dining room. After breakfast, he returned to the newsstand and bought a tour book. On his way to the street exit he was stopped several times to sign autographs, and well-wishers called out greetings to him.

Chad had not noticed a man seated on a couch, who was smoking a cigarette and reading a newspaper. The man was unobtrusive. He was small, had thick coal-black hair and an unlined boyish face. He had a thin smile on his lips. When Chad went out the door the man put down the newspaper and followed him.

Jensen hated the computer room. It was windowless, low-ceilinged, and dim. For the protection of the intricate machines the room was kept at a constant temperature of 68 degrees. Yet Jensen sat in the room and perspired. His coat was off, his shirtsleeves rolled up, his tie loosened. His eyes glazed with ennui and he drank cup after cup of coffee.

He had been at it since seven o'clock, three hours already, and he had nothing to show for his work. Even the number of names on the lists was seemingly no smaller.

McGarrity was coming in after lunch, and Jensen was looking forward to that. At least he would have someone to talk with.

First, he had put the twenty-two losers through the computer. He was looking for a clue, a path, a motive, a hint, an accident, a piece of luck: any directional signal that would point the way to the kidnappers. He was looking for a tax cheater, a securities swindler, a rich businessman who, to get a large sum of money, had written a bad check or forged a good one. Jensen was looking for anyone who had a motive strong enough to lead to an act as desperate as kidnapping a whole family and trying to fix the World Series.

Printouts on three of the losers had shown some promise. A doctor in Louisville was in deep trouble with the IRS. A stockbroker in Chicago was under investigation for a securities swindle. A motion picture producer in Los Angeles had allegedly raked money off the top of his films and was about to be nailed by several federal and state agencies for a string of charges ranging from fraud to forgery.

Using Frazzini's authority, Jensen telexed orders to the appropriate FBI bureaus, requesting immediate reports on the three men. He stipulated a forty-eight-hour answering period. This meant field agents would go immediately into action collecting raw data, including unsubstantiated rumors and hearsay, from FBI and other sources.

After the losers, he started the list of three hundred forty-seven big bettors. McGarrity would help feed these lists through the computers.

The system was simple and demanded no training. The ability to type was beneficial, though not necessary. One typed a name onto a tape, fed the tape into the machine, and waited. Like a giant pinball machine, the computer hummed and clicked and whirred and tinkled and finally, through a narrow slit, spit out its knowledge. So far, Jensen thought, the computer was a witness that "didn't know nothin'."

He glanced at the latest printout. It was a Billy Bob Schneider in Raleigh. Schneider was a realtor who had bet seventy-five thousand dollars on the Senators. The printout showed he once had been arrested for driving violations in Iowa City and once had been audited by the IRS. He had faithfully served in the United States Army, which once punished him for a day's AWOL and which later discharged him honorably. Why Schneider bet the seventy-five thousand dollars on the Washington Senators was not evident on the printout.

At 11 A.M., his work was interrupted by a call from Frazzini. "Evans invites you to lunch with him at noon."

"I'll be there," Jensen promised.

"The martinis will be ready."

"And so will I," Jensen said. He hung up and turned to the computer.

A Monday afternoon in October is not the height of the Washington tourist season, and only a few other persons were about as Chad visited one point of interest after another. He saw the Lincoln Memorial, the Smithsonian, the National Gallery. He didn't stay long at any of them. He would come back another time, with his family.

He couldn't totally shut baseball from his mind and he wondered how the kidnapper felt when he hit the game-winning home run. It had been luck. He was trying to drive in the tying run by shooting the gap in left center. He had gotten more power into his swing than he intended and the pitcher had made a mistake getting the ball in to him where he could use his power. Everyone had been unlucky, Chad thought. Most of all the kidnapper.

He hoped the guy hadn't gotten upset over the loss. Washington was sure to lose others. Chad thought the Series would go six games, maybe seven. The Senators were a scrappy ball club.

When he left the National Gallery, he hailed a taxi and asked to be dropped off in a downtown shopping area. He wanted to buy presents for his children. When he got them back they would ask him about Washington. The presents would show that he had thought about them while he was there. As if that would be necessary.

As he walked along, looking in store windows, he was conscious of passersby recognizing him. Several gave shy greetings. Chad said "hi" or "hello." He believed in the relationship between the fans and the players. He felt privileged to be a famous person and he was conscientious about his status.

Seven teenagers, seniors on Skip Day from a nearby Virginia high school, stopped him for autographs. A pencil was shoved at him, followed by souvenir programs and menus the students had collected in their wanderings.

He exchanged good-natured banter with the youths, who told

him they were for the Wonderful Washies (but wished him good luck), before moving on.

He crossed the street and entered Garfinckel's, the famous Washington department store. Before he went to the toy department he stopped in the men's shop. The salesmen recognized him and called him Mr. Chad and were very polite.

He selected a camel-colored cashmere turtleneck sweater. It cost over a hundred dollars and he felt guilty for spending so much. Most of his sweaters were lamb's wool. He rationalized that the sweater was his World Series gift to himself.

When he paid for the purchase, the salesman asked him to sign an autograph for his son Jimmy. Chad wrote it on a Garfinckel's order pad. "Good luck, Jimmy. Rosie Chad."

He gave his credit card to the salesman and looked absentmindedly at a jewelry case next to the sales desk while he waited for the sweater to be boxed. He paid no attention when the phone rang at the packaging counter. A young girl answered.

"Just a minute," she said and turned to the salesman.

Chad was bending over the jewelry case when the salesman said he was wanted on the phone. He straightened up so quickly that the blood rushed from his head and he felt a moment of dizziness.

"You can take it at the buyer's desk, sir," the salesman said, and pointed to the rear of the department. "You'll have privacy there."

"Thank you," Chad said. He was confused. No one knew he was in the store. It was only by accident that he had come in. A suspicion came over him and he quickened his step to the phone.

Shortly after twelve o'clock Jensen left the computer room and took the elevator to Evans's suite.

Frazzini already was there, standing at the bar mixing a shaker of martinis. Evans was reading the *Washington Post*. He put it down when Jensen entered. "Any luck?" he asked.

Jensen shook his head and reached out for the martini Frazzini offered him. "'Maybe McGarrity will bring us the luck of the Irish.'"

"Is it really a good idea to let him run those lists through the computer?" Evans asked.

"They're his lists," Jensen reminded the FBI director. "Without them even *I* wouldn't be in the computer room."

"We've got no worries there, John," Frazzini added. "The Mafia will play it straight when cooperating with us. It's when they're working alone that they'll try to get the advantage."

Evans pondered that. "You think they're looking for the kidnappers on their own?" he asked Jensen.

"For sure."

"How would they go about it?"

"Well, they got their own computers," Jensen answered.

"But not with our information," Evans countered.

"I'm sure they keep some information, some kind of records, on the high rollers who bet with them," Jensen explained. "And they can always run credit checks."

"You gotta remember, John," Frazzini said, "they got a lot of resources at hand."

For a moment the men sipped the martinis. Jensen broke the silence. "What the case needs, John, is wiretaps."

Frazzini immediately set his martini on the bar. Evans paused, his glass almost to his lips. He set the glass down.

"Some of the twenty-two names on the losers' list belong to very important citizens." Evans's voice was low and sober. "The Justice Department wouldn't buy tapping their phones without just cause. And theory isn't just cause."

Frazzini put both his hands flat on the bar and looked at Evans. "Do it without the Justice Department, John. You tap that list and you got your kidnappers. I'd bet on it."

"You'd bet!" Evans's voice became sarcastic. "How much would you bet, Al? Would you bet your career on it? Because that's what it'd cost if you get caught."

A knock on the door interrupted the conversation. A waiter wheeled a luncheon cart through the doorway and the men followed him into the dining room that was part of Evans's suite of offices.

The man who did order taps placed on the phones of the twenty-two losers had spent the morning listening to the first shipment of tapes from the Midwest and East Coast. In the early morning McGarrity had received a telephone call from Gotnich, who apologized that several tapes were missing. He promised they would be included in the following day's shipment.

McGarrity didn't complain. He was impressed by the efficiency with which Gotnich handled what McGarrity knew was a huge and complicated logistical problem.

All the West Coast tapes had been collected, Gotnich said, and the messenger was at the moment on a flight to Washington.

Chad's heart stopped when he heard the voice. Chad immediately knew it was the kidnapper. It was a voice he never would forget. "Is that you, Mr. Chad?"

Jensen's briefing flashed through his mind. He remembered the words credibility, reassurance, relationship. He felt confident. "It's me," he answered.

He heard a sigh through the receiver. "Can you talk?" the voice asked. It sounded tense.

"I'm at the buyer's desk. There's no one around."

"You missed a terrific chance yesterday to lose a game," the voice accused him.

"You said I might not have to," Chad replied.

"I know what I said." The voice was anxious. "But if you hadn't hit the home run, Washington would have taken a two-to-nothing lead in games."

"The Washington manager is happy," Chad countered. "He said on TV that all he wanted in Los Angeles was a split."

"The Washington manager doesn't have his life bet on this Series either," the kidnapper argued. "If he did, he'd feel exactly as I do, that you missed a good chance."

"I'll create my own chances," Chad answered.

"You better. Never forget that I have your family."

"And you never forget that I control your bet. I can win it, or I can lose it. Whether you like it or not, we're partners."

There was a pause. Chad was quietly elated that the argument given him by the FBI man had obviously struck home. "We have a deal," Chad said, pushing the point, "but it goes two ways. I plan to do my part, *my way*. I expect you to do your part and that is to take good care of my family and release them when this is over."

"I'm doing my part, *partner*, I taped a message from your mother," the kidnapper said.

"Let's hear it!"

"In a moment. I want to talk to you again tomorrow. Take a walk. Stay downtown on busy streets. I'll contact you."

"Tomorrow I want a message from my children."

"That might be inconvenient."

"It's more inconvenient doing what you want me to do."

"Okay."

Chad knew he had scored another point. "And have them include something current so I know it's up to date."

"Goddam! Anything else?"

Instinct told Chad to leave the ransom for another conversation.

"Here's the message from your mother."

Chad pressed his ear to the receiver. In a few seconds he heard his mother's voice. It sounded changed, weaker, but it definitely was his mother. "Hello, Roosevelt. We are in good health, but we miss you. God will take care of us."

The kidnapper had hung up. For a moment Chad stood at the desk, the receiver in his hand, and forced back his emotion. When he was all right again, he telephoned Jensen.

Evans, Jensen, and Frazzini were sipping coffee and cognac when the intercom buzzed. Evans answered.

"It's for Mr. Jensen, sir," a female voice said. "It's on the emergency line."

"Chad or McGarrity," Jensen predicted.

"Put them on," Evans said, and flipped a switch activating a speaker.

"Go ahead, sir," the secretary said to the unknown caller. Her voice filled the room.

"Hello. Mr. Jensen?"

"Yes, Mr. Chad. I'm here."

"He called." The ball player's voice was excited.

"Tell me about it," Jensen said.

Frazzini and Evans listened and Jensen scribbled notes as Chad related the conversation.

When he finished Jensen asked. "How did he react when you told him you could win his bet, or lose it, and that you expected him to do his part?"

"It stopped him," Chad answered. "I could tell until then he thought it was all a one-way street coming his way."

"How about the ransom?"

"We didn't get into that. I'll bring it up tomorrow."

"Mr. Chad, this is John Evans. How long today were you gone from the hotel? How long did he follow you?"

"I'd guess two and a half hours. I hope he doesn't wait that long tomorrow. I got a game tomorrow night."

"Call me immediately after he makes contact," Jensen said.

"I will. And thanks. You're right. He can be maneuvered."

Evans switched off the speaker.

For a moment the three men were silent. Frazzini spoke first and said what was on all their minds. "We'd never get him. Too much distance. Too many stores. Too many phones."

Evans nodded in agreement. "Well, at least he made contact."

"And Chad handled it beautifully," Frazzini said. "You did a wonderful job briefing him, Tom."

"He's a good student," Jensen said.

"He was awfully cool about it," Evans added. "You'd hardly think he was agonizing over his decisions."

"He's not," Jensen said.

Frazzini and Evans looked questioningly at him. "You mean he's decided to take himself out of the lineup?" Evans asked.

"No."

"Well, I doubt if he's decided to sacrifice his family," Frazzini said skeptically.

"I'm not saying that he is going to sacrifice his family, or throw a game, or take himself out of the lineup. He is in agony over his family, but he is not in agony over any decision he may have to make because he's not going to make any decisions. Not until he has to.

"People don't like hard choices. They postpone decisions on operations and die. They postpone decisions on a divorce and live in misery. They postpone getting the maturity to grow old with and instead have a facelift and make themselves ludicrous. People postpone and wait for God or fate to intervene.

"That's what Chad is doing. It's unthinkable to him to throw a single game, what's more a World Series. It's unthinkable to him that anyone could be so monstrous as to kill his family. He is immobilized. He made one big decision when he called us rather than going it alone. That's the last decision he is going to make until the kidnapper is about to lose his bet. And then he will decide if he can play his best or, if not, to take himself from the lineup and hope the kidnapper will take a ransom if the bets are lost."

"Or to do neither and try to lose the Series after all," Frazzini said.

"You got it, Al." Jensen stood up. "Well, maybe I can save him from all that by finding the guy in the computer."

After talking to Chad, Hencil walked quickly away from the phone booth to another one several blocks away. There he telephoned Helen.

"Did you threaten him?" she asked.

Hencill made a face. Her violent nature was becoming a burden. "I warned him," he said. "Chad is a bright, sophisticated guy. I reminded him what was at stake."

Mocking laughter came over the phone. "I see, you thought he'd forgotten his family had been kidnapped and you gave him a polite reminder."

"I don't believe in crying wolf," he said. "When the time comes . . . *if* it comes . . . I'll be tough. In the meantime, there's no point in yelling at him every day. He's agreed to lose. What more can we ask?"

"That he *does* lose, goddammit! That he doesn't win lost ball games with ninth-inning home runs."

Hencill closed off the argument. "All right, all right!" he said. "What's done, is done. Tomorrow I want a message from one of the children. So that Chad can be sure the tape wasn't made several days ago, he wants the child to say something indicating the tape is current. Use a sports score from a night game. I'll try to call you between eight or nine o'clock your time."

"That means I'll have to get them up early." Her voice betrayed anger. "And then put them back to sleep and get them up again in the afternoon." From the very beginning she had organized a routine in order to decrease the demanding task of caring for the family. She did not like that routine disturbed. Mrs. Chad required less supervision than the children and she had planned her days accordingly.

Hencill understood her pique. But security was more important than her convenience. He was paranoid about losing the cassette or, in his haste, forgetting the tape recorder in a phone booth. Even the thought made him shudder with fear. As nearly as possible he wanted in one moment to get the message from Helen, in the next moment play it to Chad, and in the following moment erase it.

He ignored her complaint. "A few minutes before I contact Chad I'll call you. We'll transmit exactly as I showed you," he ordered. "Hold the recorder close to the phone, wait for me to count off and then start the message."

"And what should I have the little darlings say?"

Hencill sighed. "Let them tell their father that they're in good health."

"And happy," Helen added, "and that in the afternoon we're going to Disneyland.'"

Before Hencill could retort, she had slammed down the receiver.

McGarrity was overwhelmed by the computer. "My God! No wonder the liberals are always after you guys."

"We call it Big Brother," Jensen said.

McGarrity shuddered. "Let's hope it's never controlled by an evil power."

"That's why we keep it out of the hands of the media," Jensen said.

McGarrity put a hand on the computer and patted it. "Am I in there?"

"Yes."

"Are you in there?"

"I better not be."

The men laughed.

The rest of the afternoon was not so funny. It was boring, tedious work. At four o'clock they took a cocktail break. McGarrity had brought a thermos of martinis. "I once read that FBI agents didn't drink around J. Edgar Hoover," he said.

"They didn't have time," Jensen explained. "They were too busy doing repairs on his house."

At 11 P.M. they knocked off. "The end of another glamorous day in the life of an FBI agent," Jensen said.

"Glamorous!" McGarrity snorted. "Tomorrow I'm going to wear overalls and carry a lunch pail."

The West Coast tapes were in his room when McGarrity returned to the hotel. The lawyer felt that if the kidnapper was one of the losers, he would be from the West Coast. It was a West Coast kind of crime, McGarrity thought. Freaky.

In the morning session he had developed a speed system that eliminated the need to listen to every word of each conversation. Housewife and teenager calls were quickly gotten out of the way by liberal use of the tape recorder's Fast Forward switch.

Some of the tapes were amusing, or sexy, and for those McGarrity sometimes lingered. One such set of tapes belonged to Mr. Wayne Alexander, a San Francisco attorney. A notation with the tapes indicated there were three phones at the Alexander residence. One was for general purposes. Another was for the lawyer's professional use. The third was for their teenage daughter.

Those tapes reminded McGarrity of the sex-oriented soap operas. The tap of the general-purpose phone revealed that Mrs. Alexander was carrying on an affair with one of Alexander's partners. The tap of the lawyer's professional phone revealed he was having affairs with one of the office secretaries, a client, and the wife of his partner who, unbeknownst to him, was having an affair with his wife.

The couple's sixteen-year-old daughter was not much better . . . or worse. Her phone tap revealed she was sleeping with a high-school football hero and her math instructor, and was trying to seduce a thirteen-year-old neighbor.

By midnight McGarrity had gone through three tapes. He took a break and ordered a sandwich and a pot of coffee sent to his room.

When Jensen left the computer room he drove to the Plaza Hotel, parked, and spent an hour walking the empty streets of late-night Washington. He followed along part of the path Chad had taken.

On one block he counted all the phone booths on both sides of the street. He noted the frequency of shops and small stores.

A passing police cruiser pulled alongside the curb. Jensen flashed his identification. "FBI," he said. "Out for a walk."

"A bad place this time of night, sir," the driver said.

"I'll watch it," Jensen said.

The cruiser pulled away.

Jensen walked to the end of the block, turned the corner, and passed a large discount store. Beyond it he peered into a dimestore and tried to locate all the telephone fixtures. There appeared to be three in front and three at the rear.

He moved on. He saw the police cruiser pass the intersection ahead of him and knew they were keeping a lookout.

Jensen turned another corner and ahead was Garfinckel's. He stopped at an entrance and looked inside. To the left he saw a public telephone. He wondered if the kidnapper had used it when he called Chad. It certainly would have been easier than running back to a sidewalk phone. And had he run to the street and called, and missed Chad, he'd have had a difficult time picking up the trail again.

But there were strong arguments against calling from inside the store, Jensen thought. A store had guards and house detective who were on the lookout for suspicious persons. Jensen guessed that the kidnapper probably felt suspicious as hell.

On the street the kidnapper was part of the crowd. He was free to move in many directions. Jensen decided that if he were the kidnapper he would not go into large stores or lose the anonymity of the sidewalk crowds.

He hailed a passing taxi and went back to the Plaza, where he'd left his car.

On the way he considered his plan for capturing the kidnapper on the street. Working against him was the immense area to cover and the great number of telephones. Working for him was the building relationship between Chad and the kidnapper. Jensen knew this would make the kidnapper trustful and confident, which, in turn, would lessen his caution. This, the veteran agent knew from experience, could lead to many interesting developments.

Fragments of an insight floated in Jensen's mind. He thought that if he could put them together he would have the plan he was looking for.

McGarrity had finished the sandwich and coffee and had drawn himself a bath. He had pushed his body deep into warm water. Blue bubbles floated on the water around him, releasing a mild scent as they popped. He played another tape.

It was in this comfortable, even luxurious, setting that he heard an icy female voice say, "Chad won't win any more ball games. I've taken care of that."

The statement caught McGarrity unawares and shocked him. Apparently it had the same effect on the man, for there was a pause and then the woman's voice inquired, "Are you there?"

"Yes." McGarrity heard a puzzled male voice answer. He put his right elbow on the edge of the tub and listened intently to the cassette.

"Did you hear me? We won't have any more problems with the ball player. I've fixed it."

McGarrity thought he heard a trace of sadism in the woman's voice.

The man asked, "How did you fix it?"

McGarrity would never forget what came next.

"I sliced off his daughter's ear."

McGarrity knew death and cruelty first hand; nevertheless his face flinched and he cried out, "Oh, God Almighty!"

Though encased in the warm water, his body turned absolutely cold as a man's scream emanated from the cassette.

Immediately McGarrity got out of the tub. For a moment he stared at the cassette as if it were a loathsome reptile. Distastefully he reran the tape to the beginning of the conversation. Twice he started it and turned it off. He didn't want to hear it again. There was nothing he could do anyhow about the sadistic crime, and he didn't want to hear of it again. He looked at the name on the tape cassette. It read ROBERT HENCILL, JR. Below was a Beverly Hills address.

McGarrity had found his man.

TUESDAY
Game Number Three

After the 1919 World Series scandal, it was hard to believe that Joe Jackson, a star Chicago player, had participated in the fix. He hit .375 for the Series and was the team's second leading producer of RBIs. Also, he led the team in home runs.

16.

At 7 A.M. Mrs. Sanders injected a stimulant in Billy's arm. The drug would prematurely rouse him from his induced sleep. It was a light dosage, as she wanted him to awaken only long enough to tape a short message. Then she would put him back to sleep. She didn't want the children awake at the same time as their grandmother.

What should she have the boy say? Robert would want something touching and sad, with violin music in the background. He was a fool.

She sighed and forced her mind back to the boy and the message. A thought for the message entered her mind and she spoke it aloud to the quiet room. "Daddy, we are doing what the people tell us. We hope you do too. We want to see you again. If you don't do what they say . . ."

She laughed. She'd end it right there. Let Chad think about that. Robert wouldn't like it. It would be too *brutal* for him. But for her it was too soft. The message she would like to play was the one she had recorded of the children crying and screaming. She could imagine what *that* one would do to both Robert and the ball player.

The problem with them, she thought, was that they both had had it too good. Robert had always had his money and Chad his baseball talent. All she had was her home and pension, and she had had to work hard for both. She didn't want to lose them because Robert wanted to remain a Stanford gentleman and the baseball player wanted to remain a Boy Scout hero. It depressed her that these two owned her future.

She heard a stirring in Billy's bed. The stimulant was taking affect. She looked at the screens blocking off the beds holding the three hostages. Robert and the baseball player owned her future. But she owned theirs as well.

Hencill hurried along a crowded Washington street. Ahead, at a busy traffic intersection, was a telephone booth. He glanced at his watch. It was eleven o'clock, eight o'clock in California.

He entered the booth, shoved some coins in the slot, and dialed the number of the coach house. While he waited for Helen to answer, he took the tape recorder from his pocket and put it on the shelf under the telephone.

The connection was made. "Hello." Helen's voice came strongly over the wire.

"It's me," he said. "How are they?"

"Barely alive," she answered.

Hencill cursed to himself. "Do you have the message?"

"Yes. It runs twenty seconds."

"Do you have something current on it?"

"The Monday-night football game score."

"Good. I'll take it now."

Hencill was waiting down the street and spotted Chad leave the hotel. He hated following the ball player. Every time a police car passed, his blood pressure soared. But he knew it was the safest way to make contact. Though he was not certain, he believed Chad had not gone to the police. But until he was certain, he was not making any direct phone calls into the player's hotel room. He was making no conversations into a tapped telephone. He waited forty-five minutes before he called.

He saw Chad enter a shop. In the window were models of airplanes and ships and armored equipment. A large sign over the window advertised the store as the Washington Hobby Shop. Hencill looked around for a public telephone. He saw none on the street. He had just passed a drugstore and there was sure to be a phone there; drugstores were the best places to find telephones. Each store had at least one, and usually it was in an enclosed booth. Hencill didn't like to use open booths.

He muttered obscenities as he thumbed through the directory. Under "Washington" there were first the city offices, then the District of Columbia offices and finally the federal offices. The book was heavy and hard to balance on the narrow shelf. Once it fell off, causing him to lose his place. Sweat ran from him as he slammed the book open and he began all over again to find the number for the Washington Hobby Shop.

He found it. Today he had remembered to bring lots of change, and he dropped a dime in the slot and dialed. A male voice answered, "Washington Hobby Shop."

Hencill lowered his voice an octave and attempted to make it sound brisk. "This is the room clerk at the Plaza Hotel. Mr. Chad, the baseball player, left word he would be shopping with you. Could you call him to the phone, please."

"He just left."

Hencill forgot about being brisk and official. He slammed down the phone and muttered more obscenities.

Back on the street he momentarily thought that he had lost Chad. Then, down the way, in the direction from which he just had come, he saw a clump of people. In the middle of them Chad was signing autographs.

A few minutes later the autograph session was over and Chad was on his way again.

Hencill had no fears that the ball player would break off the walk. He wanted to hear his son's message. Reassured, Hencill tapped the cassette in his coat pocket. And then Chad entered a furniture store. A sign on the window read "Five Acres Of Furniture." Hencill cursed. He would have to go into the store to be sure of getting Chad on the phone. To do so made him feel trapped. Why hadn't he learned his lesson the day before in Garfinckel's? He had been sure a store detective watched him during the entire call.

He darted between traffic and crossed the street. Above the store entrance a canvas banner flapped in the wind.

SALE
Save 17%
To 57%

The sidewalk in front of the store was crowded with shoppers pushing through the entrance. Hencill joined them.

Inside he looked around for the ball player. Chad wasn't to be seen. Remembering the autograph fans, Hencill looked for clusters of people, hoping Chad might be in the middle.

No luck. Apparently furniture shoppers were not baseball fans. Or they were more interested in bargains than in autographs. He glanced up at the mezzanine which ran completely around the barnlike building. A small group was ascending the stairs and Hencill thought he got a glimpse of Chad. If it is him, there is no way I'm going up those stairs, Hencill thought. He was not getting off the first floor. He was reluctant to be inside at all.

He exhaled when the man turned out not to be Chad.

His eyes swept the room. Signs throughout the store told shoppers where collections of furniture were located. Far to the rear Hencill saw a sign CHILDREN'S ROOM. It gave him a hunch. Nearby he saw a salesman finish with a customer. "Where are the public phones?" Hencill asked.

"How about right behind you," the salesman answered, and approached another customer.

Hencill wheeled about and three paces away was a wall phone.

A small sign with the store's telephone number was posted over the phone. He dialed, and when the store's operator answered he asked for the children's department. He couldn't help but smile with satisfaction when a saleswoman confirmed that Mr. Chad was in the department.

Hencill waited.

"Play the tape!" Chad's voice and the brusqueness of his demand startled Hencill.

"Where are you? I mean, can you talk?"

"You're not hearing sign language, pal. Play the tape!"

Hencill took a fast look around. No one was coming toward the telephone. He took the cassette from his pocket, and huddling between the two partitions which gave some privacy to the wall phone he touched the On button. "Are you ready?" he asked.

"Play it, goddammit. I've been ready since yesterday."

Hencill's face expressed annoyance. He bent forward to hear the tape himself. After a few seconds he heard the boy's voice.

"Daddy, we are doing what the people tell us. We hope you do, too. If you don't, they say we'll never see you again. Do what they say, Daddy . . . Tampa won last night fourteen to ten."

Chad's reaction was immediate. His voice, hushed, but angry, came through the receiver. "What are you thinking of, telling my son he'll never see me again? You son of a bitch."

Hencill didn't like to be called names by a man who supposedly was not in a position to call names. "Why do you think we took them in the first place?" Hencill reminded him angrily.

"I already got your message. You don't have to deliver it again through my children. Leave them out of it."

"I'm sca . . . I'm concerned, that's all."

"If anything goes wrong I'll pay you a ransom."

The thought that he could lose his bet raised fear and alarm in Hencill. "Ransom! What the hell is going to go wrong?"

"What if I hurt myself? I missed games in the Series against Kansas City, you know."

"When that happens I'll call you in the hospital."

"Just don't forget it," Chad told him.

"All right, all right." Hencill was irritated. "Tomorrow same routine except stay out of these big stores." From now on he wasn't following Chad into stores. He'd call from phones on the street or in drugstores and shops.

"Okay. And how about contacting me sooner. I don't like walking all over the city. I got to stay strong ... so I can lose ball games."

Chad hung up.

Jensen, Evans, and Frazzini had been waiting for Chad's report. The ball player called the moment after the kidnapper hung up. Now the three FBI men analyzed it.

"The guy is getting faster," Frazzini observed. "Yesterday he waited two and a half hours before making contact; today he did it in forty-five minutes."

"That figures," Jensen said. "As he loses his fear of police surveillance and his confidence builds in the relationship with Chad the contacts will come faster."

"How fast?" Evans asked.

"Ten, fifteen minutes, maybe," Jensen said.

"That sure will cut down the distance," Frazzini pointed out.

"What do you think, Tom," Evans began, "think we can wait another day and then on Thursday flood the street with undercover agents and follow Chad along? One of them ought to spot someone suspicious.'"

"That's scatter-shooting, John," Jensen told him.

"You can't do that, John," Frazzini added. "We don't know if the guy is working alone or not. If he's following on foot or in a car. If he's behind or in front of Chad or on the opposite side of the street. He'd be hell to pinpoint and if we guessed wrong we'd scare the guy off sure as hell, and you could scratch Chad's family."

Evans's face showed disappointment.

"We've got to nail this guy in a phone booth," Jensen said.

"I don't know, Tom," Frazzini said dubiously. "It's fifty-fifty that the guy has an accomplice on the street. If he's in a car, he's got to have a driver. He can't just double park while he runs to a phone. So you get the guy in the phone booth, the accomplice runs home and kills the family."

Evans shuddered.

"I agree about the accomplice, Al," Jensen said, "but I don't agree on the rest. Chad said the man who called in Los Angeles and said quote, 'I'm making a bet, a very big bet on the Series,' is the one who is calling him here in Washington. In my opinion this guy is the motivating force behind the kidnapping. I don't think he's a professional mobster. Our Mafia friends agree. I think he's a straight guy, an addicted gambler with heavy losses who has become desperate. He's working with one or two other persons. You can bet one is a woman. His wife, or girl friend, or sister or mother. She's taking care of the family. And maybe he's got a flunky to help him with the logistics, to drive him, as you suggested, Al, while they follow Chad. But if we get the man in the phone booth, we'll get the family."

"How are you going to do that without putting a couple hundred agents on the streets?" Frazzini asked.

"We may have to put that many agents on the street, Al, but I don't want to scatter-shoot them, I want to aim them."

"How?" Evans asked eagerly.

"I don't know yet, John. But there *is* a way, and I'm working on it. It's like trying to see through a lifting fog. Each time I look I see more. But there's still some haze. When it clears away, I'll tell you what I see."

"I just hope McGarrity doesn't see it first," Frazzini said dourly.

"That's the chance you took from the very beginning," Jensen said. "And you knew it."

Using the one-finger "hunt and peck" system, McGarrity typed a name onto the tape and fed it into the computer. While he waited for an answer he turned to Jensen. "I talked last night to Linda and Shirley. They miss us. I said we missed them too."

Jensen chuckled.

A printout dropped from McGarrity's computer. The lawyer

looked at it. "Would a millionaire from Buffalo who bet one hundred twenty-five thousand dollars on the Senators and who once was arrested for wearing women's clothing have any motivation for fixing a World Series?"

"What was his motivation for wearing women's clothing?" Jensen asked.

"His motivation was ..." — McGarrity serched the printout — "he's gay."

"Well, it's refreshing to know that gays are gamblers."

"I wonder how gay he'll be if he loses."

Jensen got up from his chair and walked to a stand that held a coffeepot and a plate of sandwiches and pastry. "Want a cup of coffee?"

McGarrity shook his head. "Coffee spoils the taste of the martinis." He fed a tape into the machine.

Jensen poured a cup of coffee and sipped from it. The brew was like acid. He made a face and carried the cup to the sink and poured it out.

"I FOUND HIM!" McGarrity cried.

Jensen let go of the cup. It fell into the sink where it smashed into pieces.

"I GOT THE SON OF A BITCH!" McGarrity cried again. He had leaped up from the computer and was holding his arms victoriously over his head, his fists clenched.

"Who is he?" Jensen asked, walking toward him.

"Ralph Gottlieb, and he lives in St. Louis."

"He's the kidnapper?"

"No. No. He's a goddam deadbeat who's owed me two thousand bucks for over twenty years. I lost track of him. So I'm sitting here, bored to death, and this gay's name comes up from Buffalo where Ralph Gottlieb used to live and I said to myself, 'Maybe this computer can find Ralph Gottlieb.'" He chortled. "And it did, and now I'm going to get that son of a bitch."

"I thought we couldn't use each other's information for our own purposes," Jensen reminded the lawyer.

"For our organization's purposes," McGarrity corrected him.

"Nothing was said about making personal use of the information."

Jensen shrugged. "What are you going to do to the guy?"

"The usual," McGarrity said. "Tie a concrete block around his neck and throw him in the river."

"What if he can't swim?" Jensen asked.

Ilka was restless. The uncertainty of her immediate future was the cause. She could never in her life imagine that her destiny could be tied to a stupid boy's game. In her whole life she had never been interested in sports and now she found herself waiting anxiously for the stupid World Series game to begin.

She had lunched with Renata. She wished her girl friend could have taken the afternoon off. It was relaxing to be with Renata.

Later she had shopped in Beverly Hills. Normally it relaxed her to buy things. Today she found nothing to purchase. It irritated her. She wanted sex. She had called Bjorn, but he was out. She had called a dozen times and had hung up as soon as she heard his answering service. She even had considered flying to Nashville. How nice it would be to spend an entire night with Saccente. He would relax her.

At four-thirty she had turned on the television. The game started at five. She didn't understand very much about baseball. But she understood who was supposed to win.

She drank champagne and watched the innings roll by, no one scoring anything. Every twenty minutes she telephoned Bjorn. He hadn't come home. "He doesn't know what he's missing," she thought. At the end of the fourth inning there was still no score. She opened another bottle of champagne.

The top of the fifth inning Chad came to bat with one out and men on first and third. The game was scoreless. Chad was batting right-handed against the left-handed pitcher. The defense was playing him to pull. He tried to cross them up by going to the opposite field to score the lead runner. Instead, he popped up. It was a short fly into right field, which hung up longer than the outfielder anticipated. He overran it. The ball dropped safely. A run scored. Chad was on first, a base-runner on second.

While the next hitter faked a bunt, Chad and the base-runner on second executed a perfect double steal. On the next pitch the batter flied deep to center, scoring the man on third. The inning ended with the Dodgers leading two to nothing.

As he trotted to his shortstop position Chad wished the Washington outfielder had made the play. All things being equal, Washington had a chance to win. Chad had felt this even before his family had been kidnapped. Now that they had been, and pressure was on him to lose, he hoped bad luck would not force him to. If Washington won fair and square, he told himself, he wouldn't mind.

Jensen and McGarrity worked late again to finish the lists. They had found some more leads and Jensen, using Frazzini's name and authority, had sent the appropriate requests to FBI bureaus in New York, Miami, Kansas City, Houston, and Dallas. Two of the bureaus to whom he had sent requests the day before had already reported back. The securities broker in Chicago seemed to be clean, as was the doctor in Louisville. The investigation was still ongoing into the film producer's activities.

Before they left the computer room, the two men made arrangements to telephone the next day. McGarrity had to fly to New York.

The game had already started when Jensen got home. He made a sandwich and opened a beer and watched the Dodgers score two lucky runs in the fifth inning.

The score was still two to nothing at the end of the eighth inning, and he went to the kitchen for another beer.

In the ninth inning the Dodgers got their leadoff man on. The next batter doubled him up. The third batter doubled and died on second when the next batter struck out.

The Washington crowd let out a massive roar when their team's first batter came to the plate in the bottom of the ninth. They were rewarded when he drew a walk.

The Dodger manager immediately called for a new pitcher.

The relief pitcher walked the first man he faced. The second man he struck out. The third man he hit on the shoulder with a pitch. The bases were loaded with one out.

The Dodger manager brought in a new pitcher.

The Washington manager responded by sending a pinch hitter to the plate.

With the crowd screaming on each pitch, the cat-and-mouse duel between pitcher and batter began.

The first pitch was outside. Ball one.

The batter stepped from the box and knocked imaginary dirt from his cleats. He stepped back into the batter's box. The next pitch went by for a strike.

Again the batter stepped out of the box. He picked up the resin bag, looked at the third-base coach, nodded, got back into the batter's box.

Just as the pitcher released the ball the batter jumped back from the plate and slapped his right hand over his right eye. A gnat had flown in it, he told the umpire. The umpire called time out. The pitch, which would have been a strike, exploded harmlessly in the catcher's mitt.

The mighty crowd was hysterical for their Wonderful Washies. All year long the team had won games in the ninth inning. The crowd screamed and implored them to do it once again.

The pitcher checked the base-runners, went into his motion, rifled the ball to the plate. A resounding crack echoed in the stadium. The ball sailed high and deep into left field. The base-runners tore around the field. The packed crowd held its breath.

The left-field umpire ran along the foul line. He watched the ball sail two inches on the wrong side of the foul pole.

Foul ball.

The wind went out of the crowd. The runners returned to their bases.

The count was one ball and two strikes.

The next pitch was a ball.

The next pitch was fouled behind the first-base dugout.

The next pitch was a ball inside. The count was full.

The batter stepped out of the box. He wiggled to loosen himself up. He pulled up his stockings. He tied his shoelaces. He adjusted his cap. He looked at the third-base coach.

Finally, he got into the box.

But only for a second.

He called time and motioned the third-base coach for a conference. He dropped his bat and ran down the foul line. The umpire shouted after him.

The batter conferred with the third-base coach. They stared at the pitcher.

The batter returned to home plate. He picked up the bat, picked up the resin bag, dropped the resin bag, walked slowly to the batter's box. Just before stepping in he held up one finger to tell the base-runners there was one out. A fact well known to them all.

The pitcher looked at the base-runners, stretched, pitched.

The batter swung mightily. He made good contact with the ball. But swinging downward too much, the bat made the ball spin crazily along the ground toward shortstop.

There were two, maybe three shortstops in the major leagues who could have fielded the ball and made a double-play. And Roosevelt Chad did.

The Dodgers won two to nothing and took a two-to-one lead in games.

Jensen got up from his couch, walked to the TV set and switched it off.

WEDNESDAY
Game Number Four

If God had wanted us to win, he'd have had Graig Nettles get sick. We had a good shot at the World Series after winning the first two games. Then Nettles came up with those plays in the third game.

— TOM LASORDA, manager of the Los Angeles Dodgers

Nettles turned it around. I think his play was the turning point of the Series.

— REGGIE SMITH, All-Star outfielder for the Los Angeles Dodgers

17.

In the late innings of the telecast of game number three, Mrs. Sanders began to feel that the rest of her life rested on the outcome. The broadcasters emphasized over and over that the winning team would take a two-to-one lead and this meant that if they won game number four they would have a three-to-one lead. In over a half-century of play only two teams had come back from being down three games to one. One of those teams was the Yankees of Mantle, Maris, Berra, Ford, and Larsen. The Senators, the broadcasters said, just weren't in that class.

When Chad made the double-play, Mrs. Sanders's initial reaction was despair. That quickly turned to a hate that previously she had reserved for Ilka. She hated Robert and Chad with equal intensity. Robert was a fool and Chad was manipulating him.

She was going to end this stupidity. If Robert couldn't control the baseball player, she could.

She stayed up late and when she went to bed she slept fitfully, dozing and waking. Finally, she went to sleep through sheer exhaustion.

She was awakened early by the sound of a car engine. She got out of bed and looked outside. The garage door was open and Ilka's Porsche was gone. Mrs. Sanders wondered where the German bitch had gone so early.

She put on a robe and collected the *Los Angeles Times* from the drive where it had been thrown by the paper boy. A second *Times* was for Robert. She retrieved it as well. Ilka read only the German papers.

She made a pot of coffee and toasted an English muffin. As she ate the light breakfast she read the sports page. Every writer had the same message: tonight was the crucial game. To have any chance at all the Senators had to win it. If the Dodgers won, the Series was as good as over. Jimmy the Greek had favored the Dodgers 8 to 5 to win the game and 11 to 5 to win the Series.

The violent emotions Mrs. Sanders had felt the night before returned with even a greater fury. She was more determined than ever to fix both Robert and the baseball player.

Across the country the fog lifted for Jensen and he saw what he had been looking for. When the insight struck him he realized why he'd had trouble finding a plan to get the kidnapper. He had thought of it in complex and abstract terms. The answer, when it revealed itself, was simple and logical. The plan would require detailed preparation and complicated logistics, but the idea itself was absolute simplicity. It was foolproof, and it had to be, because there could be no room for second-guessing when it was over.

He breakfasted in the FBI cafeteria and at eight o'clock he was waiting for the personnel records section to open. There he acquired the name of an agent who had grown up in Los Angeles and who worked in the building.

Jensen telephoned and made an appointment to see the man at ten o'clock.

He took along a city map of Los Angeles, which he got from the

Bureau library. The two spent an hour together, the agent pointing out locations Jensen asked about.

Jensen asked question after question and penned a small notebook full with the answers. He did not tell the agent why he wanted the information and the man did not ask why. In the Bureau one asked only about those things that concerned one.

Afterward Jensen took a long walk and put the plan together in his mind. He walked a long time. The plan excited him greatly. It had but one hitch. It could be used only if the Series shifted back to Los Angeles. And he had no control over that.

Michael McGarrity, the man who was going to have the kidnapper killed, sat with his childhood friend Jim Flynn in the office of the latter's saloon on Third Avenue in New York. They talked about an IRA gunman. McGarrity mentioned no names or motive. Nor did Flynn expect him to.

"When will you be needing the lad?" Flynn asked.

Plans would have to be made quickly. "As soon as possible," McGarrity answered. "Certainly within forty-eight hours."

Flynn nodded. "That should be no cause to worry, Mikey me boy. Let's call them in Dublin and get the man himself on the way."

Flynn placed a call to Dublin. When the connection was made he spoke in Gaelic, a language that McGarrity understood but did not speak well. There was no problem with Flynn's request. After he hung up he said, "He'll be arriving tomorrow. They'll call me back later with his flight number. Will you be meeting him?"

"Yes. So I'll need a description as well."

"You'll have one," Flynn promised. He opened a drawer and pulled out a bottle of Paddy. "You'll not have a drink before you go?"

"Just a wee one," McGarrity smiled.

While Flynn poured two glasses half full, McGarrity took out his wallet. "How much do I owe you?" he asked.

Flynn waved a hand. "You have to pay the lad himself. For meself, you owe nothin', you know that."

McGarrity took from his wallet two one-thousand-dollar bills and one five-hundred-dollar bill and put them on the table. "A contribution for the widows and orphans fund," he said.

"Now that's awfully generous of you, Mikey. It will bring them joy in Dublin to know what you've done."

Hencill was across the street at the counter of a coffee shop waiting for Chad to come out of the Plaza. On Hencill's lap was an attaché case, the handle clenched firmly in his right fist. For added security he had fastened a small chain around his right wrist and connected it to the handle. In the case was the hundred thousand dollars in cash he was going to bet in New York later in the day.

The ball player came out of the hotel. Hencill took another sip of coffee before walking casually to the cashier's stand.

On the street he walked briskly in the direction opposite the one Chad had taken. A half-block away he entered a dime store and went to a phone booth in the rear that he had previously scouted.

He placed a call to the coach house. Helen answered on the second ring. The cassette was out of his jacket pocket.

"Let's make this fast," he said. "I'm already on the street."

"I'm ready," she said. "The tape runs twenty seconds and I am starting it five seconds from . . . *now.*"

While his cassette recorded the message he looked out the door of the phone booth. Niether shoppers nor sales persons paid him any attention. Washington was a city in which a man could carry an attaché case chained to his wrist and hold cassettes to telephones and attract no notice.

After thirty seconds he turned off the cassette and put it back in his pocket. "I'll call you from New York," he said.

"I'll be here," she said sarcastically, and hung up.

As Hencill walked from the store he glanced at his watch and nodded in appreciation of his planning. Less than three minutes had elapsed since Chad came on the street.

A taxi cruised by in the direction Chad had taken and Hencill flung up an arm. "Just down the street a way," he told the driver.

At the third stoplight he saw Chad cross the street and enter a store on the corner.

"I'll get out after you cross the intersection," Hencill told the driver, and to stifle any protest at the short trip he dropped a ten-dollar bill over the seat. "I've got a bum leg," he said unnecessarily.

It was too late to call Chad at the store so Hencill loitered at a sidewalk newsstand. This was when he felt most vulnerable: when he was caught in limbo waiting for Chad to appear or to escape autograph seekers. Waiting on the street was even worse than making contact. The calls were becoming routine, and though he was cautious it didn't frighten him anymore to telephone.

Chad came out of the store and continued his walk. Hencill bought a newspaper at the stand and then followed along. Less than a minute later the ball player entered a hi-fi store.

Hencill stepped off the curb and crossed the street. He had to dodge through the equipment of a crew doing repairs on the street.

He entered a soda fountain. Three booths were to the left inside the door.

There was a telephone book in the booth but the page he needed had been torn out. He cursed and dug into his pocket for change. He got the number from information and called the hi-fi store. When he made the connection with the record department, he used the hotel clerk routine. He was getting it down pat.

The clerk was very polite and told him Chad was a counter away. He heard Chad ask if there wasn't a phone that would give him privacy. "He's getting his part of the act down, too," Hencill thought.

A moment later Chad was on the line. In the background Hencill heard rock music blaring.

"Can you talk?" he asked Chad.

"I could scream, and no one would hear me," Chad answered.

That suited Hencill. On the street came the sound of jack hammers. He felt like screaming himself and the sound muffled it. "When are you going to lose?" he cried. "You keep winning games you could lose."

"How?" Chad's voice was angry.

"How! You had a perfect chance in the ninth inning. You didn't have to make that play. You could have booted it."

"It would have been too obvious an error," the ball player said disgustedly.

Hencill swore into the receiver. "You're trying to finesse it and it's not working."

"You're goddam right I'm trying to finesse it. I'm trying to get back my family, win your bet for you, and keep myself from getting thrown out of baseball. I'm telling you for the last time. I'll do this my way. Not the way you want me to do it. But my way. Now let me hear the tape from my children," the ball player demanded.

Hencill took the tape recorder from his pocket. "Get ready," he said. He held the recorder to the phone, pushed the On button, and bent forward to hear the tape.

At first he thought the children were laughing. He put his ear next to the recorder. His blood ran cold.

"Oh, Daddy, Daddy," It was the little girl. She was crying and obviously terrorstricken. "Please come and get us." Hencill heard the distinct and unmistakable sounds of a person being slapped. The girl's cries became louder. "She won't give us anything to eat. Oh, Daddy, I'm so afraid. I hate this mean woman."

A sharp crack came from the recorder and then the boy shouted. "Stop hitting my sister or I'll kill you!"

Then there came a woman's scream. Hencill knew it came from Chad's mother. The sound chilled him.

Helen's voice came over the tape. "If the Dodgers win tonight I'm going to kill your mother the moment the last out is made. And if the Dodgers win the Series I'm going to kill both your children immediately."

The tape whirred on. Chad's voice came through the receiver. It was low, close to tears. "What kind of people are you?"

Hencill couldn't answer. He was stunned.

Chad hung up.

Once outside Hencill tried to clear his brain. The scream had unnerved him. He didn't think Helen would kill Chad's mother. She was just saying that, like she did about the little girl's ear. She was bluffing. She had to be.

The street was crowded and he almost walked up an old woman's heels. He raised his head to apologize and almost collided with Roosevelt Chad.

The ballplayer stormed by him. Several kids ran alongside, trying to get autographs. Chad waved them away. The ball player looked ahead and right into Hencill's eyes. Hencill thought his heart had stopped beating and he was going to keel over in a faint right in front of Chad. All the phone calls made him feel they knew each other personally. It took his brain a moment to sort out that they had never met.

There was no recognition in Chad's eyes. Just pain.

"What's the matter?" a youth called after the ball player. "You too important to sign your name?"

At the airport Hencill tried Helen's number. The line was busy and he knew she had taken the phone off the hook and that it would stay off until the game was over.

"Jesus Christ!" he thought. She had to be bluffing. She couldn't be that crazy. Then he remembered Ilka's dog.

Chad hurried to the privacy and solitude of his hotel room. He threw himself on a bed and buried his face in a pillow. When he was a child this was how he had reacted to sadness and now he thought of his childhood and his mother and his body was seized with pain.

When the mind is overly burdened with unhappiness it has the ability to turn itself off and Chad fell into a short, deep sleep.

He awakened refreshed and began to think.

For the first time he thought seriously ... really seriously ... about losing a game. Before he had thought of it fleetingly, flirted with the idea, toyed with the possibilities. He had not liked to think about it. Now he couldn't keep it from his mind.

It made him feel guilty that his first inclination was to lose a game and not take himself from the lineup as he had promised he would do. Something told him that if he didn't play his problems would become much larger. There would be the immense media publicity which certainly would cause the kidnapper's bets to be aborted. Perhaps the man would accept a ransom if he tried to lose a game and failed, but would the kidnapper do so if he pulled himself from the lineup? Even Jensen couldn't answer that one.

But if he tried to lose a game, lost one even, he knew the guilt would never leave him. Only a professional athlete really understood the mystique of winning, of doing your best, giving your all, never quitting, never letting your teammates down. Defeat with honor. If you never quit, never let your teammates down, you left the field with your head high. It was the American way of sports. It began in preschool, was intensified in Little League, and by the time a boy put on a high-school uniform he was professional in mind if not in ability. It was the American gospel. His mother had taught it to him, and he was teaching it to Billy. Now he was being asked to renounce it.

If that was the price he had to pay to save his family, what would they say afterward?

For the first time he saw his dilemma clearly. What price a man's honor? The scales leaned first one way and then the other. And in the end his decision remained the one he made the night the kidnapper called. To do nothing until he had to.

He got up from the bed and eyed the telephone. Jensen was waiting to hear about the contact. He couldn't tell him about the tape from his family. Jensen would be alert if later he tried to lose a game. He didn't know if he would, or could, but he wanted to keep all his options open.

He got off the bed and went to the writing desk, where he took out a sheet of hotel stationery and outlined an imaginary conversation between himself and the kidnapper.

The kidnapper had been very upset over the Dodger win, he would tell Jensen. But I convinced him that one loss did not lose a Series. Besides, I pointed out that by hitting in the clutch and performing well defensively in these early games, there would be no suspicion on misplays in later games. After all, it wouldn't do any good to lose the Series if it became known to the public. Who'd pay off on bets then?

This was an insight Chad hadn't gotten before and he thought it was a powerful argument. One he could use today on Jensen and later on the kidnapper.

Jensen would want to know why he hadn't reported immediately after the kidnapper made contact. A minute of thought gave him the answer to that one. He had tried but had been bothered by fans and had waited till he got back to the hotel.

Chad went over the imaginary conversation three times before he was satisfied it was logical and that Jensen would buy it. Then he telephoned the FBI man and offered him the story. Jensen bought it.

The flight from Dublin had just landed at JFK, and McGarrity watched the passengers debark. Flynn had told him he couldn't miss the gunman. His name was Fitzpatrick. He had flaming red hair, freckles, and a face that would not be taken for anything but Irish even if encountered in the Gobi Desert.

McGarrity did not miss him. He was as described; he looked like a rugby player. His legs were tree trunks, his torso lean and muscled. He had powerful wrists and huge hands. McGarrity knew the type. A bully boy fresh from the farm.

"Did you have a good flight?" McGarrity asked him.

"Bleedin' awful," Fitzpatrick replied, in a powerful tenor voice. "The shagging airplane bounced all over."

"Well, you'll get a good night's rest here and tomorrow we'll go to Los Angeles."

"Think I'll have a chance to see a movie star?" the gunman asked.

"Maybe," McGarrity said, and led the Irishman to a taxi stand.

"Who's my hit?" Fitzpatrick asked.

"A Los Angeles businessman. We'll arrange for you to get a look at him."

"I hope so," the gunman said. "Bejesus, I wouldn't like to get the wrong man."

If McGarrity had known what Hencill looked like, he could have taken Fitzpatrick into one of the airport cocktail lounges and introduced the two.

Hencill stood at the bar drinking a double Scotch. The attaché case no longer was attached to his wrist but rested on the floor beside him. It was empty; the money had been bet. One hundred thousand dollars with four bookies, using a different name at each place.

Originally had had planned betting on the game but the Washington defeat the night before had raised the odds on the Dodgers winning the Series to 11 to 5. It was too good to pass up and he had taken it. He reflected that not many gamblers would have made the bet. He wouldn't have either except he knew something the others did not.

Now he was waiting for a flight to Los Angeles. He would be halfway there when the ball game began. With a little bit of luck, he would be in the coach house in time to prevent Helen from killing Chad's mother. He couldn't believe she would do it. But he was taking no chances. He was an embezzler. Fine. He admitted it. He was an extortionist, a fixer, a failure, a compulsive gambler. Fine. But he was not a murderer. At least, not yet.

His flight was called and he picked up the glass and downed the last of the Scotch. He picked up the attaché case and hurried out. His small legs moving quickly gave him a scooting motion.

The Dodgers got ready for game number four. Their lead of two games to one was reflected in the dressing-room atmosphere. They joked and shouted friendly insults across the room. They had momentum. They were loose.

Chad was not. He smiled automatically whenever he heard his name mentioned. But his thoughts were not on his teammates' banter. His thoughts were on his decision to lose the game. In the hotel it had been so clear. In the locker room it was blurring. Agony and indecision tore at his heart.

Ilka had been having a day-long orgy with Bjorn. It was why she had left the coach house so early in the morning. Anxiety over Robert's bets had thrown her into a sexual frenzy.

Bjorn was enjoying it immensely. For two years their meetings had mostly been brief, hurried ones. He never had been able to get his fill of her. Today he overflowed.

She was insatiable. They had spent the entire day performing in a variety of positions.

Moreover, Ilka had discarded her streak of prudity. She had always liked sex, but in her own way with certain and many limits as to what she would do to him, or permit him to do to her. Today everything had been permitted. Indeed, she seemed most stimulated doing these things which before she had said she would never do, things she had said would make her ill. Today she had done them with enthusiasm.

Her previous lovemaking had been mechanical, unimaginative. Today she was inventive. Bjorn had a best-selling illustrated sex manual. Late in the morning Ilka had gone through the book writing on small slips of paper the page number of each illustration. They cast the slips in a box and they spent the afternoon drawing slips, performing the act depicted on the page, and drinking champagne.

She had worn him out. He was surprised when she turned on the television to the baseball game. "I thought you couldn't stand these silly games," he reminded her.

"This one is different," she told him.

In the second inning the Dodgers scored two runs and Ilka became dour and drank champagne hurriedly.

When the pilot announced the Dodgers had scored two runs, Hencill sank deeper into his airplane seat. Everything was working against him. The plane had had a minor mechanical problem and was late taking off. What if he didn't get to the coach house before the game ended?

When finally they were airborne, he thought of chartering a helicopter to take him from the Los Angeles airport to Beverly Hills. That would save time.

First class had been booked and he found himself with the peons, squeezed between two fat women who smelled strongly of cheap powder and perfume.

A stewardess came by and he stopped her. "Can you radio ahead to Los Angeles?" he asked, "I want to charter a helicopter to fly me to Beverly Hills."

The fat women looked curiously at him.

"I'll ask the captain, sir," the stewardess said. "I'm sure we can."

A moment later she was back. "The captain said it's no problem, sir."

Hencill gave her his name, which the crew would radio ahead.

Mrs. Sanders was drunk. She had taken the day off. To do this she simply had given the family extra dosages to keep them asleep. She wasn't going to bother with exercise periods and feedings. To hell with it.

After she had played the tape to Robert she had taken her phone off the hook, given the family the shots, and then gone out for an expensive lunch in Beverly Hills.

She drank a lot of wine and was high when she returned in mid-afternoon to the estate. Ilka was not at home so Mrs. Sanders went to the wine cellar in the main house and took two bottles of vintage German white wine. She carried them to the coach house and opened one and put the other in the refrigerator.

Before the game began she prepared a lethal dosage of drugs to inject into Mrs. Chad. Robert might be bluffing. She was not.

In the fourth inning the Dodgers scored a run and took a three-to-nothing lead. Mrs. Sanders opened the second bottle of wine.

She was enraged when Roosevelt Chad hit a solo home run in the fifth inning to make the score four to nothing. She walked to Mrs. Chad's cot and cursed the unconscious woman.

Jensen alternately watched the game on TV and worked on the plan for Los Angeles. A force of nearly a hundred agents would be required. He could get them from bureaus in western states. They would need lodging for at least one night and maybe three. And he wanted them under one roof, not scattered in motels all over the city. The operation had to be kept secret. He could achieve maximum security only through maximum control of his operational force. He made a note to contact the GSA first thing in the morning. As the government's housekeeper, they could recommend buildings and warehouses available. He wanted something as close as possible to the scene of the operation.

He'd have to contact the army for some logistical support. A communications van would be required and maybe they could furnish cots, bedding, and other housewares.

The plan would require considerable electronic work. He'd need the assistance of the telephone companies. In the past the telephone people had been stung several times by FBI wiretaps, but Jensen knew he could expect their full cooperation in catching an extortionist.

In the bottom of the seventh inning the Senators got their first two men on and Jensen set aside the pad of legal paper and his pen.

The Dodgers got an out and then the Washington cleanup hitter doubled-in two runs. The score was four to two. They got another out then, but couldn't retire the side before a walk and single scored the third run of the inning. Jensen reflected that Chad's home run was the difference. If the score didn't change, the ball player would have a hard time explaining that to the kidnapper.

He picked up his pen and continued working on his plan.

A strong tail wind had helped Hencill's flight to make up time. And just before they landed he was further relieved when the captain announced that Washington had tied the score in the bottom of the eighth.

His happiness was short-lived. On the way to the waiting helicopter he learned that the Dodgers had gotten their first two men on in the ninth inning. Even worse, when he boarded the copter he discovered it had no radio frequency to pick up the game. He balled his left hand into a fist and slammed it repeatedly into his right hand. Wasn't that the goddamnedest luck!

THURSDAY
Game Number Five

In the 1919 World Series, the Chicago White Sox, with eight bribed players on the team, committed a total of twelve errors; the same number made by their opponents, the Cincinnati Reds.

In the eight games the White Sox made but five hits less than the Reds.

18.

Sunlight was streaming in the window when Hencill awakened. From the slant of the rays he knew that it was still early. Probably around six.

Ilka was beside him. She had not been home when he went to bed. That he had not heard her come in attested to the soundness of his sleep. Admittedly, he had been exhausted. The fight with Helen had made him more so. It had absolutely pulled the plug on him.

He had no great feeling for her. At one time, before he was a teenager, he supposed he had. She had raised him and represented authority and security to him. Last night the final strings had been broken. It was a miracle that he had not struck her.

The fight had solved many things. The most important immediate effect was to establish his hegemony over the Chads. They now stood under his protection.

He got out of bed and walked to the window. Sunlight glistened on the water of the swimming pool. It had been a long time since he had gone swimming. It was a beautiful morning, and after the mind-numbing events of the past few days he felt the need for strenuous exercise.

He took a heavy robe from the closet and went down to the cabana. There he got a large bath towel. At poolside he removed his pajamas. He swam in the nude, something he had picked up from Ilka.

For ten minutes he stroked back and forth as fast as he could. Then he toweled off, slipped the robe on, and entered the house through the kitchen door. He fished around in the refrigerator for some bacon, set a pan on the stove, turned the heat on low, and started the bacon. While it began to cook he went to the front of the house to retrieve the paper.

He had learned the final score of the game after the helicopter landed. And Helen had told him a little bit about the ninth inning. Now he wanted to read the details of the game.

Hencill loved newspaper reviews and accounts of a sporting event even more than he liked watching the actual game. He loved to read the columns of Red Smith, Dick Young, Jim Murray, and Milt Richman. These writers were the Walter Kerrs of the playing fields. They did not gloss over a player's errors or failure to produce in a critical situation. They did not excuse sloppiness or hide failure.

The paper lay in the driveway. He picked it up and walked back to the kitchen. He turned the bacon and sat down at the kitchen table, opened the paper, pulled out the sports section. The fourth game of the Series dominated the news.

He glanced quickly over the account of the game and read some locker-room interviews.

On page two he found what he wanted to know in an article written by UPI columnist Jack Barry. His eyes glowed when he read it.

He read it again and then a third time. He got up from the table and nervously lit a cigarette, something he did not normally do before breakfast. He went back to the column once more.

Then Verban's single scored Murcer, which gave Washington a 5–4 victory and tied the Series at two games each. That run was earned but it would not have scored if Rosie Chad had converted a grounder hit by Lynn into a double-play. Chad bobbled the ball . . .

Hencill stopped there and slapped his hands together twice before continuing.

Chad bobbled the ball, allowing Murcer, who had singled to open the botton half of the 9th, to reach second. He moved to third on a sacrifice and then scored the winning run on Verban's single through a drawn-in infield.

Hencill dropped the paper on the kitchen table. He remembered the angry call with Chad. "I'll do it my way," Chad had insisted. And he had. In the bottom of the ninth inning Chad had won it for him. He put back his head and gave one long shout of joy. He *was* going to win. Impulsively, he turned off the fire under the bacon and hurried to the coach house.

Chad awakened slowly. He did not immediately get up. He looked at his watch. Nearly nine o'clock. He reached down with his right hand and touched his thigh. It was sore. In the seventh inning he had slid hard into second base to break up a double-play. It was a bad slide and he had bruised his thigh.

He pushed away the covers and laboriously and gingerly set his feet on the floor. He looked at his thigh. The bruise was just below the leg of his jockey shorts and was the size of his hand. It pained him, though it wouldn't affect his play.

He definitely did not want to breakfast in the restaurant. He did not want to see reporters or talk with teammates or coaches. He called room service and ordered a light breakfast. He'd eat steak and eggs for lunch.

In the shower his leg began to feel better. He ran the water as hot as he could stand it, and let it beat down on the bruise.

Before he toweled off breakfast arrived. He sat down hungrily at the table. He was halfway through when the phone rang. The caller's voice made him forget the bruised thigh: it was the kidnapper.

"I promised that if you did your part I'd do mine," the kidnapper said. "To prove it, you can talk to your family."

Chad's heart swelled with excitement.

"Hello, Roosevelt." It was his mother and she wasn't on tape.

"Mother!" he shouted. "Mother!"

"I'm all right, Roosevelt." Her voice told him so more than the words. It was strong and relaxed. "Billy and Camilla are all right, too."

"Mother, they played a tape. Billy and Camilla cried and you . . ."

"We're all right, Roosevelt. It has been hard and unpleasant, but we're okay. Here's Camilla."

"I love you, Daddy," his daughter said.

Tears came to Chad's eyes and his voice choked. "I love you, baby. Oh, how I love you."

"Daddy, I've been so frightened."

"Me, too, baby, but I'll see you soon."

Billy came on the line. "I haven't been scared," he boasted.

Chad broke into delirious laughter. "How much I miss you, son!"

"I miss you, too, Daddy. I miss everything. I miss hamburgers, and television, and playing with you." There was a pause. "I don't miss jogging though."

The kidnapper was back on the line. "I let you talk to your family to make up for yesterday's tape. But we still got the same deal. You lose, you get back your family. If you don't . . ."

"You get a ransom," Chad interrupted.

"Well talk again after Saturday's game," the voice said. "Ninety minutes after the last out, walk down the even-numbered side of the five-thousand block of Wilshire Boulevard. Do just as you did in Washington. Before you pass the fifty-three-hundred block I'll contact you."

"I got it," Chad said.

"Good-bye, then," the voice said.

"Good-bye," Chad answered. "And thanks for letting me talk to my family."

It was the first time the two had ever said good-bye to each other.

Chad left that out when he made his report to Jensen. Also he left out the part about talking to his family. If he had mentioned that he would have had to explain what he had withheld the day before. He told Jensen he'd heard another tape.

"You know," he said, "over the past few days this guy and I have threatened and shouted at each other, but today it was the strangest feeling . . . I felt kinship with the guy. And I think he sensed it as well. We *really are* in this thing together."

In Los Angeles, a few minutes later, Larry Cruikshank received a telephone call. Cruikshank was vice-president in charge of operations for Pacific Telephone. He knew and liked Tom Jensen from other times. "Hello, Tom," he said, "long time, no hear."

"How are you, Larry? I've got some work for you. I need some phones tapped. Legally, of course."

The men chuckled.

"How many phones, and where are they?"

"I don't know how many. They're on Wilshire Boulevard from the five-thousand block through the fifty-three-hundred block."

"The Miracle Strip?"

"Right."

"Which numbers?"

"All the pay phones, Larry. Every pay phone for four blocks. And I'll need a chart showing each location and call number."

"That's a heap of phones, Tom. Fifty, anyhow."

"That many!" Jensen's low whistle came over the receiver. "Could you take a bunch of them out? Or better yet, just leave twenty. Don't bother the ones on the street, reduce the amount in the stores. If you've got a bank of six phones, say, in a drugstore, take out four. At least put them out of order, take them off the wall, whatever. Make it look good. And you're going to have to do it fast."

"What do you call fast?"

"Today. Tonight."

It was Cruikshank's turn to whistle. "That's fast."

"But you can do it?"

"We can do it. Where will you monitor the taps?"

"In an army communications van."

"Terrific. That'll save us time. Send it to our operations center at the corner of Sunset and Gower."

"That has to be today as well, Larry."

"Not tomorrow?"

"Today it will show up as an army vehicle. Tomorrow it will be painted as a furniture van. For cover purposes I'd rather get it to you today about noon. You can have it all night."

"Roger."

"There will be some other things, Larry. Nothing pressing. I want one of your men to check out the twenty phones you leave operating to make sure each is operating perfectly and that each station is equipped with a new phone book."

"That's no problem."

"I'll be on the Coast myself in the morning. I'll give you a call first thing."

"Fine."

"And, Larry, the fewer people who know this, the better. It's top secret."

"Why else a furniture van from an army truck?" Cruikshank joked. "Don't worry, Tom. Have I ever let your cat out of my bag?"

"No, Larry, and the Justice Department appreciates your help. We're after an extortionist. A very mean man. Your stockholders will love you for helping us."

"Maybe," Cruikshank said, "but let's not tell them."

Three hours later Jensen stood in front of a blackboard in Evans's office. He had chalked in eight rectangles to designate both sides of the 5000, 5100, 5200, and 5300 blocks of Wilshire and marked twenty X's to represent the telephone locations. Another rectangle, smaller than the block designations, was drawn in front of the 5200 block. On it was lettered COMMO VAN.

"Here's how it works," Jensen began. "I've left twenty telephones on the street and in stores. The phones will be tapped into the commo van. Each will be monitored individually. Twenty taps, twenty agents with headphones. On the outside, each phone location will be monitored by two disguised agents. They will make the arrest. And here's how that will happen."

Jensen turned to the blackboard and picked up a pointer which he used to highlight his description.

"Chad walks along the even-numbered side of the street. He enters a store. The kidnapper sees Chad go in the store, he heads for a pay phone and calls the store. In the van, the monitor hears the store answer and he hears the kidnapper ask for Chad. Immediately he activates the electronic devices carried by his agents watching the phone booth. They move in and arrest the person in the booth. For further assistance, a team of five agents will be standing by on each side of the block."

Jensen put down the pointer and turned to face Evans and Frazzini.

"I've gone over it repeatedly," he said. "If it has a flaw, I can't find it. I've even arranged for a helicopter to get Chad on the street in time."

"Are you notifying Chad of the plan?" Frazzini asked.

"No," Jensen said.

"I'd think about that," Evans cautioned. "He must be wondering what the hell we're doing."

"I'm sure he is," Jensen agreed. "He can wonder a little bit longer. He'll perform better on the street if he doesn't have this hanging over him."

"How about McGarrity?" Frazzini asked.

Jensen laughed. "When my good friend Michael tells me what he and the Mafia are doing, I'll tell him what we're doing." He laughed again. "And even then I'd lie to him."

"One thing bugs me, Tom." It was Frazzini. "How do you know this guy is going to use a pay phone?"

"Because he has every time so far," Jensen assured them. "After each call Chad reported background noises related to public telephones."

"But that was in Washington," Frazzini pointed out. "What if the guy picked this section in L.A. because he has an office there?"

"With a view that covers a four-block area! I think he picked the Miracle Strip because it's an easily accessible and heavily traveled pedestrian area, of which there are not many in Los Angeles."

"But he still can make a call from a private phone," Evans argued.

Frazzini and Jensen looked at him for an explanation.

"He can go into a store, a men's shop, say, make a purchase and ask to use their phone." The FBI director looked triumphant. "I've done that."

"Me, too, John," Frazzini said. "But I goddam sure wouldn't do it if I had to hold a cassette to the receiver or to phone a kidnap message. Tom's right. The guy will be in a phone booth. Privacy will be his top priority."

"I wonder who the guy is?" Evans mused.

"We'll know Saturday afternoon," Jensen promised.

Irishmen are famed as drinkers and talkers. McGarrity took consolation that Fitzpatrick was only the latter, even though he talked constantly during the flight to Los Angeles. The killer was a nice enough chap, but not very charming company.

They arrived after lunch. McGarrity checked the gunman into a Sunset Strip motel and then they took a drive to Beverly Hills. They motored past Hencill's house. "A rich bastard," the gunman said.

"Inherited it," McGarrity sniffed. "Not a workingman like ourselves."

"Is that where I do it?" The killer nodded backward after McGarrity had driven by.

"Yes."

The Irishman yawned and looked at his watch. "It would be midnight back home."

"I'll drop you back at the motel."

"Will you be needin' me tonight?"

"No. Walk along Sunset and see the sights. Look out you don't get robbed."

A contemptuous look passed over the gunman's face. "Wouldn't I be givin' some boyo a surprise."

McGarrity had kept his suite at the Century Plaza, and when he arrived all the tapes from the night before were waiting for him.

He had considered canceling all but the Hencill tapes. But if he did, it might spotlight Hencill's name to Gotnich. He doubted that the man paid any attention to the tapes, and he further doubted if Gotnich would care one way or the other should one of the persons whose phone he had ordered tapped come up dead. Still, it was better to minimize all risks.

It touched him to listen to the tape of the little girl crying. The woman must be a beast, he thought. It was a cruel thing to kidnap children.

He telephoned Linda and made a dinner date. He went down to the bar for the cocktail hour and watched the first three innings of the game.

In the bottom of the first inning Chad hit a bases-loaded single, driving in two runs.

At the end of the third inning McGarrity left to meet Linda at the Cock 'n' Bull. The score still was two to nothing.

FRIDAY
Travel Day

The first agent of the Federal Bureau of Investigation to be indicted for a
crime while on active duty, was sentenced in Federal District Court in
Brooklyn to a year and a day in prison for obstructing justice.

He pleaded guilty Nov. 9 to a count of filing false documents to impede
a grand jury investigating charges that he had received a $10,000 bribe
from a Manhattan bookmaker and then had perjured himself when questioned about the payment.

The convicted man, an agent for 18 years before he resigned in November, asked for leniency, saying, in a near-whisper, "I made a mistake. I
shouldn't have gotten involved." But the judge said, "Because you are an
F.B.I. agent and admitted obstructing justice, you must go to jail."

— *New York Times* story, January 1979

19.

At 3:45 A.M., the jetliner carrying the Dodger baseball team
touched down at Los Angeles International. On hand to greet them
were nearly five hundred fans. This was a generous number considering that six hours earlier the Dodgers had taken a two-to-nothing
lead into the bottom of the ninth inning and then blown the game.
An error by the first baseman, a walk, and a home run by Verban
ended the game before the Dodgers could get a man out. With this
upset victory, the Wonderful Washies had taken a lead of three
games to two. They needed only one more victory to take the
World Series.

A microphone had been set up on the tarmac and Danny
Dougherty grabbed several players to say a few words to the loyal

fans. Chad was one. He thanked the fans for showing up and promised them the Dodgers would not quit.

The manager said a few words, and then everyone went home.

At eight o'clock in the morning, a Hughes Air West flight from Phoenix landed at Los Angeles International. Among the passengers was Rick Frey, a baby-faced FBI agent who looked younger than his thirty years. He wore Levi pants, a short-sleeved sports shirt, and cowboy boots. He carried a navy leave bag, which contained his navy seaman's reservist uniform.

Frey was one of the nearly one hundred agents who would arrive that day in Los Angeles. He did not know his assignment. He had been ordered to report to the General Services Administration warehouse on Grove Street right off Wilshire.

In the GSA warehouse desks and filing cabinets had been stacked next to the walls to make room for rows of army cots. The scene reminded Rick Frey of the barnlike barracks of a naval induction center.

By noon more than seventy agents had arrived. A field kitchen had been set up to prepare meals. In a typical military snafu the stoves wouldn't work in time for the noon meal and the agents were served box lunches and coffee.

At one o'clock they were assembled in a second-floor room converted to an auditorium. Folding chairs faced a speaker's stand. A man all recognized as Al Frazzini strode into the room. A voice called for attention. A quietness settled over the room. Frazzini took his place behind the podium at the front of the room. "Good afternoon, gentlemen," he said.

Almost in military fashion the agents returned his greeting.

Frazzini cleared his throat. "You have been sent to Los Angeles to participate in a secret operation. I am the administrative head of the operation; the operational part will be under Tom Jensen."

A murmur went around the room. Frazzini waited till it passed before continuing.

"Any operation can be compared to a puzzle. It has various

pieces that make it a whole. Today, each of you will learn his piece. Tomorrow, Mr. Jensen will give you the picture.

"Upon arriving you received a card that told you, among other things, your team number. In a moment the teams will meet in the rooms downstairs. There you will be told your piece of the puzzle and your part in it. Afterward, you will be sent on the streets in a rehearsal. You will stay on the streets for a limited time. Once you return to the building you are not to leave it unless authorized by your team leader. The top-secret security that went into effect when you left your bureau remains so until you are told otherwise.

"You were told to bring along reading materials. I hope you did so. If not, you are going to be in for a boring evening. A few television sets are available, though not enough to accommodate all of you. For those who failed to bring books or magazines I suggest you purchase some while you are on the street.

"I have been informed that the stoves are now working [cheers] and you will be served a hot dinner tonight and a hot breakfast in the morning.

"We have limited facilities, so each team has been assigned times to use the showers. Your team leader will tell you yours. At eleven o'clock tomorrow morning, Mr. Jensen will give you your final briefing. Now you may report to your team leaders."

The number of Frey's team was forty-seven and he sought the room of the same number. He was the sixth agent to enter. The others had taken seats and looked around when he entered. No one spoke, even though Frey recognized one agent from training days. At the head of the room stood a man Frey assumed was the team leader. Frey took a seat and waited.

Twenty persons were in the room when the man at the front asked that the door be closed. When it was he addressed the group.

"My name is Mike Haggerty, special agent in charge of our bureau in Reno. For this operation I am your team leader. We have the most important assignment."

"This operation has been mounted to apprehend a man. Maybe several; even a woman could be included — we don't know. We do know for sure there is a man. Other teams will pinpoint him. Our job is to arrest him."

He paused and looked around the room.

"We are going to find this man in a telephone booth. Each of you have been assigned one booth to observe. You will wear the disguises you brought with you."

Haggerty pulled a package of cigarettes from his shirt pocket. "You may smoke."

Several agents lighted cigarettes. Another got up and opened a window.

"I am going to assign you your stations now. I want you to go there, to the booth, and make a call. Telephone a theater and ask a show time, or an airline and ask about a flight. Anything. As you do so, put yourself in place of our man. Look around you. What will he see? If he becomes aware that an arrest is imminent, where would he try to run? What are his escape routes? If your telephone station is located in a store, look about for entrances, exits, stairwells, elevators, and fire escapes. Familiarize yourself completely with your area."

Frey was assigned a telephone booth in Wilshire Drugs. He had one hour to spend on the street, to look at the store, make his call and return.

On the way to the store he stopped at a bookstore and browsed through the paperback department. He selected two books by Joseph Wambaugh.

Wilshire Drugs was on the odd-numbered side of the street in the 5100 block. A U-shaped lunch counter was to the left as Frey walked into the store. Next to it, at the rear, was the phone booth. Frey observed that originally there had been three booths. Two had been removed, and quite recently he thought, as the construction marks were still fresh.

He sat down on a stool at the end of the counter and next to the telephone. He ordered a cup of coffee and looked at the covers of the Wambaugh books. When the coffee was served he said to the waitress, "Guard it for me, I got to make a call."

He made a decoy call to the Pantages Theater, asking show

times. Afterward, he talked to the dial tone and looked about him. There were two exits leading to the back of the store. One was marked OFFICES, the other was unmarked. He watched a clerk carrying boxes from the room and assumed it was the storeroom.

He left the booth, paid for his coffee, went onto the street, and headed for the warehouse.

Jensen had been on Wilshire Boulevard for two hours. The day was warm and Jensen removed his jacket. He had walked "the course" as he called it, four times. The first time he did so in the role of Chad. Next, he played the role of the kidnapper. The third time he checked the pedestrian flow. The last time around he compared the phone booth locations against the chart given him by Ronald Lee, the telephone executive.

He entered a sidewalk booth positioned in front of a hardware store. He took a roll of dimes from his coat pocket and began making phone calls.

Using various ruses he called first a municipal office and asked if any parade permits had been issued for Saturday afternoon. There had been two. But neither along Wilshire Boulevard.

Next he telephoned Republican and Democratic campaign headquarters and asked for campaign schedules. It was an election year and the California gubernatorial race was in full swing. He was told no speeches or rallies were scheduled for Wilshire Boulevard for late Saturday afternoon.

Fearing disruptive construction activity, he telephoned municipal engineers and asked if any projects were ongoing that would interfere with the normal flow of vehicular and pedestrian traffic. Negative.

He made similar calls to the gas, power, and light companies. Negative.

Jensen pocketed the last of his dimes and went onto the street. He stopped to get his bearings before taking off in the direction his car was parked.

He had been in the booth a half hour, and his shirt was soaked with perspiration. He was satisfied with his work. He had done everything one could do. He had checked the plan to the last detail. If anything went wrong he could not be criticized.

He watched a man approach him. The man wore robes, had a long beard, and carried a placard which read:

REPENT, THE WORLD IS ENDING

Jensen altered his course to encounter the man. "Hello," he said in a friendly tone.

The man looked at him. His eyes were wild. "Good afternoon, brother," he croaked.

"When is the world going to end?" Jensen asked politely.

"Soon, brother, soon. Repent before it's too late."

"Will it be too late Saturday afternoon, say, at about four o'clock?"

The prophet thought that over. After a moment of meditation he pronounced his judgment. "Personally, I think it will come to pass Sunday morning."

"Any time but Saturday afternoon."

"Any time is the right time to repent, brother."

"Amen," Jensen agreed, and continued on.

On his car windshield there was an overtime parking citation. He looked both ways before tearing it up.

Shortly before five o'clock Hencill stood in front of a shoe store at 5001 Wilshire. He had come to the street to record the names of all the small businesses on the even-numbered side of the street. He had brought a pocket notebook for that purpose. Later, at home, he would look up the telephone numbers and then list the businesses alphabetically. He was taking no chances. When Chad went into a store Hencill did not want to run to a phone booth only to discover there was no directory, or to learn that the page he wanted had been torn out. When Chad entered a store, Hencill wanted to have his "own" telephone directory. This would be the most important call he would make to the ball player. It had to be fast.

SATURDAY
Game Number Six

A 26-year-old Arlington Heights man has been charged with telephone harassment for threatening the life of Walter Payton, star running back for the Chicago Bears.

The first threat was received by a television station. The caller demanded to speak to a sportscaster and when informed he was not available, said that unless $100,000 was delivered by the station to his "associate" on the corner of Dearborn and Washington streets that afternoon, he would kill Payton.

— A Chicago newspaper story, October 11, 1976

20.

Ninety-three FBI agents were assembled for the eleven o'clock briefing. They stood about in clusters talking shop. Except for their disguises they could have been participants at a convention. At least a dozen of the agents were women. One was in a nurse's uniform, another dressed as an airline stewardess, still another as a nun. Men were clad as plumbers, electricians, and ice-cream and hot-dog pushcart vendors. Rick Frey was in his seaman's uniform. The majority, however, were dressed as the housewives and businessmen who normally made up the pedestrian traffic of the street.

Word rippled through the group that Frazzini and Jensen had entered. The room quieted. Some of the agents jockeyed for position to get a good look at Jensen.

The two veteran FBI men took positions at the podium. Frazzini made the introduction. "Gentlemen, Mr. Jensen will now tell you why you're here."

There was no applause as Jensen stepped to the makeshift speaker's stand. He began the briefing at once.

"This operation concerns Roosevelt Chad, the baseball player." He looked at the faces. "Is there anyone here who does *not* know who Mr. Chad is?"

Again Jensen looked about. No hands were raised. He continued.

"Extortionists are trying to shake down Mr. Chad for a half-million dollars. This sort of thing is becoming common practice. Most of you can recall news stories of threats on athletes. Rarely have the offenders been arrested.

"Previously this was a matter for local and state police. Recent congressional action has now brought federal agencies into it.

"Most of the extortionists you have read about have been satisfied to send an anonymous note or two, or make some anonymous calls. The man trying to extort money from Mr. Chad is different in many ways. For one thing, he is persistent. He telephones each day. Mr. Chad is cooperating fully with us, and here is what has transpired.

"Mr. Chad walks along crowded streets and stops randomly into retail businesses. Somewhere in the crowd an extortionist or extortionists follow along and wait for Mr. Chad to enter a store. Then they run to a phone, call the store, have him paged to the phone, and repeat their extortion threats."

A stir passed through the assembled agents. For the first time each saw the significance of his role. When the stir passed Jensen walked to a blackboard covered by a sheet. Frazzini was standing next to the blackboard and helped remove the sheet. Jensen turned to the agents.

"This is how we are going to arrest the extortionist this afternoon."

The explanation Jensen gave of the operation was a lengthier version of the one he had given in Washington to Evans and Frazzini. The information, however, was the same. One set of agents would listen to taps of public telephones. Another set would observe the phones. A third set would be on the street to offer whatever assistance needed. The man they were looking for was believed to be educated and cultured, his age in the mid-thirties.

When Jensen finished he looked around at the faces. "Have we left anything out?" he questioned. "Later, I don't want to hear that we should have done X or Y. If you have anything to say, say it now."

Three or four agents raised their hands. Jensen pointed to the nearest. "What if the extortionist doesn't use a pay phone?" the man asked.

Jensen explained why it was thought he would.

Two other agents who had raised their hands nodded to indicate that that was the question they were going to ask.

Jensen's eyes skimmed the room. No more hands were raised. "Thank you," he said.

Hencill watched the game at Casey's, a downtown restaurant. At the cocktail hour Casey's is a singles bar. The lunch crowd is more sedate, interested in food rather than fun.

Hencill ate a bowl of soup. He didn't want to eat more lest it make him sick.

Washington scored first, a single run in the top of the second. They scored another in the third.

Hencill chain-smoked cigarettes and drank soda water. He yearned for a real drink, but didn't want to be tipsy when he telephoned Chad.

In the bottom of the third inning the Dodgers got one of the runs back.

Jensen had gone onto the street immediately after the briefing. He had left the administrative details to Frazzini and didn't want to upstage him.

He walked the course, watched the crowds on the sidewalks, and the traffic flow, and checked the phone booths. As the sixth inning ended, he called the commo van. He heard a portable radio tuned to the game. An agent told him the score was five to three, Washington.

"Everything going all right?" he asked the agent.

"Smooth as can be," the agent's voice came back. "The telephone company must make a mint off these phones. They're always busy."

Jensen checked next with Frazzini at the warehouse and then he continued walking the course.

Ahead he saw a crowd watching the game on a television set in a department store window.

He stood to the rear and peered over heads at the screen. The Dodgers were coming to bat in the bottom of the seventh inning, trailing five to three.

The first two men singled, the third man walked, the fourth man tripled, the Dodgers led six to five. The street was in an uproar.

The Dodgers weren't finished. The next batter flied out, scoring the man who'd tripled. Now it was seven to five.

The next batter singled; the following man was safe on an error. Men at first and third, one out. The next batter homered and it was ten to five.

The crowd watching the department store TV set screamed and applauded as if they were in box seats behind home plate. Passing motorists slowed and called out for the score. A city bus stopped at a fireplug and the driver ran out to get the results. His passengers shrieked when he came back and joyously shouted the score to them.

By the seventh inning, the Dodgers led thirteen to five.

The Wonderful Washies couldn't come back and the Dodgers won. The World Series was tied three games apiece.

Well, Jensen thought, as he continued down the street. In a couple hours there is going to be one goddam angry kidnapper walking up and down this street.

He was wrong.

When the rally had begun, Hencill was upset. But as it went on he became philosphic. He felt exhilarated, almost sensuous.

He had always had the gambler's dream of having a million dollars riding on one event. Well, tomorrow he would realize that dream. If Washington won, he would win more than a million dollars. If they lost, he would lose six hundred thousand dollars. And God only knew what else.

He thought back to the day he lost one hundred thousand dollars on the football game. That was two weeks ago exactly. It seemed two years. It was two weeks tonight that he listened to the old man in Vegas explain his theory on how to fix the World Series.

Tomorrow Hencill would find out if the theory worked.

He paid his check and headed for the five-thousand block of Wilshire to talk to the man who was supposed to make it come true.

21

The Dodger clubhouse was in pandemonium.

"TOMORROW WE GET THEM," a voice called and was echoed by a dozen other players.

In front of his locker, Roosevelt Chad was questioned by a mob of reporters. As he answered he kept one eye on the clubhouse clock. He wanted to be on Wilshire at four-fifteen.

It was twenty minutes past three when he finished the interviews and ran for the shower. Mentally he thanked Jensen for providing the helicopter.

At twenty minutes to four he was dressed and on his way to the helicopter pad.

Shortly before Chad was due to appear on Wilshire, Jensen entered a shoe store at 5001 Wilshire. A clerk approached him, a youth of twenty-one.

"I want to buy some jogging shoes," Jensen told him.

"Any particular brand?" the boy asked.

"Let's try Puma. Ten and a half. But you'd better measure me."

Without waiting for the clerk Jensen walked to a seat which gave him a full view of the street. He kicked off his right shoe.

The clerk squatted on a stool and placed Jensen's right foot in the measure. "Right, sir, you're a ten and a half."

The clerk got up and walked to the rear of the store.

Jensen got up as well and walked, one shoe off, one shoe on, to the window. No sign of Chad. The street was filling up now that the game was over. Traffic was heavy. Jensen guessed what the freeways must be like. He was glad he set up the helicopter for Chad.

"Let's try these, sir." The clerk was behind him. Jensen watched over the clerk's head to the street as first his right foot and then his left foot were fitted with the shoes.

"Walk around, sir. See how they feel."

Jensen walked to the door and looked out. Still no sign of Chad. He heard a helicopter and looked up. A police helicopter.

Across the street was a jewelry store. A clock registered twenty-five past four. Chad had to be along soon. Jensen returned to the waiting clerk.

"How are they, sir?"

"Perfect. I'll take them." Jensen sat down and let the boy take off the shoes.

"Will there be anything else, sir? Do you need socks?"

"Just the shoes, thank you."

Jensen followed the boy to the sales desk. He pulled a money clip from his pocket and dropped two twenty-dollar bills on the counter. As the boy made change, Jensen looked out the front door. Directly opposite the shoe store Chad was beginning his walk up the five-thousand block. Jensen scooped up his change and the box and headed for the door.

"Thank you, sir. Come back again," the clerk called after hhim.

"Go get 'em tomorrow, Rosie," a voice said.

Chad nodded his head. "Gonna try," he said. He looked ahead at the stores and tried to select one to enter. It was amazing, he thought, that even in a crisis a practical person remains practical. He wanted to enter a store where he could buy something he or his family needed. He didn't want just to shop aimlessly while waiting for the kidnapper to make contact.

"Hey, Mr. Chad! How about an autograph?" Someone clutched his arm. He looked around. A middle-aged woman was standing beside him. He didn't want to take the time, but he said, "Sure."

She dug in a deep handbag for paper and a writing implement.

"I've got a pen," Chad said impatiently. He wanted to get moving.

"Just a minute," she said. "I've got a postcard in here." She ferreted about in the handbag. "Here it is." She held up a dog-eared card.

"Who's it for?" Chad asked her.

"My grandson Stephen. Call him Steve."

Chad wrote, "To Steve from Rosie Chad," and handed it to her.

"Oh, thank you very much, Mr. Chad. I wish I could say I was for the Dodgers, but I'm not. My brother was born in D.C., so I'm for the Senators. I'm not wishing you any bad luck, but I hope you lose tomorrow."

"How does Steve feel about it?" Chad asked dryly, motioning to the card he had just signed.

"He's a soccer fan," the woman said.

Hencill cursed under his breath. Why didn't Chad get moving? What the hell was he doing gassing with that old bag? Hencill had entered a ten-cent store. He stood limply at a stationery counter and looked out the window, across the street. He sighed with impatience as the old lady moved on and Chad began talking to three teenagers.

"Can I help you?" a clerk asked Hencill.

He picked up a ball-point pen. "I'll take this," he said.

"Pay for it at the cashier's stand," the clerk ordered.

Hencill nodded. "Okay." Chad continued down the street. Hencill dropped the pen back on the counter and rushed out of the store.

On impulse, Chad entered an automobile appliance store. He had been heading for a bookstore when he saw a group of teenagers coming toward him. A clerk approached him. "How you doing, Mr. Chad? Gonna win tomorrow?"

Chad forced a smile. "Hope so."

The clerk rubbed his hands together. He was Chad's age. He wore a short-sleeved white shirt. Clipped to his breast pocket was a plastic pencil holder. "What can we do for you today?"

Chad had no idea. Over the clerk's head he saw a display of rear-view mirrors. He thought of Billy. "I want to buy rear-view mirror I can put on my son's bike. Got something like that?"

"Let's take a look," said the clerk. Chad followed him to the display.

The clerk lifted a small mirror from the display. For an MG," he explained. "Nice and small. And plain. You don't want anything heavy or fancy for a bicycle."

Chad looked perfunctorily at it. "Okay," he said.

"Anything else?" asked the clerk.

"I'll look around," Chad said.

"All right. I'll hold this in case you want something else."

Chad walked to the rear of the store and looked at tires. The salesman tagged along and tried to sell him a set of Volkswagen tires.

Fans were going to be a problem. Hencill saw that right off. He should have taken into consideration that Chad would be immensely more popular in L.A. than he was in Washington. It was too late now. He watched Chad head for a bookstore and saw a group of five teenagers swerve toward him. He saw Chad escape into an auto appliance store.

Hencill looked about him. Twenty-five yards ahead was a sidewalk phone booth. As he saw Chad enter the auto store he walked quickly toward the booth. He reached into his right trousers pocket for dimes. In his other hand he clutched the notebook with the list of store names and telephone numbers he had compiled the day before.

He was two strides from the telephone booth when a high-school-aged girl beat him to it, as if by magic — one moment she was not there; the next moment she rounded the corner and was in the booth. Hencill stood helplessly outside as she dialed a number.

Through the door he heard her say, "Hiya, Debbie. Watcha doin'?"

"Goddammit," Hencill mumbled and looked around for another phone. The next booth was occupied by an old man. A dog waited outside and wagged his tail at passersby.

The old man came out of the booth and Hencill walked toward it. He decided to occupy it. No more waiting for people to finish calls.

He almost lost the booth to another teenage girl. But not quite. He beat her by a split second. "Are you going to be long?" she asked.

"Yeah," he nodded. "I got to make a long-distance call."

"Ah, shit," she responded and turned away.

Hencill telephoned his company and talked with the assistant sales manager. He tried to be coherent while waiting for Chad to enter a store.

Chad was losing his patience. He wanted to get the call over with, and here he was, surrounded by autograph seekers. It seemed he would sign his name six times and then another six persons would push pieces of paper in front of him to sign. "Listen, folks, I really got to go. I'm sorry I can't sign them all. Just a couple more and I've got to be going."

He began pushing his way through the band of people around him, doing the best he could to sign a few last autographs. Normally he wasn't so besieged. It was the Series fever.

"C'mon, Rosie, sign mine," someone shouted. "I've been standing here five minutes."

"Me, too," echoed other voices.

"Catch me at the ball park," Chad retorted.

"When? Next year?" moaned a disappointed voice.

Crowds attract crowds and other persons coming along the sidewalk stopped to see what was going on, swelling the crowd around Chad.

He stopped signing his name. He realized he was only worsening the situation. "Good-bye, everyone," he called out. "All the Dodgers appreciate your support. See you at the ball park." Like a plunging fullback, he burst free of the crowd and headed for the corner.

The traffic light was changing and he put on a burst of speed. He hit the curb as the light turned yellow. He was two strides deep into the intersection when the red light came on. Spurred by the blare of horns, he leaped ahead. Behind him the crowd of fans and well-wishers stood helplessly on the curb, their pursuit momentarily cut off by a stream of vehicles.

Agent George Dean had been assigned a sidewalk telephone booth in front of a vacant storefront at 5025 Wilshire. As a cover he was washing the store windows. When Chad began his walk the booth was occupied by an old man whose dog waited patiently outside. Dean did not think whether the man with the dog looked like a kidnapper. Ten years in the Bureau had taught him there is no such thing as a typical-looking suspect.

He tensed when Chad entered an automobile appliance store and was disappointed when Chad came out. Dean would liked to have made the arrest. An agent needed arrests like army officers needed battles. They were often the key to promotions.

After the old man and the dog left the booth Dean watched two persons, a high-school girl and a short, baby-faced guy, race for it. The short guy won. Across the street Chad was becoming surrounded by fans.

"Rosie Chad is over there giving autographs," a voice called out.

Dean saw the ballplayer break through the crowd and run for the corner. The people on the sidewalk in front of Dean began crossing the street. The short guy came out of the booth.

Hencill was left behind when Chad made his break. He had expected Chad to stay in the five thousand block. When the ballplayer broke free of the crowd, Hencill could not be sure the booth he was occupying would give him a view of the store Chad entered. He dashed from the booth and ran to the corner.

Hencill hated his size. He couldn't see Chad. He stopped and jumped into the air. He felt like a fool but he had to know where Chad was. He didn't see him. He ran forward a few steps and jumped again. There he was. In front of some kind of a boutique. He ran a few steps further. An open space at a no-parking zone gave him a clear view of the other side of the street. His eyes ran like rifle sights down the street. There he was! Going in the sporting goods store.

Hencill looked quickly about for a telephone. Ahead was Wilshire Drugs. He skimmed over the sidewalk like a student moving in a hallway where he was not supposed to run; arms at his sides he ran while trying to give the impression of walking.

He entered the drugstore carrying the notebook with the telephone numbers in his right hand. At one side of the room was a lunch counter. Beyond it he saw a phone booth. Sweat was pouring from him. He walked along the lunch counter and slipped inside the booth. He put the notebook on the tray beneath the phone and traced his finger down the names until he came to California Sporting Goods. The number was 469-9987.

He reached in his pocket for a dime and jammed it at the slot. It fell to the floor. He cursed and quickly bent down to retrieve it.

The next time he inserted the coin carefully in the slot. The dial tone was slow in coming and he resisted an impulse to slam his fist against the phone box. Then it was buzzing in his ear.

He had forgotten the number and he referred again to the list. He got the number and dialed it. His heart pounded as he waited for the sporting goods store to answer.

The number ran once, twice, three times, four times, five times, six times, seven times, eight times.

"Hello." The voice was that of an old woman.

"Who is this?" Hencill asked.

"Who's this?" the old woman replied.

Hencill realized he had dialed a wrong number. It was the tension and all the goddam fans and running about. He took another dime from his pocket.

Before dialing he glanced across the street. He saw a small crowd of people in front of the store. Chad was still inside. He referred to the list and held his finger on the number for the sporting goods store. 469-9987.

He dialed 4. He dialed 6. He dialed 9. He dialed 9. He dialed 9. He dialed 8. The final number, 7.

He hung up immediately. Chad had come out of the shop.

Hencill slammed open the door, walked past the lunch counter, and left the store. As he came onto the street a yellow school bus stopped in front of the sporting goods store. Black lettering on the side of the bus identified it as property of Saint Patrick's Academy. The bus was jammed with students of high-school age. Hencill remembered they had played the National Anthem before the game.

Within a minute after the bus stopped there arose a great racket — shouting, and musical instruments being played. The bus blocked Hencill's view, and he couldn't see what was happening. A cheer rose into the air. Pedestrians on Hencill's side of the street began jaywalking to see the cause of the excitement. Hencill could see students in band uniforms. They swirled around the bus and into the center of the street, blocking traffic. Now automobile horns mingled with the cacophony of sounds.

The students wore red uniforms and carried brass instruments. Hencill heard the pounding of a bass drum, followed by the staccato beat of smaller drums. Then, above it all, came the shrill cry of a bugle sounding "Charge."

"CHARGE!" the crowd echoed.

And from around the bus came a wave of students. On their shoulders was Roosevelt Chad. Again the bugle sounded. And the students, with Chad on their shoulders, his face reflecting total shock, charged down the street.

22.

Chad was almost ill with frustration and disappointment when the students had set him down.

Rather than being surprised when Jensen appeared suddenly

from the mass of people, Chad felt relief to see the FBI man. "Stay close behind me," Jensen told him.

The crowd seemed to part for the broad-shouldered FBI man, and it was a moment before Chad realized they were in the middle of a wedge of men, whom he supposed to be FBI men as well.

They burst into a side street and Jensen opened the door to a sedan and motioned Chad to get in. The FBI man went around the car and got behind the wheel. Magically, the escorts disappeared.

Jensen headed for Dodger Stadium. Once firmly in traffic he turned to Chad. "Well, it didn't go the way I planned it."

Chad listened silently as Jensen explained the trap the FBI had set. Despite his frustration, Chad could not help but be impressed by the try the FBI had made. They had gone the extra mile to catch the kidnapper, and only an incredible stroke of fate, or bad luck, or whatever one wanted to call it, had spoiled the plan.

Chad turned his head from the car window. "Well, what now?"

"He still has to contact you."

"Tonight?"

"Or in the morning. Sometime before the game. He'll want to talk to you about your play. You'll want to talk to him about your family. And concerning them: we'll have an ambulance and doctor standing by. A special room has been set aside at the Veterans Hospital. The moment your family is released, or their whereabouts are known, we'll go into action."

"He'll turn them loose, won't he?"

"The chances are that he will."

"But you're not certain?"

"Nothing is certain."

"But if the relationship is there, what would stop him?"

"The recognition factor."

"He'll be frightened that my family can give you a description?"

"Precisely."

Jensen pulled off the freeway. Several hundred cars were still standing in the parking lot. "It's the red Volks," Chad said.

Jensen pulled alongside the car and stopped.

"So what about my family tomorrow?" Chad persisted.

Jensen turned to look Chad in the face. "Let me tell you what experience tells me the kidnapper is going to think. If the Dodgers lose he wins his bet and he will be ecstatic, euphoric. In his mind you will be the greatest man who ever lived. You've kept your promise. The relationship between the two of you is at its highest. He will release your family.

"An hour later he will begin to have doubts. How much did the family learn about him while they were his hostages? Did they know where they were hidden? Can your family identify him or his accomplices? In the end, he will wish he hadn't let them go."

The two men sat silently for a moment.

Chad stirred. "And if the Dodgers win and I have to pay a ransom, he has a lot of time to think whether he really should release them or not."

"Or he might not call at all. He hasn't specifically agreed to a ransom."

Chad's heart sank.

"I'm sorry," Jensen said, "but that's the way it is."

Chad looked away. For a moment he was lost in thought. Then he turned back to Jensen. "I don't have that problem if we lose."

"Are you planning to throw it?" Jensen asked.

Chad turned angrily to the FBI man. "I told you people in the beginning that the moment I can't produce I'll take myself out of the lineup."

"You'd do that tomorrow in a clutch situation in front of a television audience of eighty million persons?"

"I would."

Jensen looked the ball player in the face. The two stared at each other. Chad refused to lower his eyes.

Chad went home and waited for the kidnapper to make contact.

He broiled a steak, drank a couple beers, and watched television. The variety show he was watching had a skit on the World Series, so he switched to an adventure movie. He couldn't get interested.

He switched off the TV and played his stereo. Twice he thought he heard a car stop in front of the house. Both times he went into the darkened dining room and peeked through the drapes. Once there was no car; the other time it was a boy bringing home the girl across the street.

At ten o'clock the telephone rang. Chad knew instinctively it was the kidnapper. He snatched up the receiver. "I couldn't help it today," he said. It never occurred to him that the caller was other than the kidnapper.

"I don't care about today," the voice said tersely. "It's tomorrow that concerns me now. You know what you have to do." It was a question.

"Yes."

"Then I have no worries." Again it was a question.

"I can't do anything about games like today when we score ten runs in an inning."

"I understand that," the voice said. "But if the Dodgers score ten runs tomorrow, you better not figure in any of them."

"I don't think it will happen," Chad said. "But if it does, how do I pay a ransom?"

"Monday I want you back on Wilshire. Five P.M., same place. This time cover yourself up a bit. Wear a hat, or dark glasses. I'll recognize you. Have the money with you."

"In small bills?"

"Hell no! I'm not a weight lifter. All in hundreds. Five hundred thousand dollars."

"And if Washington wins, how do I get my family back?"

"I'll call you ten minutes after the game, in the Dodger clubhouse. Give me the number."

Chad told him, and the man hung up.

For a moment the ball player held the receiver to his ear. Then he telephoned Jensen and told him of the conversation.

"I haven't got that kind of cash," Chad worried. "Can you help arrange something?"

"I have already," Jensen said.

Across the city Red Fitzpatrick, the IRA gunman, was walking a dog. He had bought it earlier from a pet shop and now he had it on a leash and was casually approaching Hencill's estate. He turned in at the drive and walked the long distance to the main house and to the coach house, which sat near it. The buildings were dark. But Fitzpatrick was prepared, should anyone appear unexpectedly, to drop the leash and pretend the puppy had escaped him. That shouldn't be hard to fake, since the young animal had been pulling on the leash the moment it was slipped on. It also had barked frequently. It gave that up soon after it learned that each bark earned a rough kick in its hindquarters.

Cautiously the gunman approached the houses. He noted the doors and windows, the hedges and trees, and the garage. He walked around to the pool side of the estate. There, in the back rooms of the house, he saw light. Through a window he saw the giant-sized TV screen. The puppy let out a whimper, and the gunman nudged it with his toe to remind the animal of things to come if it didn't shut up.

After taking a look at the rear of the estate, Fitzpatrick retraced his path to the front driveway. He had counted three doors on the main house and one on the coach house.

Once again on the street he walked quickly toward Sunset Boulevard where he had parked the rental car. When he got to the car, he knelt down and unleashed the puppy. The animal wagged its tail and sat on its haunches, waiting expectantly. The Irishman got into the car, started the engine, and drove off.

The puppy chased after the car. A hundred yards later it gave up. The animal stood for a moment on the curb and then started across the street. Halfway across, a passing automobile struck it, killing it instantly.

23.

Hencill was sincere about releasing the family. He didn't want to kill them. Furthermore, he knew he couldn't do it personally. But Helen could.

He had considered the best ways to release them and had decided on leaving them in a motel room. He had made reservations at an old motel on the Pacific Coast highway. It was a favorite trysting place for lovers and the management paid little attention to who came and went.

It was midnight when the van pulled into the driveway of the Beach Motel. The building was designed in a T. The room Hencill had reserved was at the bottom of the T. Next to his was one other room. The shades were up in it, the curtains not drawn. Hencill looked into the window. "It's empty," he said.

Mrs. Sanders kept watch as he quickly carried the family into the room they had rented. The children were in their street clothes and wrapped in blankets.

"Okay?" Hencill muttered the question before he carried in Mrs. Chad.

"Okay," Mrs. Sanders assured him. It was safe. She was wearing a jumpsuit and gloves, a scarf tied over her hair. She was leaving no clues. She'd even brought a small vacuum cleaner and cleaning supplies.

The two of them carried Mrs. Chad into the room and put her on one of the beds. Hencill straightened up and flexed his arms once and looked around the room. "You know what to do?" he said to Mrs. Sanders.

"Me knowing what to do has never been the problem," she answered bitterly. "It's you and the ball player who are confused about what's happening."

"Let's not go over that again," Hencill snapped.

"What did Chad say when you telephoned?"

"He said I didn't have any worries."

Mrs. Sanders laughed mockingly. "Isn't that fine! The Dodgers win tomorrow and you have no worries."

"I told you, I get a ransom."

"And what do I get?" she lashed back. "That doesn't solve my problem."

Without another word, Hencill left.

Mrs. Sanders began preparations for her stay. She was taking no chances on leaving fingerprints or other clues in the room. She took a sheet of brown wrapping paper from her suitcase and unrolled it on the dresser top. On it, she placed her toilet articles and the drugs for the Chad family. Robert had made sure she had only enough drugs to last through Sunday's game. If the Dodgers won, and he had to accept a ransom, he would bring her additional drugs Sunday night to last through Monday. She knew he was taking no chances with her. No matter, she had her own plans.

If the Dodgers lost, she would follow Robert's instructions. If they won, she would not.

Who knew what the family would remember? Who knew what they had seen or heard which later they could tell the police? She did not want one day to answer the ring of her door bell and find detectives waiting at the threshold, the Chad family standing behind them, prepared to identify the coach house. Besides, they'd all gotten a good look at her the day of the kidnapping, before she began wearing the ski mask. And she hadn't disguised her voice. They'd remember *that* for sure.

It would be bad enough to turn loose the family if the Dodgers lost. To turn them loose if the Dodgers won would be absolutely stupid.

She had no intention of being stupid. She had brought with her a large bottle of sleeping tablets. If the Dodgers won the Series, the ball player would never again see his family alive. He — and Robert — could suffer for it.

She turned on the television to a program of all-night movies and settled down to the long wait.

Chad couldn't sleep. He wished he would have taken a sleeping pill before going to bed. He had gone to bed at eleven o'clock and now it was two-thirty and he still was awake. It was too late to take a pill now. He was afraid it would leave him groggy at game time.

What did it matter? He was supposed to lose the game anyhow. Could he do it? If he did, he knew he could never play the game again. If he intentionally lost the game, he'd announce his retirement in mid-winter when no one could make any kind of a connection. That would be his own personal punishment, his self-imposed sentence.

Chad sat straight up in bed. This was crazy! Was he really thinking about throwing a World Series, retiring from baseball? Was this all real? Was his family really gone? Was he really lying awake the night before the seventh game of the World Series seriously thinking of throwing the whole thing? For a moment he considered getting up and looking in his children's rooms. Certainly they were there. This was a dream.

He knew it wasn't. It was true, all of it, and that's why his mind was crowded with unbelievable thoughts.

What if he did have to throw the game? How would he do it? He couldn't know until the time came, until the exact moment the chance presented itself.

He didn't want to make an error. He'd rather lose with his bat. A thought occurred to him. If Washington were ahead and he came to bat and struck out, it wouldn't be as if he had lost the game, as if the Dodgers had been ahead and he had done something to put them behind. If he didn't produce at bat, it didn't mean he had lost a game. It meant only that *he had failed to win.* He threw back the covers and put his feet on the floor.

If it came to it, he hoped that would be the way it would be . . . with his bat in his hand. God knows, he had literally won two games single-handedly. No one could blame him for not producing just once, even if it was in the seventh game.

He stood up and walked to the window and looked out into the night. No one there. No one watching him. He turned back to his bed.

He hoped it would not come down to him, the responsibility for winning or losing the Series. What he hoped . . . what he really hoped . . . was that Washington would win and the kidnappers would get away and he would be rid of this awful burden.

There! That was it. That's what he really wanted.

Guilt tore at him and he became angry. He didn't want to feel guilty. Why feel guilty about treasuring one's family more than a baseball game? The guilt pushed at him, and he hated it.

"I HOPE WASHINGTON WINS!" he shouted to the empty house.

SUNDAY
Game Number Seven

Since 1946 nearly half the final World Series games have been decided by one or two runs.

24.

Chad awoke cross and tired shortly before eight o'clock. He was lying on his back. He rarely slept on his back, and when he did he slept poorly and had bad dreams. Once, in the middle of the night, he awoke shouting. He couldn't remember the dream, but he remembered the shouting and the fear, and his heart racing wildly. The covers were on the floor and he got up to put them back on the bed.

Now he lay on his back, his eyes fixed angrily at the ceiling. He shoved back the blanket and sheet and set his feet on the floor. He balanced his elbows on his knees and rested his chin in his hands as he stared at the floor. His mind was angry, but blank of purpose.

In a few minutes he got to his feet and poked desultorily in a hallway closet for his jogging clothes. He had to take a run, if only one lap around the school track, to clear his mind and wake himself up.

The morning air refreshed him. It was going to be a beautiful day for a baseball game. The haze and smog of the day before had been replaced by cool, dry air from the northwest.

On the street in front of his house he broke into a trot. By the time he reached the school track he felt awake and the anger was passing from him. He trotted twice around the track.

He walked home. Four doors from his house he saw Mrs. Granter watering her flowers. Mrs. Granter was a beautiful old woman who was very good to his children and who was great friends with his mother. The two exchanged recipes and Chad's mother often drove Mrs. Granter shopping. In turn, Mrs. Granter had knitted afghans for the children's beds. This morning, in an apron and sunbonnet, she was a Norman Rockwell painting. "Good morning," Chad called out.

She turned and shaded her eyes. "Oh, Mr. Chad, it's you. Good morning. How is your family?" She turned off the hose. "I miss them very much. Will they soon be back?"

"Yes. Soon."

He wanted to change the subject. "Your flowers are beautiful," he said.

"Thank you. Let me cut some for you."

"Ah, they look so nice in your yard, Mrs. Granter."

"And they'll die here. Come, I'm going to cut a bouquet for your mother. She should have flowers when she comes home."

Chad turned off the sidewalk and crossed the lawn to the flower garden. As he approached, Mrs. Granter put out her hand. "It's nice to see you, Mr. Chad. You've not been around much lately."

He shook her small hand and was surprised at the strength of her grip. "The team has been on the road quite a bit in the past couple weeks," he explained.

She took a pair of garden shears from the porch and began cutting flowers. "How is your team doing this year, Mr. Chad?"

Chad smiled inwardly. "So far, so good," he replied.

As he walked home he bent his face into the flowers and smelled their bouquet.

Hencill hadn't been able to sleep. He had awakened in the middle of the night. Fearful that his nervousness would wake Ilka, he had gotten up and gone downstairs. He drank two beers, turned on the television set, and watched the final half hour of an Andy Hardy movie. How simple life had been in those days.

He went back to bed and still couldn't sleep.

"What's the matter?" Ilka asked. Sleep made her voice sultry.
"I can't sleep."

"It does no good to worry," she advised him.

"I know all the philosophic arguments," he said. "I just can't sleep. Maybe I could if we made love."

Ilka sat straight up in bed. She was awake now. She switched on the lamp and looked at Hencill and began laughing. "I think you are completely crazy. You don't want to make love for more than a year, you lose all your money, you make this crazy bet which you for sure are going to lose, and now — suddenly — you want me to make love with you." Her laugh was sarcastic. "I give you good advice. Go in the shower and make love to yourself."

Now it was mid-morning and pain compressed his chest and fear made him perspire. He was seated on a bar stool and he climbed down, walked to the window, and looked out. Below him Ilka was working in the garden.

He went to the bar and poured a glass half full with Scotch. He took two long sips from it. He hadn't wanted to drink, but he couldn't help it. He was trembling violently and was frightened that he would lose control.

There is no sporting event in America that matches the drama of the seventh game of the World Series. At one o'clock the crowd was pushing into Dodger Stadium. Brilliant, clear sunlight washed the field and the stadium with its brightness. A gentle breeze, carrying on it the smell of flowers, sought its way through the crowd and ruffled the red, white and blue bunting spread around the stadium railings.

Souvenir vendors outside the stadium sold record numbers of pennants and balloons and baseball hats and miniature bats. Ticket scalpers sold their illegal wares as fast as customers learned of them. Box-seat tickets went for two hundred dollars a pair. The smart scalpers held their tickets until game time. Then they went for two hundred dollars each!

The press box was overflowing. Reporters shared typewriter

space and telephones. A half-dozen betting pools had been organized. New York sportswriters watched the crowd move politely to their seats and several wrote that a lesson could be learned by New York fans.

The Dodgers and Senators took turns working out. The players were strangely quiet. The usual chatter was not present, nor was the good-natured bantering between the opposing teams.

The fans sensed the tension and turned their own excitement and apprehension inward, until the stadium was charged with human electricity so strong it seemingly could have run giant turbines.

The two o'clock game time drew nearer. The introduction of the players was at hand. Officials cleared the field of photographers. Television reporters broke off their interviews. Club executives left the field and went to their private boxes.

The Washington players were introduced. The Los Angeles crowd applauded politely.

Then came the Dodgers. Each team member was greeted with heavy applause. The crowd thundered when Rosie Chad was announced.

On the field Chad reacted as if he were in a dream. His movements seemed in slow motion. Sound came to him as from an overseas broadcast, first rushing over him then fading away.

Dinah Shore sang the National Anthem. As she drew to the end, a roar went up, erasing "home of the brave."

The sound receded. A television producer had asked for a shot of the stadium with the field completely cleared. For a moment it lay empty, like a field before the battle.

An umpire stepped out of a dugout.

The crowd began to roar. The sound slowly grew, like an avalanche of boulders and thick soil and tree trunks shaking loose from the earth and starting its first ominous movements.

The rest of the umpiring staff appeared.

The avalanche moved ahead, rumbling louder, gaining movement and picking up new weight.

The umpires walked to their positions and stood momentarily

alone on the field, looking in their black suits like crows in a new-mown field.

The Dodgers ran on to the field.

The avalanche passed. In its place came an explosive thunder that rattled windowpanes a mile away.

Dick Riecks, the Dodger pitcher, began his warm-up throws. Boyd Simpson, the first baseman, tossed a ball across the infield to Don Reimer, the Dodger All-Star third baseman. Reimer deftly fielded the ball and tossed it back to Simpson, who lashed it back across the infield, bouncing and skidding, toward Roosevelt Chad.

Chad stooped and the ball hit the heel of his glove and dropped to the field. When he picked it up it seemed there was no feeling in his fingers and the ball dropped back to the infield. He reached again, picked it up and flipped it to Boone Sevening, the Dodger second baseman.

In the bathroom off the bar, Hencill bent over the toilet and threw up. In his mouth was the taste of Scotch, bacon and eggs, and fear.

When he felt certain nothing more would come up, he rinsed his mouth at the sink and gargled with a mouthwash. He splashed water on his face and dried it and put on after-shave lotion. He went back into the bar.

In the Beach Motel Mrs. Sanders watched the game on television. Mrs. Chad and the two children lay face down on the two double beds. Their breathing was regular and easy. Mrs. Sanders pulled a chair in front of her and rested her feet on it.

Plate umpire Toughy Twitchell watched Dodger catcher Goff Unser take the last warm-up pitch and throw it to second base. Twitchell looked at Elmer Verban, the Washington leadoff hitter standing in the on-deck circle. Verban was holding two bats. He dropped one to the ground and looked at Twitchell.

"Play ball!" the umpire cried.

Verban stepped to the plate. He had hurt the Dodgers more than any other Washington Senator player.

The first pitch thrown by Riecks clipped Verban on the right shoulder.

"Take first base," Twitchell yelled.

Verban tossed his bat toward the Washington dugout and, rubbing his shoulder, trotted down the first-base line.

Goff Unser, the Dodger catcher, ran toward the mound and shouted encouragement to his pitcher. " 'At's all right, Dick baby, get the next one."

Riecks did not get the next one. The batter was Elton Tuttle, Washington's switch-hitting left-fielder. On a two ball, two strike count, he hit a hanging slider over the left center-field wall.

For the first time, apprehension came over the standing-room-only crowd. The buzzing stopped. A silence fell upon the stadium.

In the bottom of the first inning the Dodgers went out in order. At the end of one it was Washington, two to nothing.

In the GSA warehouse a television set had been brought into the room that Frazzini had set up as his office. Jensen watched the game with him. The two sat silently and sipped coffee.

In the bottom of the second inning Jensen watched Chad loop a single over the second baseman's head. The next batter, with Chad attempting to steal second base, swung at a bad pitch and popped out. Chad returned to first.

Jensen refilled his coffee cup and watched the third hitter take the first pitch for ball one. The television picture was split, one half showing the batter, the other half showing Chad taking a lead from first, dancing back and forth.

On the next pitch he broke for second. He stumbled slightly on his first step and Jensen, watching the screen closely, thought Chad would be thrown out. He was saved by a wide throw from the catcher. Jensen laughed to himself. What if someone else had gotten to the Senators' catcher? He reflected that it was on plays just like these that games were won and lost and quite suddenly he felt an admiration for the kidnapper's theory. Also, he wondered if Chad's brief stumble, which had cost him a split second, had been intentional or accidental. Jensen had a great interest in the game. He wondered if Chad really would try to lose it. The ball player was still on second when the inning ended.

The tension had lifted from Chad that moment in the first inning when the Washington batter struck the two-run homer. It had been all Chad could do to keep from racing out to home plate with the Washington team and shaking the man's hand.

No longer was the burden on him to lose the game. It now was on him to win the game. And that would be a much harder task.

McGarrity watched the game in his hotel room. At the same time, he listened to the taps of the phone calls that had been made before midnight Saturday at Hencill's residence and at Mrs. Sanders's coach house.

At the end of the Hencill tape he learned that the Chad family had been moved. A call from Hencill to Mrs. Sanders at the Beach Motel revealed the location.

His attention went to the game. Hencill's team was winning two to nothing in the bottom of the fourth inning. The Dodgers got their leadoff man on. The next two men were out, one advancing the runner to second. With Roosevelt Chad on deck, the Dodger hitter flied deep to center field, ending the inning.

The game had a dreamlike quality for Chad. Sounds seemed far away, sights were often blurred. He moved and played by instinct, like a battered fighter.

As he took the field for the top of the seventh inning, he could not help but be satisfied with his performance. In three at bats he had singled, doubled, and flied out deep to center. That's not exactly the kind of day one would expect from a player who was supposed to lose a game.

In the bottom of the seventh inning he was the third man up. Washington had brought in Lefty Otto, who already in the Series was credited with one win and two saves. He easily retired the first two hitters. He stared long and hard at Chad before throwing his first pitch.

The first two pitches Otto threw to Chad were high and outside, a favorite place for pitchers to tempt Chad with a bad pitch. The third pitch from Otto was high and outside, but a fraction closer than the first balls. Chad heard Otto call out an oath as soon as the ball was released. Chad's body exploded into it. His bat whipped around like an angry cobra. All his weight, the strength from his shoulders, arms, and wrists whipped the bat into the high, outside pitch. At the crack of bat and ball Chad knew it was a home run.

Hencill could hear car horns from the well-traveled Sunset Boulevard a quarter-mile distant. Chad's homer made the score two to one. The fear that he had felt before the game was back again. A heavy gravitational force settled over him, pressing him downward on the bar stool. His whiskey glass was empty and he wanted to pour it full, yet he couldn't lift it.

At the Beach Motel Mrs. Sanders watched the game on TV. As she watched she crushed sleeping tablets into a fine powder that could easily be absorbed in orange juice. She had more than enough of the tablets to put the Chad family permanently to sleep.

She was convinced now that the ball player had been trying to win from the first inning of the first game. He never had intended to lose. The threats, the tapes, the phone calls . . . all were useless. She should have sent him his daughter's ear.

She was sure he had notified the police. He was the type, the Boy Scout hero. He probably was playing over his head to prove to authorities that he wasn't losing any games.

Grinding up sleeping tablets, she watched the eighth inning pass scorelessly by. When the ninth inning began, she filled a large glass with the deadly powder.

J. R. Oberreuter, Washington's ace relief pitcher, was thirty-eight years old. He was born and raised in Woodbury County,

Iowa. He had pitched professionally for nearly twenty years, since the Cardinals had spotted him in American Legion ball and signed him to a contract. He was an old campaigner who had played with a half-dozen teams. He'd pitched in three playoffs and a World Series. The Washington manager had saved Oberreuter for this spot.

As he took his warm-up pitches, Oberreuter knew he had one mission . . . to keep Roosevelt Chad from coming to bat. He had to get three men out before the fifth man came to the plate. For that fifth man would be Roosevelt Chad.

An eerie stillness had come over the stadium. Once, when Oberreuter was a little boy, a tornado had struck the farm where he lived. Before the tornado there had been a frightening stillness. He felt this same stillness as he stood on the mound ready to face the first Dodger hitter. He took his sign, made his windup, threw the ball. The batter topped it weakly to first base. One out.

The second Dodger hitter was their leadoff man. He got a lot of walks. He did not get a walk against J. R. Oberreuter. Instead, he crossed up everyone, dumping a bunt down the third-base line and beating it out for a hit.

The stadium exploded with sound.

Oberreuter turned his back to home plate and stared out to center field. A helicopter appeared, flying low and fast. Oberreuter strained to hear the motor. The crowd roar was too great. He thought of the tornado of his childhood. After the stillness there had been wind.

He drew a deep breath and turned to face the next hitter.

Three times Oberreuter threw to first base to hold the runner close. He wasn't frightened the man would steal. He wanted to keep him close in case of a hit-and-run play. The fourth pitch he threw was popped up behind the plate. The catcher circled, waited, took it.

Two outs.

Like air rushing from a giant balloon, the noise of the crowd swooshed out, leaving the stadium silent again. But Oberreuter was not deceived. Kneeling in the on-deck circle was Roosevelt Chad. Oberreuter had to get the man out at the plate. If he didn't, he knew that the tornado, poised in the on-deck circle, would strike.

The batter was Don Reimer, the Dodgers third baseman. Reimer was one of the toughest outs in the National League. Oberreuter's first two pitches to him were balls. On the second pitch Oberreuter had shouted at the umpire — the pitch had been close; he didn't want the umpire calling any more like that.

Pony Rogge, the Washington catcher, called time. He dropped his mask and trotted toward the mound. Oberreuter came a few steps to meet him. "J.R., boy, throw this guy nothing but strikes. Make him hit it. Goddam, J.R." The catcher jerked his head toward Chad, who had stood up in the on-deck circle. "Let's not get Superman there up to bat."

Oberreuter nodded. His mouth was dry and cottony.

He threw a strike to Reimer. And then another strike. The third pitch was a ball.

The count was full. He saw the manager standing on the top step of the dugout. The stadium was absolutely silent.

Oberreuter looked in at Reimer. The latter took a deep breath and blew it out. He straightened his batting helmet, went into a crouch.

The next pitch was a strike. But Reimer fouled it back. Oberreuter threw another strike. Reimer fouled it behind third base. Oberreuter threw another strike. Reimer fouled it behind first base. Oberreuter threw a ball and Reimer trotted to first base. The batter on first base trotted to second.

Roosevelt Chad walked to home plate.

From somewhere clouds appeared. The day had been calm and bright and now Oberreuter looked to the sky and saw clouds. A breeze passed over his wet body and made him shudder. He watched Chad standing at the plate. The crowd had begun to roar.

The noise hurt Oberreuter's ears. He bent to tie a shoelace. The crowd's roar passed over him in waves. He remained bent down and looked around the infield. His teammates stood frozen at their positions. Reluctantly he stood up.

So far in the Series Oberreuter had pitched three times to Roosevelt Chad. He'd gotten him out every time. Once by a strikeout;

twice Chad had popped up. Oberreuter raised his shoulders in a sigh. He looked at the runner holding close at first, he looked over his shoulder at the runner on second. He had a comfortable lead. Oberreuter had no fear the man would try to steal. The Dodgers weren't taking the bat out of Chad's hands.

Oberreuter got his sign and pitched. Chad swung. And missed. Strike one.

Oberreuter took the throw from the catcher and shook his body, trying to free it from tension. He looked at the runner on second. Still the comfortable lead. The runner at first was holding closer. Oberreuter looked at both runners and then pitched to Chad. Ball one.

The crowd noise became a shriek.

Again Oberreuter checked the runners. Again he pitched to Chad. The superstar swung ... and missed. Oberreuter swore he could feel the breeze caused by the bat. Strike two.

The freshening wind tugged at Oberreuter's cap. He swung his left arm in an arc to keep it loose. He wanted the next pitch to be a strike. In his twenty years of baseball he had thrown thousands of strikes. He would have traded all his strikes of yesteryear for one more strike to Chad.

His next pitch was a ball. The count was two and two.

Oberreuter saw the umpire call "time out" and he saw the manager leave the dugout.

They met at the mound. Oberreuter, Verban, the catcher, the shortstop, and the manager.

"Walk him," the catcher said.

"Pitch to him," Verban, the second baseman, said. "Don't walk the tying run to third and the winning run to second. Jesus Christ, we're still ahead in this game, you know."

"If we go down, let's do it with all guns firing," the shortstop said. "Pitch to him."

Toughy Twitchell, the home-plate umpire, walked up. "Let's play ball, gentleman."

"Don't be in a goddam hurry," the manager said. "This isn't a sandlot game. Nobody's going home."

Twitchell walked a few paces away. The discussion on the mound continued for a minute and then Oberreuter was alone. He was so nervous he could hardly see Chad standing at the plate. His eyes blurred. The wind brought tears to them. He thought he heard thunder. It was only the crowd.

But the tornado was coming. Oberreuter could hear it rumble somewhere in the stadium. The roar grew louder and more intense.

He glanced at the runner on first. Holding close. He swiveled his head and looked at the runner at second. Comfortable lead.

Oberreuter blinked, clearing his eyes, and looked down at his catcher to get the sign. He began to count: "One thousand one. One thousand two. One thousand three."

In one motion he spun and threw the ball at the second-base bag. There was no one there.

But two men were on their way. There registered in Oberreuter's mind the face of the Dodger base-runner, his eyes wide with shock and fear.

The second baseman dove, arm outstretched for Oberreuter's throw. The ball, the second baseman's glove, the base-runner's spiked shoe arrived seemingly at the same time.

"YER OUT!" the umpire roared.

Washington, the Wonderful Washies, had won the World Series.

Oberreuter careened from the mound toward his onrushing catcher. Just before he delivered himself to a crushing embrace, he looked at Chad.

Oberreuter was never to be sure if it was the excitement of winning, the carryover of tension of the moment before, but it looked like Chad was smiling. Or was it that his face was twisted with disappointment?

Oberreuter never knew.

WORLD SERIES AFTERMATH

If you want a sure thing, pick the Dodgers to lose the World Series.
— *The Sporting News,* November 4, 1978

25.

Exactly ten minutes after the game ended, Chad got the promised telephone call in the clubhouse from the kidnapper. The voice gave the name of the motel and the room number where the family would be found. Under his breath, Chad repeated the information. Afterward there was a pause on the line. Both realized there was nothing more to say and the kidnapper hung up.

Immediately Chad called the information to Jensen, who in turn called Frazzini. The latter was standing by at the Veterans Hospital in Sawtelle. He was to collect the family. Jensen would bring Chad to the hospital.

The hospital administrator knew only that an FBI operation of some sort was going on. If he was curious, he kept it to himself. It wasn't the first time the FBI (or the CIA or the Secret Service) had used his facilities. He was a good civil servant and he did as he was told. He minded his own business.

Frazzini wanted an ambulance, a doctor, three nurses, and two connecting rooms. He personally picked the staff. The ambulance driver was Russian-Armenian, the doctor was Pakistanian, the nurses Korean.

A look on the wall map in the drivers' room showed that the motel was but a ten-minute drive. Frazzini and the doctor crammed in the front seat with the driver.

The pickup was as low-key as possible. There were no sirens and police escorts. At the motel Frazzini flashed his identification to the manager, who looked at the ambulance and then got the room key himself. When he asked politely what it was all about, he was told politely that it was none of his business. Frazzini told the manager to keep his personnel, a desk clerk and a handy man, away from the room or he, Frazzini, would arrest them.

He paid two additional days' rent on the room and told the manager that no one was to enter. Frazzini would have to do a crime-scene investigation and he didn't want a maid vacuuming up any possible evidence. Though he doubted he'd find anything. It had been a well-planned kidnapping.

A quick check of the records revealed the room had been rented by a Mrs. Betty Williams. A call was made to the home of the night clerk, who said he didn't remember much about the woman. She was middle-aged. Or old. It was hard to tell. She had rented the room in the middle of the night and the clerk had been half asleep. (And drunk as well, Frazzini suspected.)

The business with the manager took five minutes, then Frazzini joined the waiting doctor and ambulance driver and went to the rear of the motel where the room was located.

There were no other guests about. Most of the motel rooms seemed to be unoccupied.

Frazzini anticipated that the family would be drugged, so he was not apprehensive when they opened the door and saw three inert forms on the bed. The doctor checked their pulses and pulled back their eyelids. He said there was nothing he could do until he examined them at the hospital. They seemed to be in reasonably good condition, he said.

The family was loaded in the ambulance and taken to the hospital. There, towels were placed over their faces to prevent identification as they were wheeled quickly through the corridors. Two rooms in a seldom-used wing of the hospital were ready. In front of the rooms was a small waiting room where Frazzini sat while the doctor and his staff worked.

The world did not know about the kidnapping, and Chad, as impatient as he was, was expected to stay in the Dodger dressing room to do game interviews. He didn't arrive at the hospital until two hours after the game.

Frazzini stood up when Jensen and Chad entered. "They'll be awake soon," he told the ball player. "The doctor says that in twenty-four hours they'll be as good a new."

"Maybe I can stay here with them tonight," Chad suggested.

Frazzini and Jensen exchanged looks. "That's out of the question," Frazzini said. "It'll only be another day, and then you'll have them home again."

He motioned to one of the closed doors at the rear of the waiting room. Chad looked questioningly and Frazzini walked to the door and opened it. Inside was Chad's family, unconscious. Frazzini stood aside to let Chad pass. Tears streamed down the ball player's cheeks.

"We'll wait for you out here," Frazzini said, and stepped back into the waiting room, closing the door behind him.

Ten minutes later Chad came into the room. His eyes were swollen. "It's just like they're sleeping," he marveled.

"I'm happy for you, Mr. Chad," Frazzini said.

"Thank you," the ball player said.

The room had a table and two straight-backed chairs. Jensen waved at a chair. "Sit down a moment, Mr. Chad. We want to go over a few things with you."

"Sure," Chad said. He rubbed his eyes.

Jensen turned the other chair backward and straddled it. "We are not going to announce that your family was kidnapped." He said it quickly and then stopped to let Chad comprehend it.

He didn't. "Why not?" he asked.

Jensen leaned forward on the chair. "For the safety of your family."

Chad felt a pain shoot through his chest.

"You see," Frazzini explained, "right now, the kidnappers feel safe. We'll frighten them if the newspapers get hold of the story.

The only ones who can make *positive* identification of them are your family. Tom said he discussed this with you. So you'll understand that this puts them in danger if we release the story."

"And it will make it easier for the FBI to catch the kidnappers if they're not on the run," Jensen added.

"When will you catch them?" Chad asked. He looked at Frazzini.

"Maybe next week," Frazzini answered. "Maybe next year."

Jensen got up from the chair. "There's another side to this. If we go to the press before we've caught the kidnappers, it casts doubt on the legitimacy of the World Series." He paused. "And perhaps even your play in it," he added significantly.

Chad swallowed. He wanted to be angry, to show outrage. But he couldn't. Not after all his thoughts on losing. "What do you mean?" he asked weakly.

Jensen told him quickly what he meant. "The fourth game. The error in the ninth inning that set up the winning run."

"I made an error," Chad admitted. "But to score, Washington needed a sacrifice and a hit. How could I anticipate that?"

"Well," Jensen said, "I'm not debating it with you. I'm simply pointing out the possibilities for a sensational press."

Chad looked around the room. "What about the hospital staff? Won't they talk?"

"We've handled that," Frazzini said. "The doctor, and he's a very good one, is Pakistani. He is very interested in cricket, totally absorbed in soccer, and has no interest whatsoever in baseball. The three nurses are Korean. They've never seen a baseball game in their life."

"We showed them your picture along with those of other sports figures," Jensen added. "Neither doctor nor nurses recognized any of them."

"One of the Korean nurses thought Joe Namath looked like the American soldier who got her sister pregnant in Seoul," Frazzini said dryly.

"And they won't talk?"

"Not unless they want to go back to Asia," Frazzini said.

"We can handle everything but your family," Jensen said, coming back to the point. "Can you explain it to them so they won't talk? They've had a rough time of it."

Chad looked at the floor. "That's no problem. In a million years my mother wouldn't say a word."

"What about the children?" Jensen asked.

Chad got up. Strain filled the small room. The three men were almost as strangers clinging to the straps in a subway car.

Chad thought of Billy and Camilla. Camilla would be no problem. He would have to make it a game with Billy. "Okay," he said at last. "I can handle it. Kids forget fast."

"We've registered you and your family here under a phony name." Jensen looked at Frazzini. "What is it, Al?"

"Gilbert Martin."

"Your family can go by their first names," Jensen said. "We don't have to change those."

"Okay," Chad said.

Jensen got to his feet. "In a couple weeks we'll have to release something to the press to the effect that an extortion attempt was made. Mr. Frazzini will help you get the story straight." He put out his hand. "Well, Mr. Chad, I'm flying back to Washington tonight. Next week I retire from the FBI. Mr. Frazzini will Godfather you now."

Impulsively Chad grasped the veteran agent's hand. "Thank you, Mr. Jensen. From both my family and myself."

"Have a good life, Mr. Chad," Jensen said.

The ball player went back into the room with his family.

Frazzini walked Jensen to the door. "When are you seeing McGarrity, Al?" Jensen asked.

"As soon as I leave here. He's waiting at his hotel."

"Tell him I'm sorry I didn't have a chance to say good-bye in person."

"I'll explain it," Frazzini promised.

"And I think it would be a good idea for you to call Apicelli." Frazzini looked questioningly at Jensen. "It'll take the heat off McGarrity," Jensen explained. "He cooperated fully and it would be better if we, rather than McGarrity, talked to Apicelli. After all, we telephoned in the first place."

Frazzini nodded. "Okay, Tom. I'll call him from McGarrity's room." He put out his hand. "Will we see each other before you leave Washington?"

"I'll make it a point, Al. Nice working with you this time . . . and all the other times over the past twenty-five years."

The two men shook hands and Jensen walked out of the room, closing the door on the last case in his FBI career.

Frazzini let Chad stay fifteen minutes with his family and then he hustled the ball player out of the hospital.

"You can pick them up tomorrow," he told Chad.

"What time?"

"After supper," Frazzini said. "It might be better if your neighbors don't see their return. Give you an evening to get your stories organized."

Chad nodded. "Okay. How about eight o'clock?"

"See you here then," Frazzini said, and drove off to meet McGarrity.

McGarrity was disappointed that he wouldn't be able to say good-bye to Jensen personally. "For Tom's sake, I wish we could have brought it off," McGarrity told Frazzini. "It's a shame he had to retire on a losing case."

"He's a professional," Frazzini said. "He won his share."

"You're keeping the case open, of course," McGarrity said.

"Absolutely. I'll review everything and see where we go next."

"If we stumble across anything, someone will let you know immediately," McGarrity promised.

The telephone rang. "That's Apicelli calling back," McGarrity said.

He lifted the receiver. "McGarrity," he said. He looked at Frazzini. "Yes, sir. He's here." He handed the phone to Frazzini. "It's Apicelli," he confirmed.

"Hello, Iggie," Frazzini said. "Well, the Dodgers lost and so did you and I. As we used to say in Brooklyn, 'Wait till next year.' "

A soft chuckle came over the line.

"But we're not giving up," Frazzini continued. "We may get this guy yet. We want to thank your organization for its cooperation, and in particular we want to thank you for Mr. McGarrity. He did everything we asked him."

Apicelli's voice came back slow and soft. "Alberto, I, too, am sorry. But as you say, we catch him yet. There is an old saying in Sicily, 'The rabbit who escapes the hunter often gets caught by the fox.' "

"We have the same saying in Naples, Iggie. Thanks again."

"May I speak now with Michael?" Apicelli asked.

"Absolutely. Here he is." Frazzini handed the telephone to McGarrity.

"Yes, sir," McGarrity said into the receiver.

"Will you be alone soon, Michael?"

"Yes."

"I'll wait for your call."

"Fine," McGarrity said, and hung up.

He escorted the FBI man to the door. "Good luck to you, Frazzini."

"All the best," the FBI man replied.

The two shook hands, and Frazzini went out.

McGarrity returned to the phone and dialed Apicelli, who answered on the second ring.

They discussed the kidnapping and the bet tersely, and then Apicelli said, "Come to my home for dinner before you leave for Ireland. You'll get no noodles over there. Only potatoes."

The two men chuckled together and hung up.

McGarrity sat for a moment in thought. The conversation had gone well.

THE WEEK AFTER THE SERIES

In December of 1978 five jockeys and two trainers were found guilty in New Jersey of race fixing.

— *The New York Times*, January 1979

26.

For one night all the past problems and differences at the Hencill estate were forgotten, lost in the joy of the Washington victory that afternoon. Hencill took Ilka and Helen to the Polo Lounge for dinner. The women treated each other civilly. Helen never acted more positively; Ilka was charming and never looked more beautiful. Several movie stars turned to give her an extra look and then glanced questioningly at Hencill, wondering, perhaps, what he had that could attract such a beautiful woman.

After dinner they caught the late show at The Comedy Store on Sunset. The acts were so funny that even Ilka had to smile a few times.

When they went home, Hencill walked Helen to the coach house and kissed her good night. Ilka came along and shook hands.

The betting coup released a sensuality in Hencill that he hadn't experienced since his early teens. Instead of going straight to bed, he wanted to drink a bottle of champagne with Ilka in the bar. She consented. He surprised her, shocked her, even, by taking off her clothes and making love to her on the floor in front of the TV set. She had to admit that he didn't do it half badly. Afterward, he stalked about the room like a rooster. He acted so pleased with himself that Ilka thought he might crow. She didn't mind. Sex would be her reward to him for winning the bet.

In the middle of the night he awakened her and they made love again. The same when they woke early in the morning to prepare for their trips east to collect the winnings.

She reflected that her husband was becoming a sexual athlete a little late in their marriage. She planned to tell him of the divorce as soon as they had returned and the money was safely in the bank. All this lovemaking would not make the divorce news any easier. But it had to be done. It would be only a matter of time before he began betting again. And losing. An attorney had to get a freeze on it quickly.

They were going their separate ways to pick up the money, but would meet in Las Vegas afterward. He was going to take his airplane to Vegas and then fly commercially to New York and back. After Ilka made her rounds, they would meet in Vegas. She would help him with the collections there, and then they'd fly back in his plane with all the money to Los Angeles.

McGarrity waited. He stayed up Sunday night to get the latest tap from Hencill's phone. He was rewarded with a call from Hencill to Carmichael. Hencill made an early appointment Monday to pick up his six hundred thousand dollars.

Monday morning McGarrity was waiting in his rented Chevrolet as Hencill parked his car in front of Carmichael's office. McGarrity noted that Hencill drove a black Mark IV.

He watched Hencill carry a grip from Carmichael's office, and then followed him to the bank. He guessed quite accurately that the gambler was returning the embezzled money which had been mentioned in an angry conversation with the woman Helen in an earlier tap.

McGarrity would liked to have had the money, but he knew the embezzlement could not come out in the papers. That might be all the smoke the FBI would need to lead them to Hencill.

After Hencill left the bank, McGarrity drove to a Lincoln dealer and arranged to rent a Mark IV, the exact year, make, and color as Hencill's.

Tuesday morning, while listening to the Monday tapes, McGarrity got a highly crucial piece of information. Hencill had called from New York. His pickups were going perfectly. "You'll have your fifty thousand Thursday night," he told the woman confidently.

"What time will you be back?" she wanted to know.

"I've filed a flight plan from Vegas for late Thursday. I'd guess around midnight we'll be home."

"You can pay me the next morning," she said.

Hencill laughed. "You're getting old."

"Recent events have not helped to keep me young," she replied tersely, and hung up.

Monday and Tuesday nights McGarrity and Fitzpatrick, the Irish gunman, each made a turn driving past Hencill's estate. They made the sweeps in different cars to get a feeling for the neighborhood.

It was a quiet street. As McGarrity drove by on one of his swings, he focused on the coach house. He mused that a quiet street worked better for holding kidnap victims than for what he planned. No matter. The risk was small that something could go wrong. And the profit would be so great.

On both days they looked for a place to get rid of the body. They considered trash dumps above the Hollywood hills. McGarrity finally discarded that idea. Human bones had a way of turning up that would bring FBI labs in on it. McGarrity wanted no corpus delicti. He wanted the body simply to disappear from the face of the earth.

He chose the ocean.

Ilka experienced no problems with any of her four collections. The men didn't seem reluctant or angry about paying her the sums of money. Instead, they laughed and joked with her. It was the American mentality, Ilka gueessed. They didn't care about money. That's why their dollars were no good in Europe.

In each city she collected one hundred fifty thousand dollars. It passed her mind more than once that after the final pickup in Nashville it would be an easy matter to continue on to New York and catch a Lufthansa flight to Frankfurt. She tried to convince herself that running off would solve her problems. She knew, though, it would only aggravate them and give her a host of new ones. Perhaps even more serious ones.

In each city she briefly checked into a motel. She used the privacy of the room to pack the money. She was exceedingly nervous after the first city, but then she noticed that no one paid attention to her or to the suitcase. As far as people on the street were concerned, or airline personnel, or the security people who disinterestedly x-rayed the suitcase, the contents could have been dirty laundry.

She was a bit disappointed at not seeing Saccente, who was out of town. Gallantly he had left her a sweet note and a red rose. She couldn't understand — she was suspicious almost — that he wasn't there. How could he have missed the chance to be with her? At the airport she tossed the rose and the note in a trash can.

Robert was still playing his role of sexual athlete when he picked her up in Vegas Wednesday afternoon. He embraced her and stroked her several times in the passenger lounge. In the car he kissed her passionately and ran his hands over her body. She knew what was expected of her when he got her to the hotel room. It was as if he were trying to make up for all his years of impotence.

She considered telling him in Vegas of the divorce. No. She had to wait until the money was in the bank. In the meantime, she had to play his game.

At the hotel she stood obediently as he took off her clothes and put her on the bed.

Afterward she joined him in the collections. He gave her betting slips and a list of casinos. By now she was experienced and relaxed and had lost her self-consciousness. She had learned that gambling is a very impersonal business. She suspected that might be one of the reasons her husband was addicted to it. He never had been much for people.

They met back at Caesar's at seven o'clock. They were going to stay overnight, catching a show, having dinner, and resuming the collections on Thursday.

He had brought a large suitcase to carry the money. He placed it on the bed and opened it. In it was the money he had already collected in New York. He added the six hundred thousand she had collected from the four cities, plus the money they had just picked up in Vegas.

While they were on the town he would leave the suitcase in the vault the hotel provided guests who wanted to lock up luggage. Many women checked furs, jewelry, and gowns they didn't want to leave in their rooms.

The stacks of bills were filling the suitcase. Ilka had never seen so much cash. The sight thrilled her. "How much is there?" she asked huskily.

Hencill giggled. "Over a million dollars."

They stood by the bed staring at the neatly wrapped bundles of money. "How does it look?" he asked.

Her throat was thick, and a thrill went through her body.

"How does it look?" he asked again.

She shifted her feet, opening her legs slightly. "Sexy." Her voice was filled with lust.

27.

Late Thursday afternoon McGarrity picked up two tickets for Friday morning flights from Los Angeles to New York. He would remain there. Fitzpatrick would continue on to Dublin.

In early evening they had dinner and went over their plans. The main thing was flexibility. The men knew what they were going to do and where they were going to do it. How and when they did it depended on other people: Hencill, his wife, and Mrs. Sanders.

After dinner the two men smoked cigars, drank brandy, and dawdled away another forty-five minutes. McGarrity figured that by ten o'clock the last dog walkers and joggers would be off the streets.

At a quarter of ten McGarrity paid the check. A few minutes later the men were driving toward Hencill's estate in Beverly Hills. They rode in the newly acquired Mark IV.

At ten-thirty Mrs. Sanders turned off the TV. She went to the bathroom and ran the water for her nightly bath. While she waited for the sunken tub to fill she went to the kitchen and took the dishes from the washer and placed them in the cupboard.

A few minutes later she heard a car in the drive and glanced at her watch. A quarter of eleven. She glanced out the window. Robert's car was parked in front of the main house. He was home earlier than expected. She finished with the dishes, went into the bathroom, and took off her clothes and put on a robe. After the tub filled, she turned off the water. She was preparing to take off her robe when the telephone rang. It would be Robert.

She belted her robe again and walked into the living room. She glanced out the window toward the main house. The garage light had been on; now it was out.

She answered the phone. No voice answered hers and she said again, "Hello."

A voice came over the line. It made her heart skip; she sank back on a chair. A high-pitched moan came from her lips. She clutched the phone to her side as the sound of Camilla's tearful voice came through the receiver: "Oh, Daddy. I'm so afraid. I hate this mean woman. I hate this mean woman. I hate this mean woman."

Mrs. Sanders shrieked and slammed down the phone. "Robert!" she screamed. "God damn you." She ran to the door, flung it open, and ran toward the main house. She had not gone five strides before she was struck down.

Hencill touched down his plane at the Hollywood–Burbank airport and headed for the parking area. He shot a glance at a hangar clock. Exactly midnight. He'd made good time.

He was dead tired. The traveling, the time changes, the strain, and (he looked at Ilka) the sex with her had drained him.

Ilka went after the car while he went through the formalities of the tie-down. He placed an order for the plane to be serviced and then walked toward the auto-park road. Ilka was waiting in the Lincoln. He got in beside her, put his head back on the seat, and let her drive them home.

"You take the money to the bank tomorrow?" she asked.

He thought a moment. "No. Not for a while."

She turned and looked sharply at him. "Why not?"

"Somebody might get suspicious if I dump all this cash at one time." After a minute he added, "It'll be there soon enough."

"Not for me it won't," Ilka retorted.

A few minutes later she pulled off Sunset Boulevard and then they were on their street.

"I'll put the car in the garage," he told her.

Ilka stopped at the front door. She left the engine running and got out of the car. Hencill slid into the driver's seat and set the car in gear. He pushed the button for the electric eye, which opened the garage door. Behind him he saw the light go on over the front door.

He pulled the car into the garage, shut off the engine, locked the doors, and walked to the house. The suitcase of money was clutched securely in his right hand.

The light over the door was on and Ilka had left the door open. The interior light was off. With the light in his eyes and walking into the darkness, he was temporarily blinded. He stood on the doorstep and reached around the door to the light switch. His hand scrambled over the wall.

Suddenly a clamping grip fastened around his wrist. He felt himself propelled through the doorway. He opened his mouth to shout, and a cloth was jammed into it.

The door closed behind him and the suitcase was jerked from his hand. He was conscious of his muffled sounds of protest. Tears welled in his eyes at the thought of losing the money.

In the shadows he saw two men. Behind them, on the floor, Ilka lay outstretched. He didn't know if she was unconscious or dead.

His arms were savagely bent behind him and he heard something snap. The pain was overpowering; he thought he might faint from it. He tried to talk through the gag. All that came out were muffled, incomprehensible sounds.

One of the men loomed before him in the dim light. "You cheated us," the man said quietly.

Hencill knew it was the Mafia. He had fixed the World Series and the Mafia had ended up winning. They must have known from the beginning. He knew he was going to die.

The second man held something in his hands. Hencill was sure it was a gun. He thought his heart would explode with fear. Tears blinded him. The second man raised his hand and Hencill felt no more pain.

Fitzpatrick had sewn pieces of canvas into a body bag. To sink it, he used weights from a weight-lifting set. McGarrity held the bag upright as the gunman stuffed the woman's body in, head first.

McGarrity regretted that she had to be killed. But she was crazy. Uncontrollable. Hencill would die before he talked. His wife knew very little of what had happened. But the woman Helen knew everything and she was uncontrollable. Besides, she was cruel to children.

Each took hold of one end of the bag and swung it off the cliff. They watched the bag strike the water and disappear under the surface of the ocean. According to ocean depth charts, the bag still had a way to go before it finally settled.

The two men got into the car and McGarrity drove them to the Irishman's hotel. McGarrity had checked out of the Century Plaza and left his luggage in Fitzpatrick's room.

By the time the two had showered and changed clothes, light was breaking over Los Angeles. Ninety minutes later they were on a flight to New York.

TWO WEEKS LATER

A career agent of the F.B.I. . . . has quietly been compiling a catalogue of allegedly illegal and abusive practices within the bureau.

The allegations assembled thus far range from . . . untruthful public statements by F.B.I. officials [to charges that] agents who recently testified in a Los Angeles criminal case covered up illegal activities by the bureau.

— *The New York Times*, January 20, 1979

28.

Ilka looked out the window of the jetliner. The sky below was cloudy.

"Would you like another glass of champagne?"

Ilka looked up. The stewardess was standing beside her.

"How soon before we reach New York?" Ilka asked.

"You have time," the stewardess answered. "Another forty-five minutes."

Ilka held up her glass and the stewardess filled it. Afterward, she paused a moment before attending to the other passengers in first class. "Where do you buy your clothes?" she asked. "They're magnificent."

"Europe," Ilka answered.

"They're magnificent," the stewardess repeated.

Ilka looked out the window. She didn't feel like talking. The events in California had left her both terrified and exhausted.

She was just now beginning to understand what had happened. Some parts of it were clear, other parts confusing. It hadn't taken much for her to figure out that Robert had tried to cheat a gang of bookies and they had found out about it and had taken their money back.

More than once she wondered if Saccente had played a role in it all. He was no fool. And why wasn't he in Nashville when she picked up the money? What could have occupied him that was important enough to miss her?

The thing with Saccente was, Ilka thought, that if he had had anything to do with it, it would have been Robert who was missing, not Helen.

She didn't understand about Helen. Robert believed the woman had been killed. But why? Robert wouldn't say. And why hadn't they killed Robert? Maybe because he was too good a customer.

Helen's absence was missed by no one. She had no close friends and only a few acquaintances. Once, when one called, Robert said that Mrs. Sanders had moved back to the Midwest. He told the caller to try again in a month or so. By then he hoped to have an address. He was simply putting the person off.

It was easy to convince someone that Helen was seeking a new home, especially after a small story appeared in the *Los Angeles Times* about Robert resigning his job. The story, quoting a press release, said that Robert had quit in order to devote himself full time to other interests. She knew that was true in a sense. Now he could gamble full time so long as his resources held out, whatever he had left over from their divorce.

The company had forced him to quit. She remembered that night in Vegas when he admitted he was broke and was going to borrow the money for the bets. The company apparently had found out where he had borrowed it. To save face for all concerned, it was announced that Robert would remain as a consultant. It was all done in a very dignified manner. No one wanted bad publicity.

As for herself, she could only color herself lucky. She wasn't going to get the million she wanted, but after Robert's property was liquidated, the estate, the airplane and the automobiles were sold, she stood to clear several hundred thousand dollars. That was better than nothing. And she knew how close she had come to nothing

Robert had reacted docilely to her demand for a divorce. He even seemed glad to be rid of her. The day after that awful night, she had moved in with Renata. She had seen him once since, several days ago in her lawyer's office. After the meeting, they had gone together to the street. There, in German fashion, they shook hands. That was it. He had turned and walked away. She knew she would never see him again.

She wondered what would happen to him. Whatever happened, it wouldn't be good. He was a very sick man.

She drank her champagne and looked at magazines until a voice on the intercom announced the airplane was on final approach to New York City. Ilka straightened her seat back and looked down at the city. In a few hours she would be on her way home to Germany.

In one of the apartments in a chic East Side building, another person was preparing to go to Europe. He was Michael McGarrity. He had just returned from the bank, where he had left in his vault a bundle containing six hundred thousand dollars. On a coffee table was a small leather suitcase containing an equal amount in cash. He would take that to the airport with him.

His apartment was naked. His best paintings and favorite pieces of furniture had been sent to Ireland. Bookshelves were bare, a Persian carpet had been taken up. Tomorrow the new owners would take possession.

He went to the kitchen and put on water for tea. While it heated, he went to the bedroom to do his final packing. A week before he'd sent two steamer trunks, leaving only a small supply of suits, furnishings, socks, and underwear.

The teapot whistle brought him walking quickly from the bedroom. He brewed the tea, waited three minutes, stirred it again, and poured a cup. He added milk, took the cup and went to the living room. From fifteen stories below, on Fifth Avenue, he heard a siren. He walked to the terrace and looked down. Two fire trucks went by.

He stood on the terrace and sipped the tea. It was a cool, late fall day. The park looked dead: the leaves were off the trees and the grass was brown. Still, it was an incredible view of the city, the park, the skyline. He had been born in New York and he had loved it. But time had passed and now a new life awaited him.

He drew in a deep breath. He still had one hurdle: the airport.

He had had dinner in Apicelli's home. It had been a gay evening filled with good wine, excellent food, fine conversation.

Several times he caught Apicelli observing him. If it was because he was suspect, or simply because the old man was bidding farewell and thinking sentimental thoughts, McGarrity didn't know. If he got on the Aer Lingus flight to Dublin, he was home free.

He felt a chill and turned from the balcony and walked into his ghost apartment.

Tom Jensen could have sympathized with McGarrity on his apartment. Jensen had just sold his home in Washington. Now he was flying to New York on the three o'clock shuttle. On his lap was a morning newspaper. He turned to the sports page. Just before he left Washington, Evans had telephoned to mention the story to him.

EXTORTION ATTEMPT
ON ROOSEVELT CHAD

WASHINGTON (UPI)—The FBI revealed today that during the recent World Series, an attempt was made to extort money from Roosevelt Chad, the superstar shortstop of the Los Angeles Dodgers.

An FBI spokesman said the extortionists demanded $500,000. He said the crime may have been an attempt to influence Chad's play.

"In either case," the spokesman said, "the extortionists failed. No money was paid out, and Mr. Chad set new records for home runs, runs batted in, and he had the third highest batting average in the history of the Series."

In recent years threats and extortion demands on professional athletes have increased dramatically. It is believed by many sports authorities that most threats are hoaxes. The FBI has a different view.

"Any cases reported to us," the spokesman said, "we treat as very real."

He said the FBI had mounted an operation to catch the extortionists, but that it had failed "because of a once in a lifetime accident." He refused to ientify the accident. He also declined to tell how many agents had been involved in the operation which he described as "very large."

The spokesman said that they had no suspects in the Chad case but added, "We haven't closed the file."

Mr. Chad was not available for comment. The ball player is on vacation with his family in Africa.

In New York City, an aide to the commissioner of baseball said his office will conduct its own investigation. However, the aide played down the seriousness of the Chad incident.

"Some guy in a neighborhood bar loses $20 on a Series game and then gets drunk and starts making nuisance calls to a star player. I'd be very surprised if we found anything."

The aide said no importance should be placed on the Dodgers' recent Series loss to the 2-to-1 underdog Washington Senators.

"They won't like this in the Dodger front office," the aide said, "but the truth is, the Dodgers are the worst World Series team in baseball. Since 1940 they've been in sixteen Series and won only four. Everybody beats the Dodgers."

Mr. Chad recently made news with a history-making contract which made him the first baseball player in history to earn $1,000,000 a year. The contract runs for three years.

It was a few minutes past four o'clock when the flight landed in New York. Jensen got in the taxi queue and when his turn came he gave the driver an address in Manhattan.

The building porter had already collected McGarrity's luggage and promised to have a taxi waiting at five-fifteen. At five o'clock McGarrity was taking a final, sentimental look around his apartment. By the door stood the small suitcase containing the money.

The bell rang, and McGarrity went to the door and opened it. There stood Ignazio Apicelli and his bodyguard, Frankie Fedullo. The bodyguard was built like an ape. Though McGarrity hastily covered his surprise, he knew Apicelli's radar had already picked it up. Nevertheless, McGarrity continued his performance. Once the curtain goes up, the show must go on. "What a surprise," he told Apicelli.

"I want to give you a ride, Michael," Apicelli smiled.

"I had already ordered a taxi," McGarrity countered.

Apicelli waved such a thought away. "Taxis are for tourists. You're a member of the family. You ride with us." The old gang boss turned to his bodyguard. "Take Michael's bag, Frankie."

The apeman grinned and picked up the suitcase.

Apicelli led the way to the elevator.

The ride down gave McGarrity time to think. He mentally complimented Apicelli on the timing of his move. Everyone knew he was flying to Dublin, so he wouldn't be missed. Apicelli probably had someone ready to take the seat. He glanced at the bodyguard. Maybe even Frankie.

He thought of making a break in the lobby. He discarded the idea. Frankie would kill him by the time he got to the door. Same on the street. Besides, Frankie had the money.

An idea struck McGarrity. The other half of the money was in his bank. It was a bargaining chip. It could save his life.

The brisk dry air hit them when they came onto the street. Apicelli slapped his arms across his body and breathed in deeply. "Great weather. Why do you want to leave it, Michael? Stay with us. In Ireland it rains."

"It's green," McGarrity said.

"Like money," Apicelli answered. He laughed uproariously. Frankie joined in.

Frankie opened the door to Apicelli's limousine. Apicelli got in, McGarrity behind him. Frankie followed and sat on the jump seat facing them. His hands were plunged deep into his overcoat pockets. He looked at McGarrity and smiled.

The driver, another apeman, named Rico, turned and smiled a half-toothless smile at McGarrity. "Hey, Mr. Mike."

"Hello, Rico," McGarrity said.

Rico laughed again before turning around and putting the heavy automobile in gear. The engine roared and they shot forward.

"We have a surprise for you, Michael," Apicelli joked. "Right, Frankie?"

The apelike bodyguard nodded and laughed. Rico shot a glance over the seat. Frankie had a look on his face as if he had a secret. McGarrity knew Frankie well. He'd also known well some of the people Frankie had killed.

The car raced up the East Side. As soon as they crossed the bridge, Rico slowed the limousine and a moment later he steered it off the main route to the airport and onto a side street. From the side street he turned into a blind alley. Halfway down he stopped. He turned off the engine and twisted so he could look over the seat. He showed his half-toothless smile to McGarrity.

There was an embarrassed silence in the car. McGarrity thought it was time to mention the money in the vault. "I have a surprise for you as well," he said.

Apicelli cleared his throat. "Ours comes first, Michael."

Frankie dug his right hand deep into his coat pocket.

"Give it to him, Frankie."

"Wait a minute," McGarrity protested.

Frankie giggled and pulled his hand from his pocket. Dangling from his huge fingers was a gold pocket watch on a chain.

"Congratulations on your retirement, Michael," Apicelli said. "The family thanks you for thirty-five years of loyal service."

"Forrrr heeee's a jolly goooood fellooooow," Rico sang.

Frankie handed the watch to McGarrity. "The boys took up a collection, Mikey," he said shyly. "Everybody chipped in. Even the Brooklyn mob."

"This is the nicest surprise of my life." McGarrity delivered the line with more emotion and sincerity than he had any line since he sat on the lap of a department store Santa Claus.

"You like it, Mr. Mike?" Rico asked.

McGarrity nodded and smiled broadly. "It's beautiful."

"It ought to be," Frankie said. "It set us back three thousand bucks."

"I can't tell you how happy this makes me," McGarrity said, his voice still filled with honest emotion and sincerity.

"Another thing, Mr. Mike," Rico put in eagerly. "You can wear the watch anywhere. It ain't hot. I mean, we *really* bought it."

"Full price," Frankie added sadly.

"You shouldn't have done it," McGarrity protested.

"See!" Frankie snarled to Rico. "I told you we should have bought a hot one."

"That's enough, boys," Apicelli cut in. "Michael has a plane to catch."

They shook hands around. McGarrity attached the watch to his vest. Rico started the engine, backed quickly out of the alley, and headed back to the main route. Thirty minutes later he slammed the limousine to a halt in front of Aer Lingus.

Frankie got out and held the door. When McGarrity got out, Frankie handed him the suitcase filled with money.

A final farewell, a handshake, a wave. McGarrity turned and walked into the terminal. Behind him the limousine sped away. Rico tooted the horn once. McGarrity lifted his left arm over his head. Too late he remembered he hadn't told them his surprise, about the money in the bank, which he was going to use as a chip to barter for his life.

McGarrity walked to the ticket counter and checked in.

"Do you want to check the bag?" the girl said, motioning to the suitcase, "or is that carry-on luggage?"

"I don't want to check it," McGarrity said.

The girl handed him his boarding pass. "You have a half hour, sir, before the flight will be called. The bar and restaurant are out the door and to the right."

"Thank you," McGarrity said.

He picked up the suitcase and turned around. He had walked five paces when Tom Jensen was beside him. "I'll take that off your hands now, Michael."

Jensen took the suitcase and tested its weight. "I wonder if six hundred thousand dollars is twelve times heavier than the lousy fifty thousand Evans was going to pay me."

"We had a great idea, Tom."

"You inspired it, Michael."

The two walked toward the entrance.

"Do we have any future worries from your organization, Tom?"

"None. They just reviewed the case and they ended up exactly where I did, on Wilshire Boulevard watching the students carry Chad away. And," he said pointedly, "they did not learn that the bus driver who put the students up to it is your favorite nephew."

"A status he would have lost had he arrived one minute later."

"Especially considering that he was supposed to have the bus and students on Wilshire as Chad *began* his walk."

"Were you frightened by his lateness?"

"Frightened? No. I was panic-stricken."

The men smiled. They were at the entrance now. Two stewardesses came in the door and shot them admiring glances.

"Makes one think of Shirley and Linda," Jensen said.

"Weren't those the days," McGarrity reminisced.

"How about your former organization, Michael? Will we have any future worries there?"

McGarrity stopped. He turned back his coat and pulled the gold watch from his pocket. "From the family," he said.

Jensen stared at the watch for a moment, then he turned back his coat and pulled a watch from his vest pocket. "From the FBI," he said.

The men laughed. They shook hands and Jensen went out the door. McGarrity turned and headed for the bar.

At five minutes past 7 P.M., Aer Lingus flight number eighteen to Dublin took off from Kennedy Airport. On board was Michael McGarrity, a retired attorney.

At thirteen minutes past 7 P.M., SAS flight number one twenty-three to Stockholm, with an intermediate stop at Copenhagen, took off from Kennedy Airport. On board was Thomas Jensen, a retired government official.

At twenty minutes past 7 P.M., Lufthansa flight fifty-two to Frankfurt took off from Kennedy Airport. On board was Ilka Hencill, estranged wife of Robert Hencill, the man who tried to fix a World Series.